THE BLAME GAME

SANDIE JONES is the author of *The Guilt Trip*, *The Half Sister*, *The First Mistake* and the bestseller *The Other Woman*, which was also a Reese Witherspoon pick. Previously a freelance journalist, she has contributed to the *Sunday Times*, *The Mail on Sunday*, *Woman's Weekly* and *Hello!* magazine, amongst others. She lives in London with her husband and three children.

Also by Sandie Jones

The Other Woman
The First Mistake
The Half Sister
The Guilt Trip

SANDIE JONES

THE BLAME GAME

PAN BOOKS

First published 2022 by Macmillan

This edition first published 2023 by Pan Books
an imprint of Pan Macmillan
The Smithson, 6 Briset Street, London EC1M 5NR
EU representative: Macmillan Publishers Ireland Limited,
The Liffey Trust Centre, 117–126 Sheriff Street Upper,
Dublin 1, D01 YC43
Associated companies throughout the world
www.panmacmillan.com

ISBN 978-1-5290-8639-3

1 3 5 7 9 8 6 4 2

A CIP catalogue record for this book is available from the British Library.

Typeset by Palimpsest Book Production Ltd, Falkirk, Stirlingshire
Printed and bound by CPI Group (UK) Ltd, Croydon, CR0 4YY

MIX
Paper | Supporting
responsible forestry
FSC® C116313

Visit www.panmacmillan.com to read more about all our books
and to buy them. You will also find features, author interviews and
news of any author events, and you can sign up for e-newsletters
so that you're always first to hear about our new releases.

For Oscar
Watching you grow into a wonderful
young man is my greatest pleasure
Follow your dreams and I'll be
right by your side

PROLOGUE

She wants to be everything to everyone, but making yourself indispensable is dangerous.

It means you're party to secrets that others don't want you to know. It means you'll go to any length to keep your own close to your chest. It means that everyone around you becomes collateral damage.

But she'll not bring me down. I'll get to her, before she gets to me.

Her need to be essential is about to make her an accessory.

PART ONE

PART ONE

1

I'm sure, as soon as I see the door ajar, that something has happened. I never leave my garden office unlocked overnight, not because there's anything in there worth stealing, but there's been a spate of petty shed burglaries around here recently and I don't need my clients' files strewn across the manicured lawns of Tattenhall in the hapless pursuit of a mower or power tool.

Though you'd have to be pretty stupid if you honestly thought that the sprawling estate was tended to by a hand-held strimmer kept in my pimped-up shed. The fifty acres of rolling land that surround our cottage are maintained and nurtured by a team of three full-time greenkeepers, who you're more likely to see astride a sit-on John Deere than hovering a Flymo.

I remember Leon showing me the barn where all the machinery is kept, when we first moved here after he'd become the estate's manager. My eyes had stood out on stalks, as I'd always been a tomboy growing up and one of the best days I remember having as a child was being taken to Diggerland, where I was allowed to operate a JCB. I'd patiently waited in line for over an hour, just so I could pick up dirt from one pile with the giant bucket and move it onto another. My dad was infuriated that a theme park would charge for such an inane. activity, but I'd been delighted.

Pushing the memory to the back of my mind, before it turns sour, I tentatively pull the door open and peer inside the converted outbuilding I've grown to love. I expect to see my desk upturned and its drawers thrown across the room in frustration, as the low-life realized that there wasn't as much as a skateboard on which he could make his getaway. But my workstation is still upright; the framed certificates proving my right to prac- tise as a psychologist still hang, dead straight, on the wall, and the vase of flowers that I'd been sent by a grateful client still blossom, their optimism jarring against the unnerving sensation that is coiling around my stomach.

My eyes travel to the salmon-coloured couch, where many a life story has been shared, but its cushions remain perfectly plumped and the magazines on the coffee table are fanned out just as I had left them after my last appointment on Friday.

Nothing looks to have been disturbed and I allow a little frisson of relief to ease its way across my shoulders, loosening the knot that has so quickly tightened there. Maybe I had carelessly left the door unlocked and the breeze had just taken it off the latch, leaving it swaying in the brisk morning air.

I admonish myself, promising that I will pay more

attention in future. There might not be anything in here to entice an opportunist looking for an easy grab and sell, but there is still incredibly sensitive information held within the drawers of the cabinets that, in the wrong hands, could have far more damaging consequences.

I take a sip of my coffee and turn the electric heater on, just to take the edge off. It's forecast to be a warm day, but the overnight coolness has made its presence felt. *Not helped by leaving the door open*, I say scathingly to myself.

I shiver involuntarily as I open my diary, though I can't tell whether it's because of the very real chill in the air or seeing who my first appointment is.

Jacob.

My chest tightens and I ask myself for the hundredth time whether I've done the right thing by him. I know I certainly haven't done right by Leon, but then I wonder if that's not his own fault.

If he hadn't been so distracted lately, I would have found it easier to tell him. But the job that we thought would give us more time together has actually resulted in exactly the opposite. Because even when he's home, he's on constant call, and the summer concert that he's spent the last four months organizing is fast approaching, leaving him with even less time, and certainly less patience.

I've wanted to tell him about Jacob; tried to several times, but he's never listened long enough for me to get to the important part. But maybe that's just me choosing to see it that way, because I know how he's going to react when I do. He'll no doubt take me to task for caring too much and going beyond the call of duty. But there's a reason for that.

I knew as soon as Jacob started coming to see me three months ago that his story was different. Although he, like all of my clients, had reached the point where he felt able to put his pride aside and bravely ask for help, the irony of his situation was that he wasn't looking to save himself; he wanted to save the woman who had been abusing him for ten years.

'If I don't get out now, I'm terrified of what I might do,' he'd said when I asked why he'd come to see me, during our first session. 'For the first time ever, I was going to retaliate and it scared me because I didn't know what I might be capable of.'

I'd looked at him, curiously, unable to recall another client who thought they were the one who needed help, instead of the person who'd been making their life hell.

'Can you tell me what happened to make you feel this way?' I'd asked softly.

He'd looked down at his intertwined fingers in his lap. 'She stayed out last Saturday,' he started. 'All night.'

'OK,' I said. 'And do you know where she'd been?'

He'd laughed cynically. 'Oh, she made sure to tell me all the details.' He shifted on the sofa, pulling a scatter cushion onto his lap, as if it were a metaphorical barrier.

I'd sat back in my chair opposite him, giving him the time and space to decide whether he wanted to elaborate.

'She'd been with another man,' he'd said eventually. 'Having the best sex she's ever had.'

I'd recoiled inwardly, unable to imagine how it must feel to be told something like that by the person you thought you were going to spend the rest of your life with.

'She told you that?' I'd asked incredulously, seemingly still capable of being shocked by the sadistic behaviour of some people, despite being in the job for over ten years.

He'd nodded. 'Yes, just before she straddled me and attempted to force herself on me.'

'And what happened?'

'Absolutely nothing,' he said. 'I could still smell him on her, for God's sake. But regardless, I could no longer convince my body that making love to her was what I wanted to do. It had listened to the call to action for so long, ever ready to perform when she wanted it to, but eventually, my brain just said, "Enough, I can't do this any more."'

His lips had closed and he'd grimaced. 'She told me I was an embarrassment to mankind, unable to perform the most primitive of functions.'

'How did that make you feel?' I'd asked.

'Less of a man,' he said. 'Though I guess she's ingrained it in me to such an extent that it's impossible to feel any other way.'

'So your relationship has affected your masculinity?' I'd asked.

'Of course,' he'd said, sighing. 'How can it not? The stereotype is that a real man should be in charge, be the breadwinner.'

I couldn't help but cringe at his misguided definition. 'Don't you think that's a rather outdated stereotype these days?'

'Is it?' he'd asked, seeming genuinely out of touch. 'That gives me some hope then, as I'm not like that.'

'I think masculinity's more about how you feel.'

'Well, that morning, I couldn't have felt any less of a man if I'd tried. Maybe that's why I almost did what I did.'

He'd wiped a tear away and I pushed the box of tissues on the table closer to him.

'What did you *almost* do?' I asked.

His jaw tensed, the bristles of his beard pulsing.

'When she got off me and walked towards the bathroom, I reached for the baseball bat that we keep beside the bed. I've let her rain down blow after blow, insult after insult, without so much as a retort, but that morning, everything that I've held in over the years just rose to the surface.'

'What were you thinking you would do?' I'd asked.

10

He took a deep breath. 'I wanted to kill her,' he said, before looking at me as if to gauge my reaction. When I didn't give him one, he'd forged on. 'It felt like the only way out and I remember thinking that all I had to do was swing it once and it would all be over. I was walking up behind her, having this internal dialogue with myself, wondering how bad it would be if I just did it.'

'So what stopped you?' I asked.

'As much as I so desperately wanted to do it, all the time I was rationalizing it in my head, it wasn't going to be an instinctive act, was it?'

'I'm going to ask the question that I'm sure you've asked yourself a thousand times,' I'd said.

'Why haven't I left her?' he sighed, beating me to it. I'd nodded.

'I will, but it's going to take some organization. I've been applying for new jobs in Canterbury as I can't risk her finding me once I've gone.'

'What is it you do?' I asked.

'I'm a school teacher,' he said. 'For my sins.'

I'd offered a small smile.

'And what about accommodation?' I'd asked.

'I haven't got anything lined up, but if I get offered any of the positions I've applied for, I'll have to get something sorted out pretty quickly, even if it's just something temporary, until I'm able to get myself properly settled.'

I'd been tempted to offer him our flat, which was standing empty just a few miles down the coast, there and then. We were planning on decorating it, ready for the onslaught of tourists that descend on Whitstable for the holiday season, but somehow summer is already upon us and we haven't got around to it yet. It's in a great little spot, just two roads back from the beach, and has served us well these past six years whilst Leon and I have been commuting into nearby Canterbury: him to his job as events manager at the cathedral and me to my grey little windowless box in the council offices.

But when the opportunity to live in a grace and favour cottage at Tattenhall had presented itself, it had been a no-brainer. Not least because it gave me the chance to set up my own practice in the outbuilding, which, seeing as I was embroiled in a stand-off with my line manager, couldn't have come at a better time.

'You've crossed the line,' he'd said, when he discovered I'd helped a woman seek sanctuary from her violent husband in the middle of the night.

'She was in imminent danger,' I'd retorted. 'Are we really such slaves to bureaucracy that we're prepared to risk a woman being killed?'

'Red tape's there for a reason,' he'd barked as I walked away.

Well, if it was there, I chose not to see it when I slipped out of the house and drove the four miles to where Sarah lived. That's not to say fear wasn't coursing through my veins as I sat there with my lights and engine off, surrounded by what felt like an invisible trip wire that would set off a deafening alarm as soon as she crossed it. But my stomach was in knots for her, not myself.

I watched with my heart in my mouth as she came out and carefully closed the door behind her. Just one forced error, and her husband would be down those stairs and dragging her back up to give her the beating of her life.

'You can do this,' I'd said out loud, as she momentarily hesitated in the porch. 'Come on, Sarah, just a few more steps.'

She silently ran towards the car without looking back, but just as she reached the passenger door, an upstairs light went on.

'Get in, get in,' I whispered, my voice hoarse with terror.

I'd managed to get her to the safehouse, but two days later her husband had paid me a visit in the underground car park at work, demanding to know where she was.

I wasn't going to tell Leon, but I was still trembling when I got home, unable to shake the memory of a double-barrelled shotgun being pressed against my temple.

'Promise me you'll never do anything like that again,

Naomi,' he'd said, as he pulled me close and wrapped himself around me. Right there, nestled in my safe place, I never imagined I would.

Yet here I am, once again, with the weapon's indentation not yet forgotten, finding myself unable to deny someone in need.

'Are we still going to rent the flat out?' I'd mooted to Leon a few weeks ago, when Jacob told me he'd been offered a new job.

'Yeah, as soon as the concert's out of the way,' Leon had said. 'I'll look at getting it ready for the summer season. I think it will do well as a holiday rental.'

'Yes, but that could be unpredictable,' I'd said. 'Not to mention hard work for me and you. Wouldn't it make more sense to rent it out on a six-month contract, or even three? At least we'd know we had that guaranteed income.'

'I'm not sure there's anyone around here who would take it on that basis,' he said, his tone already distracted by something he was looking at on his laptop.

'Well, one of my clients might be interested,' I said, turning my back, conscious of what I was plotting being written all over my face.

'I don't think that's a good idea,' he'd said. 'Do you not think it would be better to keep your work and the flat separate?'

'Not when it's someone as desperate as he is.'

'*He?*' Leon repeated, suddenly giving me his undivided attention. Was that what it took these days?

'Yes,' I said, wishing I'd kept Jacob gender neutral.

'So what's his story?' he'd asked, his interest piqued.

'He's been abused by his wife for the past ten years and he's finally had enough,' I said. 'Whenever he dares to fall asleep before her, she'll pour freezing cold water over him or run razors across the soles of his feet. They leave just the tiniest of nicks that can barely be seen by the naked eye, but you try walking on a hundred paper cuts.'

Leon had looked at me with confusion etched across his brow. 'And you want him to live in our flat?'

I'd nodded.

He'd shaken his head. 'She sounds like a complete nutter.'

'She is,' I'd said, thinking he was finally beginning to understand the need to get Jacob somewhere safe.

'I don't think that's something you should involve yourself in,' he said. 'God knows what she's capable of.'

My heart had sunk. 'But she won't know where he is.'

'Yeah, but still – it's probably best we stay out of it.'

'He doesn't have anywhere else to go,' I said.

'Why is that suddenly your problem?'

'I just want to be able to help, that's all, and the flat's sitting there empty . . .'

'I think you do enough for your clients,' he'd said. 'You're paid an hour for just that; an hour.'

15

He'd made it sound so easy, but I defy anyone with half a heart to listen to what my clients say, and not think about it for long after they've left. It's a bit like reading a book. You know that feeling you get when you're so fully invested in the characters that you have to read one more page? And then another and another, until you find out what happens to them, even when you know you can't do anything to change their fate and what the author has already written on the pages.

But what if you *could* change the end of the story? What if you had the chance to change somebody's life, at no cost to your own? You would, wouldn't you?

2

'Hello?' comes a timid voice, as if nervous to announce his arrival.

I turn from watering the orchids on my bookshelf to see Jacob's bearded face peering around the Crittall door.

'Hey,' I say. 'Come on in.'

He hesitates and my eyes follow his to the handkerchief he's cradling in his hands.

'What's that?' I ask.

'I found it just outside,' he says as I go towards him. 'I don't think he's going to make it.'

I peer into the cotton nest Jacob's created to see a stricken bird, lying there perfectly still.

'Oh, poor thing, where was he?'

'Right outside your door,' he says, tilting his head towards the stone paving by the threshold.

'I didn't see it when I came in,' I say.

'You couldn't miss it,' he says. 'It was right there.'

I shiver in an unconscious attempt to shrug off the menacing cloak that's wrapping itself around me. I've always found dead birds to be rather sinister; I think it stems from a horror movie I saw when I was a kid and ever since, I've questioned their mortality. How can there be so many birds in the world and yet we see so few dead? Where do they go to die?

On my doorstep, it seems.

'It's still warm,' he says, stepping back outside.

I wonder how I could have missed it, unless it had just happened. But how? Birds don't just drop out of the sky.

I remember the door being ajar and feel a growing sense of unease as I watch Jacob dig in the soil with his bare hands before tenderly placing the bird, still wrapped in his handkerchief, into the hole. He comes back in with sad eyes, and dirt caked under his fingernails.

I could pretend not to notice – it seems the easiest thing to do, otherwise I'll have to offer him the kitchen sink in the cottage to wash in. But I can tell by the way he's holding his hands out in front of him that he's about to ask.

'Would you mind . . . ?' he says.

It's crossing another line, but I force a smile and hope that the house is empty, as the last thing I need is Jacob eulogizing about how grateful he is to be living in the flat when Leon knows nothing about it. I consider telling Jacob not to mention it as I lead him up the path, but that will only unsettle him, so I decide to fly by the seat of my pants and hope for the best.

The house is still as I open the back door and I dare to imagine that Leon has already gone to work, but as

I turn the tap on and silently gesture for Jacob to use it, I hear footsteps overhead. I hand Jacob a tea towel before he's even wet his hands and head back to the door, but it's too late; Leon is at the foot of the stairs with a surprised expression on his face.

'Oh,' he says. 'Everything OK?'

I stand there, not sure what to do for the best. In any other situation, I'd normally introduce the pair of them without a second thought, but I feel compelled to get them as far apart as possible, as quickly as I can.

'We just needed to use the sink,' I say. 'There was a dead bird and . . .'

'Oh, right,' says Leon, coming towards us with an extended hand. 'Hi, I'm Leon, Naomi's husband.'

I tense up, but force a smile. Leon will be able to sense my awkwardness a mile off.

'Jacob, good to meet you.'

I will him to leave it there and usher him towards the door.

'Thanks,' Jacob says, 'for—'

'Come on,' I interject. 'The clock's ticking.'

I can feel Leon's eyes burn into the back of my head, but I keep looking forward, intent on getting Jacob back in my office, where I get to control the narrative.

He steps inside and shrugs off his jacket, throwing it onto the coat stand.

There's an energy about him that he didn't have when I helped him move into the flat last week. Back then, he'd seemed almost grief-stricken, and I wondered if he was doing the right thing. If *we* were doing the right thing. But seeing the cigarette burns on his arms as he'd lifted a box down from the van convinced me we were.

'Why are you helping me like this?' he'd asked, as I'd hung his suits up on a rail and put his online food shop away in the kitchen cupboards.

I'd thought about it for a moment, asking myself the same question. Why did I feel compelled to cross the line of duty?

I guess the answer is right in front of me now. Jacob's brow is less furrowed and his eyes brighter than I've seen them before. There's a semblance of hope there that no matter how long I'd listened to him for, he would never have been able to muster, all the time he was going back to a woman who kicked and scratched him for not having her dinner ready on time.

'So how are you feeling?' I ask, as I go to the cabinet drawer where I know surnames beginning with M are kept.

Jacob sighs contentedly. 'I can't even begin to tell you,' he says. 'It feels like a weight has been lifted off my chest. That crushing feeling that I felt constantly has all but gone.'

I'm trying to listen to him and smile, as if encouraging him to go on, but my mind is becoming entrenched in doubt and confusion. My fingers work deftly as they swipe the files back and forth, looking for the one between

Langley and Mulville that I know to be here – well, at least it was a couple of days ago. Because I'd seen it – with my own two eyes – when I'd taken Melanie Langley's folder out and briefly found myself wondering how Jacob Mackenzie, the man whose life was enclosed in the next manila foolscap, was doing, since leaving the wife he'd become enslaved to.

I look and look again, but it's not here.

'I . . . can't seem to find your file,' I say.

Jacob laughs. 'I think you know me well enough not to need my file any more.'

'You're probably right,' I say, as I sit down on the high-backed leather chair opposite him. I reach for my bound notebook on the desk behind me, sighing at not being able to spot a pen.

'Here,' says Jacob, handing me his from the front pocket of his shirt.

'Thanks,' I say, taking it from him. 'I'm not quite as organized as I normally am this morning.'

'It's probably because I caught you off-guard with the bird,' he says. 'It's my fault, sorry.'

I lean in and look at him. 'Not everything is your fault,' I say softly. 'You don't have to apologize whenever something doesn't quite go to plan.'

He shrugs his shoulders forlornly. 'It's force of habit, I suppose.'

'She spent a long time making you feel that way.'

'It's funny,' he says, twiddling his thumbs. 'But now

that I'm out of it and with the wonderful benefit of hindsight, I can already see how messed up it all was.'

'Why do you think it was so difficult to see when you were still together?' I ask.

He shrugs. 'I just think that it went on for so long, it became normal. I knew that it wasn't right and that other people's relationships weren't like the one she and I had, but I think my coping mechanism was to normalize it. Or even tell myself that it was nothing less than I deserved.'

'There's nothing you could have done that warranted her treatment of you,' I say.

'I'm beginning to see that now,' he says, his jaw tensing. 'But it's going to take me a while to get used to the fact that not everything I do will result in my getting berated, or ridiculed, or worse.'

'Are you already learning to enjoy the simple pleasures in life?' I ask. 'The ones that before would have seen you get punished?'

His expression softens and his face breaks out into a grin he couldn't stop if he tried. 'I can't tell you what a joy it is to walk down the street, without having to worry about what time it is.'

I let him continue.

'Time was my greatest enemy. She used it as a weapon against me. She'd send me to the shops to buy something, and I'd be standing on the high street, looking at my watch, wondering if I could get away with popping into the butcher's to get some of the sausages the children liked. Would it take too long? Would she accuse me of loving them more than her?

'I wanted to visit my mum's grave. I wanted to browse the library. I wanted to stop and talk to the person whose dog was being over-friendly. But I didn't have time for any of that – not if it was, quite literally, on her watch.'

His pained expression is back as the memory takes hold. 'Do you have any idea how mentally draining it is to have to second-guess everything you do? To question whether it's going to cause a problem if you go the long way home because it's a nice day. It's utterly exhausting.'

I nod, as if I understand. 'Aside from needing to learn that you're not to blame for everything, what else did she take away from you that you'd like to get back?'

He takes a deep breath and sinks into the sofa as he begins to relax. I sometimes wish I had a time-lapse camera set up, so that I and, more importantly, my clients, could see how far they've come. So many of them beat themselves up because they don't think they've moved on, or that it's taking too long to feel better about themselves. But they'd only have to compare their first visit, when they would undoubtedly be perched on the very edge of the sofa, straight-backed and furtively looking around, nervous and distrusting, to a few weeks later, when their body language would tell a completely different story. With every session, they sit further back, their shoulders come down from their ears, and they allow the sofa to take their weight.

'My relationship took away my sense of self,' he says. 'I don't know how to change it. I don't know what it takes to be me – does that make sense?'

I nod. 'I think it's about being comfortable in your own skin. Just being who you want to be.'

He looks at me cynically, as if I'm trying to convince him of something that's just not possible.

'I don't think I even know who I am any more.'

'Because that's how you've been conditioned to feel.'

'But I can do no right,' he goes on.

'Being in the wrong is your default position now, and we just have to keep working to de-program the way your brain has been re-wired and take it back to factory settings.'

He shakes his head solemnly. 'I don't think even you can do that.'

'I'm prepared to die trying,' I say with a smile.

'You're a very special person,' he says, the edges of his mouth curling upwards. 'I don't know what I've done to deserve you in my life.'

His words catch on my conscience, making me feel uncomfortable. He makes it sound as if we're more than we are; more than we should be. I shift in my chair, sitting up straighter in a futile attempt to make me feel more professional. Though it only serves to shine a light on the line that I've crossed.

Jacob looks at me, his eyes soft. 'Why are you helping me like this?' he asks.

'I help a lot of people,' I say, careful to strike a balance between making him feel special and not singling him out too much.

'So do you put them all up in flats you happen to own?' he says, smiling.

'Not all of them,' I say. 'Just my star pupils.' I instantly regret it.

'It makes a nice change for me to be the teacher's pet. Normally I'm being accused of having my own.'

'How's the new teaching job going?' I ask, eager to get the conversation back on more of an even keel.

'It's different,' he says. 'I'm used to dealing with boys, so a mixed school is a whole new ball game.'

I offer a smile.

'Boys just want to play sport and video games,' he goes on. 'Well, that's certainly what my own were like when they were younger. They were addicted to football and the PlayStation.'

His face clouds over and I can see him flinching at a memory his words have evoked.

'How do the children feel about you leaving?' I ask. 'Have you spoken to them?'

He allows himself a little smile. 'I went up to Leeds at the weekend to see Will at university. And do you know what he said when we hugged goodbye?'

I shake my head and smile because I can feel it's going to be something that melted his father's heart.

'He said . . .' chokes Jacob. 'That he'd never seen me

like that before. That it was as if being away from his mother had finally allowed me to be me.'

'How did that make you feel?' I ask.

'Happy and sad in equal measure,' he says. 'Happy that I'd finally made the break, but sad that it had taken me so long.'

'You were trying to do right by your children,' I say.

He nods. 'I couldn't have left them on their own with her,' he says. 'I had to wait until they were old enough to look after themselves.'

'Your wife is a pillar of the community, a supposedly good mother, at least to those on the outside, looking in.' He nods. 'Do you think how she was perceived by others also played a part in you not leaving her before now?'

'Probably,' he says. 'I mean, obviously I knew exactly what she was capable of, but nobody else did. She had perfected such a polished public facade and it very rarely slipped. And even when it did, invariably off the back of me doing something wrong, you'd get a split-second flash of fire in her eyes before she got it back under control.'

'So you felt you needed others to see who was really behind the mask?'

He knits his fingers together, looking deep in thought.

'I guess . . .' he starts, before wiping a single tear that escapes onto his cheek. 'Because without other people seeing it, I didn't think I would be believed.'

I wish I were shocked that a grown man would ever

doubt that his experience would be deemed credible enough to be believed. But unfortunately, it doesn't matter whether you're young or old, male or female; the greatest fear, apart from the abuse itself, is that nobody will believe you.

'I was scared that I would be made a social outcast if I said anything against her.'

'Would it have mattered if the people who held her in such high regard had wrongly cast you aside?' I ask.

'With the benefit of hindsight, probably not,' he says. 'But back then, when I couldn't see a way out, I thought I'd be called a liar, that I'd lose all contact with the children and then I'd be even more isolated than I already was.'

I nod, understanding his predicament.

'So I decided that the life I had with her was better than the life she would construct for me if I left.'

'But her taking a lover gave you the impetus to do what you wanted to do . . .'

He nods fervently. 'It was what I'd been waiting for,' he says. 'It meant that everyone else could finally see the cracks in the picture-perfect version she presented. His other half found out and suddenly people at my wife's gym, church choir and the stables where she keeps her horse were gossiping about it.'

He moves the cushion aside and pushes himself up and off the couch, stretching his arms towards the wooden slatted ceiling.

'I got a new bed delivered yesterday and I woke up with chronic back pain this morning. It's Sod's Law that just when I'm allowed to sleep, I'm still unable to.'

'It'll probably take you a while to get used to it,' I say.

'You're probably right,' he says. 'It just needs to be broken in.'

I can't stop my skin from flushing as I picture him falling back against fluffy pillows. A woman rolls into him, resting her head on his chest, and it's only as he brushes her brunette hair away from her face that I see it's me.

'What have you got planned for the rest of the week?' I ask, in an effort to change the subject.

'Well, actually, I got a text from a very old friend yesterday – someone I haven't seen in years, asking if we can meet up tomorrow.'

'That'll be nice,' I say.

He grimaces. 'Mmm, I don't think so,' he says. 'He told me he's terminally ill.'

'Oh, I'm sorry,' I offer, never knowing quite what the right thing to say is. 'It's so sad it's taken that to rekindle your friendship.'

'Well, Kyle was more my wife's friend than mine,' he says. 'But we always got along – until she severed the relationship.'

'Do you know why?'

'I've always had my suspicions,' he says. 'Which I fear are about to be realized – he said he had something to tell me.'

'That he doesn't want to take to his grave with him?' I ask, careful to curb my mounting alarm. Jacob's still on very shaky ground and the last thing he needs is someone to come along and throw a hand grenade at his feet. Especially if it's just to assuage their own guilt by burdening him with it instead.

'Mmm,' he murmurs thoughtfully.

'Just be careful,' I offer. 'And whatever he has to say, try not to let it affect you.'

He forces a smile. 'I don't think there's anything that anyone can say that will shock me any more.'

'I wouldn't bet on it,' I say to myself sceptically.

'I've never noticed that before,' he says, changing the subject and nodding his head in the direction of the print of the New York skyline hanging on the wall.

'It's been there a month or so,' I say, clearing my throat. 'A client bought it for me.'

'I was pretty sure you were from the east coast, but thought it might be Philadelphia.'

'No, born and bred in New York,' I say. 'Well, Long Island, to be specific.'

'Ah, I remember going there when the kids were little,' he says, smiling fondly at the memory. 'It was a great day. Until we couldn't find the restaurant we'd booked, and then all hell broke loose.'

He looks at me, his eyes full of sadness and regret that the good memories he has are so quickly marred.

'When you think of her now, how do you feel?' I ask.

He sighs and sits on the sofa again. 'Deep down, I know she is a bitter, twisted woman, who at best is psychotic and at worst downright dangerous.'

A small step forward.

'But I must have been the driving force of her anger and temper,' he goes on. 'It started with me and finished with me – and I will never forgive myself for what went on in between.'

Two steps back.

'You did everything in your power to protect the children,' I remind him. 'The fact that you still have a relationship with them now, when she barely sees them, is testament to that. They don't blame you for what she put them through, so why would you?'

He shrugs his shoulders and looks at me with sad eyes. 'As I said, I guess it's just going to take me some time to stop taking the rap for her behaviour and apologizing for everything I do.'

'How do you think she's holding up?' I ask. 'Do you think about that at all?'

He nods. 'I keep wondering what's going through her head. She must have been so shocked when she came home to find me gone. She wouldn't have believed it possible, and the fact that she doesn't know where I am will have her going out of her mind. Everything in her life is controlled; we all have our place in it and if we're not where she wants us, there's hell to pay.'

'Do you honestly believe she would come looking for you?'

'As I say, I'm sleeping with one eye open.' He forces a smile. 'But when I think about it rationally, I know she's going to have to look really hard to find me because, thanks to your help, I couldn't have covered my tracks any better than I have.'

He looks at me as if searching for confirmation and I nod. Even with the keenest eye and the most dogged determination, she'd have a job to find him.

But as I think of the lengths we have gone to, I'm struck by the thought that *she*, the woman who doesn't even have a name, might be prepared to go one step further.

I glance at the cabinet that holds my clients' deepest secrets, the drawer that should have protected Jacob's thoughts and fantasies still ajar, and a sudden chill wraps itself around me.

'So again,' he goes on, oblivious to my rising panic, 'it's just going to take some time for me to relax and know that she'll never find me.'

A breath catches in my throat as I wonder if she already has.

3

As much as I hate to admit it, I barely hear anything my next few clients say, so distracted am I by the sickening realization that someone might have been in my office.

As soon as I'm alone, I hastily lock the door and set about trying to quieten the thumping in my chest that's reverberating in my ears. I go through the L–R drawer again in a desperate search for Jacob's file. It has to be here somewhere.

I check every other drawer, allowing for the possibility that I'd somehow put it back in the wrong place. But it's not been haphazardly thrown amongst the A–Ks or the S–Zs, which, for someone who has a set place for everything, is somewhat of a relief. I can't believe I'd rather the file have been taken than have my normally meticulous business practices questioned.

I try to convince myself that I might have taken his folder up to the house, though even as I'm walking up the path I know how unlikely that is, especially with what's been going on. I wouldn't have risked Leon seeing it, even in all its innocence, as whether I want to admit it or not, I have gone out of my way to avoid talking about any of my clients in the past week, for fear of the conversation turning to the man who needed somewhere to stay. Would I confess that the same man was currently ensconced in our flat? That I'd valued Jacob's safety more than Leon's wishes?

I sometimes wonder why Leon can't see it from my side, especially after everything I've been through. He knows that this is more than just a job to me; that it's my life's work to save everyone I can from situations they don't deserve to be in. But, like my clients say, 'You'll never understand what it feels like to be in that position until you've been there yourself.' Little do they know that I have, and Leon would do well to remember that every once in a while.

Perhaps then, I wouldn't feel the need to keep things from him; to hide the fact that I got Melanie Langley pushed up the emergency rehousing list, by agreeing to take on three Women's Aid cases in return. Or that I voluntarily man the Domestic Abuse national helpline one afternoon a week.

He can't understand why, when I've come from where I have, I would want to take myself back there, through someone else's experience. But that's exactly why I do it. I couldn't sit by and do nothing, any more than Santa Claus could stay at home on Christmas Eve.

'I just want to be able to protect *you*,' Leon had said to me after my run-in with Sarah's husband. 'You can't chase all the monsters away. You've put paid to your own – he will never darken your door again – but you can't save everyone.'

But couldn't I at least try?

Though now, as I sift through the disarray of paperwork on the dining table, seeing no sign of Jacob's case file, I can't help but wonder if he was right after all.

Could Jacob's wife be so driven to know where he is that she'd come to my office and steal his file? It's unlikely; she doesn't know I even feature in her husband's life, least of all that I've been privy to everything that she's done to him.

Whenever he came to see me, he had gone to painstaking lengths to get here without been seen or followed. He always made sure to leave the school by the back door and had taken two buses, so as not to move his car from its prominent parking space in front of the assembly hall.

He'd leave his phone at work too, so that she couldn't track him, because as soon as he was on the move and going in any direction, she'd be calling him, asking where he was going. He couldn't even go to get a sandwich without her questioning him, so there was no way he was going to let her find out he was seeing me.

I rifle under Leon's books and papers, which have taken up residency on the dining table over the past few weeks. I lift my laptop up and check the chairs, all the time trying to quell the sense of unease that is snaking its way up from my stomach to my chest.

'What you looking for?' asks Leon, taking me by surprise. I hadn't even realized he was in the house.

'I'm missing a file,' I say, holding a hand to my head, willing myself to think where else it can be. 'I can't find it anywhere.'

'Well, it must be here somewhere,' he says. 'Do you need it urgently?'

'I'd just like to know where it is,' I say. 'I can't bear to lose things. What are you doing here anyway?'

'There's been a cock-up on the lanterns for the concert and they're not going to get here in time, so I'm going to take the van and pick them up myself.'

'Where have you got to go?' I ask.

'Birmingham,' he says.

I look at my watch. 'But it's three o'clock already – you're surely not going to get there and back tonight.'

He grimaces. 'No, it'll be too late, so I'll stay over and head back first thing in the morning.'

My chest tightens at the thought of spending tonight on my own. What if whoever broke into my office last night didn't find what they were looking for and comes back again tonight? Might they try the house this time?

I'm already dreading the hours stretched out ahead of me, knowing that as soon as night falls, I'll be imagining what could be done to me, without anyone else in the world being aware of it until the morning. I'll count down those minutes and seconds whilst lying there, my eyes fixed on the ornate ceiling rose above our bed and my ears ever alert to the tiniest of creaks and things that go bump in the night. My sane brain reminds me that exactly the same things go bump in the day too, but it's easy to forget when you're in the grip of fear and anxiety.

I hate that I've turned what is likely to be my own mistake into something more sinister. Though a dead bird doesn't help.

'Have you been to the flat recently?' asks Leon, blind-siding me.

'No,' I snap, far too quickly. 'Why?'

'It's just that we really should start to think about getting it decorated, if we want to rent it out over the summer.'

'There's no rush,' I say. 'And besides, it's good enough as it is this year.'

'Yeah, but still, there are some odd jobs that are going to need doing. I might try and pass by today or on my way back tomorrow morning.'

My heart stops and my vision blurs as I aimlessly rifle through a pile of paperwork I've already looked at.

I picture Leon letting himself into what he thinks is an empty flat, only to be confronted by Jacob's belongings, or worse, Jacob himself. I have to stop him from going, or else come clean and tell the truth. But I don't even know where to begin.

I try to convince myself that he'll be happy I've used

my own initiative; be glad of the extra money that will be coming in every month, but if I truly believed that, I would have told him by now, wouldn't I?

'I . . . I . . .' I stutter, as he looks at me expectantly.

'What?' he asks, with raised eyebrows.

'I'll go and take a look,' I say quickly. 'You've got enough on your plate. I'll start making a list of what needs doing, then we can take a look together, once you've got the concert out of the way.'

'Is your client still looking for somewhere to live?' he asks.

'Maybe,' I say, looking anywhere but at him. 'Why do you ask?'

'Is it the guy who was here this morning?'

Heat travels up my neck; I can only hope and pray it's not leaving its mark on my skin.

'Yes,' I say, my voice sounding more high-pitched than normal, or maybe that's just my imagination.

'You seemed nervous around him.'

I instinctively tighten my ponytail and brush imaginary hair away from my eyes, in a pathetic attempt to divert Leon's attention, though by the intense look on his face, I've done the exact opposite.

'Are you OK?' he asks, coming towards me. 'Is this guy a problem?' He takes hold of my elbows and looks into my eyes. He may as well be staring into my soul.

'Of course not,' I say, shrugging him off.

'So what was the deal this morning then?' he asks,

following me to the sink. 'Neither of you could look me in the eye.'

'You're being ridiculous,' I say, forcing a laugh.

'Am I?' he asks. 'Because to me, it felt like I was interrupting something.'

'What, just because it was a man?'

'No, because of the way he looked at you.'

There's nothing I can do to stop my cheeks from blushing and the more I try, the hotter they burn.

I can't deny that it feels as if Jacob and I have crossed an invisible line; the one that makes you feel as if it's just a matter of time before it's either re-drawn or erased altogether.

'He's a client, who happens to be vulnerable right now,' I say. 'He'll anchor himself to anyone or anything that gives him stability.'

'And that's you, is it?'

'Once a week, yes,' I say impatiently, omitting to tell him that at Jacob's request, it's now going to be twice. 'Are you sure you've not seen one of my folders? Might you have picked it up with your stuff?'

'I'll check, but I doubt it,' he says. 'Can it wait until the morning?'

No! I want to scream. I need to know now, so that I don't spend the night fretting unnecessarily. At least if Leon has picked it up inadvertently, then my imagination only has an open door and a dead bird to work itself up over. But if Jacob's folder is missing . . . ? That ratchets the likelihood of it being something more ominous up a notch.

'Yeah, sure,' I say casually. 'It's no big deal.'

'Will you be OK?' he asks, leaning in to kiss me.

''Course,' I say, though my stomach is tied up in knots. 'Drive safely.'

'I'll see you tomorrow,' he says, with a tight smile.

I want to make myself a cup of coffee before my next client arrives, but I need to know if there are more files missing first. So I fill a jug with water and head back down the garden.

The promised sun is peeking through the clouds, and the buttercups that line the window boxes of my office shine a bright yellow, going some way to lifting my darkening mood.

But it doesn't last long, as all five of the clients I randomly select have files matching their names, in perfect alphabetical order. I put Anna's parchment-coloured folder on my desk, ready for our appointment, and try to force myself to remember what I might have done with Jacob's.

'Hey, how you doing?' Anna's head pops around the door, her familiar American accent instantly wrapping itself around me, making me feel closer to home, even though it's not been home for a long time.

I'd recognized it as soon as she introduced herself at our first appointment and I immediately felt an affinity with her; an unseen tie that bound us together by our shared nostalgia for a time and place gone by. Though having been here for a little longer than I have, she's definitely picked up more British traits; her vowels are softer than mine, her duty is dewty, whereas *my* duty is still dooty. Her dance is darnce, whereas mine is danse. I'd order the check where I'm sure she'd ask for the bill, and I most definitely still wear sneakers whilst she wears trainers.

I'd hazard a guess we're about the same age, and just knowing that we'd walked the same streets, smelling the same smells and seeing the same sights, had taken me straight back there.

It was bittersweet, of course – it always is when I take myself back across the Pond, both literally and metaphorically. Because as much as I try to remember the happier times, I only ever have a few seconds, a minute at most, before my world comes crashing down around me again.

'Hey,' I say, ushering her in. 'How are you today?'

'Oh,' she says, shrugging her shoulders despondently. 'You know . . .'

'Here, sit down,' I say, conscious that she sounds even more troubled than she normally does. 'Is everything OK?'

She falls down heavily on the sofa and the world feels like it's falling with her. 'I just don't know how much longer I can carry on like this,' she says meekly, as if she's frightened of her own voice.

'What do you mean?' I ask, leaning across the coffee table to steady her shaking hands.

'I just . . . I just can't imagine going through the rest of my life without him,' she cries. 'I mean, how is any mother supposed to do that?'

Her shoulders convulse and I move around to sit beside her on the couch.

'Because you have no other choice,' I say, softly but assertively. 'You have two other children who rely on you.'

She nods. 'If it weren't for them, I would have done something a long time ago.'

'That may be so, but you have to think about them now. They're your priority – they've already lost their little brother. How will they ever recover from losing their mother as well? You're their world.'

'But I just can't . . . *we* can't go on like we are. Nick and I can barely even look at each other. We don't talk any more. We certainly don't laugh. How is that right? We've gone from being the perfect, happy family to just existing in two hollowed-out shells, shuffling through life as if we're on autopilot. How is that fair on the children?'

'It isn't,' I say. 'But you're all still together and that says a lot about your resilience and strength. Most couples would have buckled if they'd lost their child in such tragic circumstances. You're stronger than you give yourself credit for.'

'But what are we doing it for?' she asks, her tear-filled eyes looking at me imploringly. 'What are we trying to prove? Do we want other people to look at us and say, "Ah, haven't they done well?" Is that more important to us than being stuck in an empty marriage? Does what other people think mean more than our own happiness?'

'Are you saying you'd be happier on your own?' I ask.

'But I wouldn't be on my own, would I? I'd have my children with me and they'd be free of the toxic environment that my marriage has created.'

'Do you think the children are conscious of that?' I ask.

She gives a cynical laugh. 'We don't eat together. We don't sleep together. We don't do anything together. It's either him and them or me and them. They're not stupid. They can still remember when it was the five of us and all the fun and exciting things we used to do.'

Another tear escapes onto her cheek.

'My eldest was just asking the other day why we don't go up to London any more,' she cries. 'He remembers us going up just after Christmas last year and spending the money his grandma had sent over.'

Anna flinches as a lightning bolt of pain crosses her face, but she quickly pulls herself together.

When she first came to see me a couple of months ago, she wasn't even able to say Ben's name, so frightened of the feelings it would evoke. But I've spent a long time gently coaxing her into talking about him.

Convincing her that the best way to keep his memory alive is to think about him often and talk about him even more. It's what she's wanted to do ever since he died last year, but she seemingly hadn't given herself permission to do it with anyone else; assuming that they too wouldn't be able to cope with the emotions it would elicit in either themselves or her.

'Tell me about your trip to London,' I say gently.

She wipes her cheek. 'It was that period between Christmas and New Year, and we took the children up to the pantomime. It was the first year all three of them were able to enjoy it; Ben was just two so was able to sit through a performance and I wanted to do it before the others thought it was too babyish.

'So we stayed overnight in a hotel and went to Hamleys, where they were enraptured by the entertainers on the street outside performing magic tricks and riding unicycles. They had twenty pounds each to spend, which doesn't buy you very much in that store, but they rushed off in awe, exploring all the floors as if they were in Willy Wonka's chocolate factory.'

Suddenly her soft features become pinched as the flashback takes on a new direction.

'The older two were far too fast for Ben, so I went off with them whilst Nick stayed with Ben. By the time we came back together again, Ben had the sugary remnants of pink cotton candy stuck to his face and a gleaming red toy car clutched in his chubby little hand.'

I smile at the vivid image playing out in my head, but Anna's face is still set hard.

'That was his one and only time trying cotton candy,' she says tightly. 'And I wasn't there to see it. And that red car was his pride and joy, right up until he died. He wouldn't go to bed without it being on the pillow beside him. But Nick was the one who was with him when he chose it and Nick was the only one who got to give him cotton candy.'

'Do you resent him for being there at moments in Ben's life when you weren't?'

'It should have been me,' she cries. 'I should have been there with him, sharing every single second with him, sharing his joy and excitement as he experienced new things . . .'

'Perhaps that's how Nick feels too?' I chance. 'Maybe he's holding in his own bitterness at what he missed out on whilst Ben was with *you*. Could you not share those experiences? Open yourselves up and embrace the memories rather than tally up who was there at the time and use it against each other.'

'It's too late for that now,' she says. 'We've gone past that point. We're slowly destroying each other. The only thing keeping me there is the children.'

I immediately think of the misery Jacob endured for fear that it would destroy his relationship with his children. But sometimes the damage caused by staying is far greater.

'It might not always be best for the children,' I moot. 'To stay in a toxic relationship.'

'Where else would I go?' she asks, looking at me, wide-eyed.

'I can help you find a place to stay, somewhere you and the children will feel safe.'

'Like a hostel, you mean?'

I nod.

She looks at me sceptically. 'I can't go to one of those women's refuges,' she says. 'As much as I hate being with him, I'd rather stay than subject the children to one of those.'

'They're not quite the same as they used to be,' I say in their defence. But my mind is already racing through what else I can offer her. If I had my way, I'd give her sanctuary here. We have two spare bedrooms in the house, one set up as a home office for Leon, and the other where I keep all of Mom's stuff, having inadvertently turned it into a replica of the room I remember her having when I was a little girl.

There's a cherrywood bedstead and matching wardrobe where I keep the blouses that Aunt Meryl managed to salvage from my mother's closet, and her red-starred sneakers that I'd refused to leave the house without. And I'd found a vintage bedspread in a flea market in Ramsgate that reminded me of the floral quilt my sister and I used to sneak under whenever we wanted 'cuddles with Mom'.

Just the thought of it hurts, the memory of my mother's comfort and assurance still so close to the surface.

I cough, batting away the tug at the back of my throat, and pull myself back to Anna.

'But we've got other options,' I go on. 'There's always the possibility of you staying here for a couple of days – just until you sort yourself out.'

It's out before I can stop it. *Shit*. I can already see the look on Leon's face when I tell him. The look that says I've finally lost my mind.

'I can't possibly expect you to get involved,' she says. 'The last thing you need is me and my kids camping out on your doorstep.' She attempts a smile. 'Especially when you've got children of your own, no doubt?'

'No, I haven't actually,' I say, feeling like I always do when posed with this seemingly acceptable, yet searingly personal question. I should be able to leave it there, yet I feel expected to elaborate. 'We've chosen not to have children.'

'Oh,' says Anna, in the same way that everyone else does when faced with this response. 'Well, I'm sure your husband could do without us destroying your peace and quiet.'

I offer a tight smile. 'He'd be delighted to help out in any way he could.'

'That's very kind,' she says. 'It certainly gives me something to think about.'

'Well, you know where I am if you need me. I'm happy to help, night or day.'

She smiles ruefully. 'I wish I was back there,' she says, getting up from the sofa and slinging her handbag onto her shoulder.

I follow her gaze to the picture of New York she'd bought me. Perhaps she thought I was homesick. I didn't have the heart to say I couldn't feel any less homesick if I tried. Even in all its beauty, the Manhattan skyline stacked up against the banks of the Hudson River evokes nothing but bad memories, so I'd discreetly hung it behind me.

'I thought you'd put it over there,' she says, pointing to the opposite wall. 'So that you could see it all the time.'

'I know what a wonderful place it is,' I say, attempting to laugh. 'So I thought my clients might want to look at it.'

'Don't you ever wish you were back there?' she says, her eyes alight.

'Sometimes,' I lie.

My phone vibrates on my desk and I give it a cursory glance to see who's calling. A breath catches in my throat when I see Aunt Meryl's number on the screen. I FaceTime her in America at the same time every Friday evening, so if she has cause to ring me midway through a Monday, it means something's wrong.

'I'm sorry, but I need to get this,' I say to Anna.

'Of course,' she says, turning to leave. 'I'll see you next week.'

I offer a tight smile, but already my mind is with Aunt Meryl, imagining every worst possible scenario.

'Hey, Aunty,' I say, my voice already cracking. 'Everything OK?'

'Well, no, not really,' she says.

'What is it?' I ask, panicking that this might be the call I've spent my entire life dreading.

4

'I don't really know where to start. It's still just as much a shock to me as it will be for you.'

I take a sharp intake of breath. Aunt Meryl may well be seventy-six years old, but I'm no closer to being able to accept her mortality than I ever was.

'Woah, slow down,' I say, my pulse quickening. 'What's going on? What's happened?'

'Oh, darn it,' she says tearfully. I wait for her to blow her nose into the tissue she always keeps in the sleeve of her sweater. 'Your father . . .' she starts. 'Your father's been released.'

My legs immediately give way and I collapse onto the couch, as every breath that had, until just a second ago, sat deep within my lungs, is sucked out of me by an unseen force.

No, no, no.

I can't tell if I scream it out loud or if the deafening cry of anguish is in my head. That isn't possible. This can't be happening.

I blindly stab at my phone, my trembling fingers typing words that don't exist, before Google eventually recognizes enough to take me to the Federal Bureau's website.

I don't know why I'm doing it because I *know* that my father is still incarcerated in Upstate New York.

Just typing his name into the Inmate Locator makes me feel sick. I trail a finger across the screen, expecting to see Green Haven under Current Location – as it's been every time I've checked over the past twenty-six years. But it's not there. My eyes blur and lose focus on the word that's replaced it.

Released.

I blink furiously, in an effort to shock my pupils into only seeing what's there instead of the morose prank they're trying to play on me. Taking a deep breath, I squint along the line, careful not to cross into another inmate, but it still says *Released.*

'Naomi, honey, are you there?' asks Aunt Meryl, through the clouds of cotton wool that my head feels encased in.

I draw my legs up onto the couch and rest my head upon my knees, trying so desperately hard not to cry. If I allow the floodgates to open, they'll never close again.

'How . . . how did you . . .' I mumble.

'Your sister's been to see me,' she says.

My heartbeat stills in my chest. That wasn't what I was expecting. '*Jennifer?*' I ask, as if I have more than one sibling.

I picture the little blonde girl with ruddy cheeks who I'd last seen as I tucked her into bed in our foster home

50

a couple of months after our mother's death. Her eyes had grown heavy as I read her a bedtime story, desperate to play mom because I was the nearest she'd ever have.

'You'll still be here tomorrow, won't you?' she asked, like she did every night, just before she fell asleep.

'I'll never leave you,' I'd promised as I stroked her hair.

The very next morning, she'd gone, with only the pink bunny rabbit she couldn't be without left on her pillow. I was terrified that she'd screamed for me as she was dragged away, and that I had been in too deep a slumber to hear her.

'She's gone to her forever home,' my carer told me casually over breakfast.

'But why haven't I gone with her?' I asked.

'You'll *never* find a forever home,' she'd said cruelly. 'Nobody wants a thirteen-year-old.'

And she was right, as after being in the system for over a year, I was still being passed from pillar to post. If it hadn't been for Aunt Meryl taking me in, just as soon as she recovered from the stroke that she swears my father had caused by snuffing out her baby sister's life so violently, I dread to think what would have become of me.

It was too late to save Jennifer though.

Just as soon as I was old enough, I immediately set about trying to find her, desperate to have my sister back with me, where she belonged. But every door I knocked on was slammed noisily in my face. 'She's a minor.' 'She's happy and settled.' 'She has all the family she needs,' were the resounding words of social services.

So why did she turn up at Aunt Meryl's as soon as she turned eighteen to find the family she'd lost?

By then, my 'happy and settled' sister had become a drug addict, who had left her adoptive home and was in and out of trouble with the law. She was also looking for someone to blame.

'She abandoned me,' she'd spat, when Aunt Meryl told her I had gone to live in England. 'She promised she would never leave me then, and now she's done it all over again.'

Could she not see I had my own demons that I needed to silence? That I'd had no choice but to get away from the grief and shame that clouded my every moment in New York. Grief for the mother and sister I'd loved and lost. Shame that I'd not been able to save them.

Yet despite all that, I'd gotten on the first plane back home, desperate to be reunited with her. By then though, she'd disappeared into the black abyss of the subway system and every time I got close to her, she'd slip through my grasp.

Aunt Meryl had given her my email address, and every week I wondered if she would ever reach out. And just when I'd convinced myself I'd never see that little girl again, a note popped into my inbox, telling me that she had to come to England because she needed to be with me. I didn't have to be told twice. I wired five hundred dollars to the account she quoted and waited at Heathrow airport for her flight to land. But to my surprise, though I imagine not to anyone else's, she was nowhere to be seen and I haven't heard from her in almost fifteen years. But as much as it hurt, I've made my peace with it, because it gave me closure on my past. At least it had, until now.

'How . . . how is she?' I ask.

'Oh, *so* much better,' says Aunt Meryl. 'She's not long out of rehab and looks really well. She's got herself a job too – it looks like she's finally turned her life around.'

I want to believe her, but there's a nagging doubt that's pulling me back. 'Where is she now?' I ask.

'She's back out on Long Island,' she says. 'She's got herself a condo, just a rental, but it's a start.'

I couldn't ever imagine going back to where it all happened. I'd rather be *anywhere* than there. *Even the metro system?* I ask myself.

'She was asking about you,' Aunt Meryl goes on.

That's what I feared, though I don't know if I'm more frightened of the past or the present. 'I can't go through that again,' I say.

'I know how disappointed you were, sweetheart, but I really do think it will be different this time.'

'Has she seen him?' I ask, unable to say his name.

'Yes,' says Aunt Meryl.

Hot, angry tears instantly jump to my eyes at the

thought of my vulnerable sister and manipulative father together. I imagine her sitting opposite him in a booth at Daisy Gray's, open-mouthed as he tells her his version of what really happened that night. What would she make of the lies he'll tell her I told the judge? How would she feel if he tells her it was my fault we went into care and if it weren't for me she'd have lived a very different life? She hates me enough already and with a little help from him, she'll hate me even more.

'She thinks he's paid his penance,' says Aunt Meryl, her words only adding to my spiralling despair.

'And what do *you* think?' I dare to ask.

There's a heavy sigh at the end of the line. 'I so want to try and forgive him. You and I both know how exhausting it's been to hold on to the anger and rage for all this time.'

And hatred and grief, I want to add. *And all the other emotions you experience when your father kills his wife; a sister to Meryl and a mother to me.*

'So *have* you?' I force myself to ask.

'Have I what?'

'Have you forgiven him?'

'He sounds like he's a very different person to the one who went into prison,' she says, and in that instant, so too is Aunt Meryl. No longer is she my advocate; our combined force for good, who protested on the streets of New York, bearing placards with the slogans *Stop Violence Against Women* and *Love Shouldn't Hurt*.

While I've been fantasizing about avenging my mother's death, she's been practising forgiveness for the very man who caused it.

'She wants to see you,' Aunt Meryl goes on, as I do all that I can to shut out what she's saying. 'She knows how much she hurt you last time and she wants to start building bridges.'

My insides feel as if they're being twisted, tying me up into tight knots. Whilst there was a time, not so long ago, when that would have been what I'd wanted, more than anything else in the world, now I can't help but wonder what her motivation is. Is she looking for sisterly love? Or is she looking for revenge?

'Have you told her where I am?' I ask, unable to stop the involuntary shiver that runs through me.

'Well . . .' she starts, coughing to clear her throat; a sign I've long since known precedes an awkward truth. 'She wanted to know how you were and what you were doing with your life.'

I swallow the bitter taste that is beginning to sour my mouth.

'I told her that you were doing really well in England and that she'd be proud of everything you've achieved.'

'So you haven't given her my number or address?' I ask, though why it suddenly bothers me, I don't know. I used to give my contact details to literally anyone on the street, if it meant there was a chance of them being passed on to her. *She's your sister, for Christ's sake*, I say to myself, in an attempt to assuage the inexplicable panic that's rising in my chest.

'I would never give your personal information out to anyone without asking you first,' says Aunt Meryl.

My breathing steadies as the image of Jennifer striding through Heathrow airport, looking to avenge the misery I've bestowed on her life, fades away.

'But she did ask to see a photo of you,' she says. 'Apparently not a day has gone by when she hasn't imagined what you look like.'

Her and me both. Even when I thought she was thousands of miles away, it hadn't stopped me from eyeballing every woman I saw, wondering if I'd be able to recognize the little girl she once was.

'So you showed her one?' I ask, as anxiety flutters its wings again.

'Only the newspaper cutting you sent me about your award,' says Aunt Meryl. 'I wanted her to see how well you've done and how far you've come.'

I pull myself off the couch to look at the same clipping that hangs proudly in a frame on my office wall. My smile is wide as I stand beside the President of the British Psychological Society, with both our hands clutching my red-stamped certificate for my outstanding contribution to clinical psychology.

I was as happy as I could ever remember being in that yellow dress, which I'd found in a vintage shop in Tunbridge Wells, knowing that Leon was just to the side of the camera, the pair of us eager to get out of the stuffy surroundings of the assembly hall and into a pub garden.

I'd finally escaped my past; stepped out from underneath the black cloud that had shrouded so much of my life, and into the sunshine. How could I possibly have known that that moment might prove to be my downfall all these years later?

I could pretend that it's impossible to see the calligraphy on the certificate that says the award is presented to Naomi Chandler. That the writing is too fancy to be able to read that my practice is called Chandler Associates. That you'd need to be Einstein to be able to then search for my website that gives my Tattenhall address.

As Aunt Meryl's faux pas resonates and the recriminations evolve in my head, each more terrifying than the last, my body folds in on itself. I hold on to my desk to steady myself, forcing breaths in and out of my lungs.

'I'm sorry,' says Aunt Meryl, blithely unaware of exactly how grave her error of judgement may have been. 'I couldn't see that it would do any harm.'

You have no idea, I think to myself, but say, 'It's fine, I've got to go,' instead.

'OK, Angel,' she says. 'I'll speak to you soon.'

5

I always know when I'm feeling insecure by what I eat – it's called comfort eating for a reason – and I'm halfway through making meatloaf before I even realize what I'm doing. I chop an onion whilst trying to dislodge the fear that my father and sister have formed an alliance to wreak revenge. I crack an egg whilst imagining one or both of them in my office this morning and the next thing I know, I'm knuckle-deep in mince, whilst desperately trying to stop my over-active imagination from running away with me. Though there's no denying that the door was open, a dead bird lay on the threshold, and at least one client's file is missing.

I will myself to stay calm, telling the part of me that's prepared to listen that this is crazy. After being inside for a quarter of a century, the last thing my father's going to want to do is waste the precious time he's got left coming after me.

I can't remember the last time I made my mother's signature dish, but just the smell of the sage and mustard takes me back to sitting around the dinner table in our Colonial out on Long Island.

When I was younger, when I thought the only nutrition

I needed came in the form of Twinkies and peanut butter sandwiches, my father would make me sit at that table until I'd eaten all my greens.

Looking back, I'm sure I only ever had four mouthfuls to endure before I could get down and go and join my cabbage-loving sister in the yard. But at the time, it felt like an eternity, and I would retch and gag whilst my father kept a watchful eye on any scraps I was managing to feed the dog.

It shouldn't be a memory that reassures me when I feel unassured, yet just the thought of the four of us being together, before our world was blown apart, wraps itself around me like a weighted blanket.

I'm still kneading the mixture when the shrill ring of my phone transports me out of my childhood home and back into the one I sometimes still don't feel grown-up enough to live in.

I brace myself for Aunt Meryl, having remembered to tell me something else I don't want to know. But as I quickly rinse my hands and take the tea towel across to the island where my phone is charging, I'm surprised and mildly alarmed to see Jacob's number flashing incessantly on the screen.

For a split second, I consider not answering it. And perhaps, if Leon were here, I wouldn't feel able to, but Jacob and I have already crossed into a more personal relationship and I can't expect the blurred lines to come into sharp focus whenever it doesn't suit me, or Leon.

'Jacob?' I answer, my voice heavy with concern.

There's a frantic intake of breath at the other end as if he'd resigned himself to me not picking up. 'She knows,' he blurts out. 'She knows where I am.'

'*What?*' I ask, though why, I don't know. I understand exactly what he's saying and it chills me to the bone. 'How? How can she?'

'I . . . I don't know,' he stutters. 'She just does . . . she's called me and . . .' His voice tails off.

'Jacob?' I ask frantically. 'Jacob, are you still there?'

'Y-yeah, but how the hell . . . ? I mean, I've been so careful. There's no way she could have . . . if she knows, then . . . I don't know . . . she'll . . . I don't know what she'll do.' He's rambling and becoming more incoherent with every syllable.

'OK, try to stay calm and tell me what's happened,' I say, in an effort to get him to take a breath.

The sudden intake of air sounds like it's disguising a sob.

'Jacob, it's going to be OK,' I say gently. 'Just tell me what's happened.'

'Sh-she called me,' he says. 'About ten minutes ago, and said that she knew where I was and was going to come for me.'

'OK, where are you now?' I ask, praying that he has had the wherewithal to get away from the apartment.

'I don't know,' he says. 'I'm just walking around. I don't know what to do.'

'Listen to me,' I say, going into the hall and picking up my purse and keys from the console table. 'Can you get a taxi to the Royal Garden hotel in Canterbury?'

'Y-yes,' he says, hesitantly. 'I can get an Uber.'

'No!' I snap, more abruptly than I mean to. 'If she has access to your Uber account, she'll be able to see where you are and where you're going.' I grab my leather jacket from the newel post of the banister and shrug it on. 'Call a cab and I'll meet you there.'

A dampness has formed under my arms by the time I've parked the car and am striding along the high street. I briefly wonder about calling the police, but then almost as quickly, I ask myself what they'd be able to do in this situation. Jacob's wife hasn't done anything. *Yet.*

I'm waiting outside the hotel entrance when a white Vauxhall pulls up and Jacob almost falls out of it. It's as if his wife is in there, quite literally kicking him to the kerb. His face is ashen, and as I take his arm and guide him through the revolving doors and into the lobby, I can feel his whole body trembling.

I tense up as I look around the bustling reception, wondering if I'll see Andy, my old boss, or any of my other former colleagues from when I used to work here as a receptionist. I can't help but wonder if I'm not also keeping half an eye out for a woman I won't be able to recognize.

There's an attractive blonde talking to the concierge and I manage to convince myself that it might be Jacob's wife. That she's somehow beaten us here. It's ridiculous, I know, but still I quicken my step and manhandle Jacob towards the bar, where I know a whisky will settle his nerves.

'So, what else did she say?' I ask, as I head for the far end of the bar, out of view of the doorway. 'Did she say anything specific about your whereabouts? Did she threaten you in any way?'

He forces a laugh. 'She doesn't need to say much for me to know what she actually means.'

'But perhaps she was calling your bluff,' I offer. 'She might not know where you live. She might have just said it to intimidate you.'

He looks at me as if I'm a child who hasn't grasped something they've already been told a million times. 'She has my phone number,' he says bluntly. 'If she's been able to get hold of that, then she would have been able to find out where I live.'

'Yes, but . . .' I start before trailing off, at a loss for words for once.

His eyes flit around the room like a cornered wild animal, assessing the risks and trusting no one. 'And besides, Vanessa isn't in the habit of bluffing,' he says eventually. 'She tends to follow through.'

It's the first time that he's mentioned his wife by name – only ever having previously referred to 'her' or 'she' – and, now that she has a name, I can picture her more easily.

I imagine how they would have looked when they were a couple; a supposedly happy couple. Jacob with his dark hair flopping down over his blue eyes, and a dimpled school-boy grin that spreads wide across his face. Vanessa, elegant, serene, with highlighted hair piled on top of her head; a thin-lipped, contained smile, giving her a distinguished air that she clearly doesn't deserve.

Despite my better judgement, I order a whisky for each of us and the first swig burns the back of my throat, but the potent liquid instantly desensitizes my jangling nerve endings. Or maybe I've just watched too many movies and am imagining it.

'So, what am I going to do?' asks Jacob, grimacing, after downing his in one hit.

'Well, you obviously can't go back to the apartment,' I say. 'You're going to have to stay here, at least for tonight, until we work out a way around this.'

He surreptitiously signals to the barman for another and raises his eyebrows at me in question.

'No, thanks,' I say. 'Not for me.'

'Something else then?' asks Jacob.

I look at my watch, though I don't know why. I have nowhere to go and nowhere to be, but being here doesn't sit easy either. Not that I'm doing anything wrong – I'm just having a drink with a friend in need, but I already know I won't be able to tell Leon about this, so perhaps I am?

'I'll have a gin and tonic,' I say, without meaning to.

Clearly my brain's not telling my mouth the right thing to say.

'How the hell could she have found out where I live?' he muses, as we both watch the barman slice a sliver of cucumber into a fishbowl glass. 'I couldn't have been any more careful.'

I shudder as I remember the open door of my office this morning and Jacob's missing file. I honestly can't remember what information might be in there – would I have mentioned the apartment? Noted the moving date? Jotted down his new telephone number? Could I have handed such sensitive information to his estranged wife on a plate?

'Is there any way she could have known you were seeing me?' I ask, whilst keeping everything crossed that he shoots even the mere suggestion down in flames.

'Absolutely not,' he says, before sinking another whisky. 'I quite literally went out of my way whenever I came to see you. And still checked behind me at every step.'

'And there's no way she could have found out from your old school where your new job was and followed you home from there?'

He shakes his head vehemently. 'I didn't tell anyone where I was going. I've treated this whole thing like a military operation because I was so terrified I was going to leave myself open . . . to this.' He looks at me and I feel unnerved, troubled that he's gone to such lengths, only for me and my security lapse to undo all his efforts.

'I left home and my job on the same day,' he goes on. 'She wouldn't have known it was coming, so wouldn't have had a chance to track me.'

'What about if someone from your new school recognizes you? It would only take an old colleague or friend from the past to have called her.'

He gives me a look that suggests I'm grasping at straws. He's not wrong.

'Can I get another?' he says, signalling to the bartender.

'I guess the issue is less about how she found you than what you're going to do about it,' I say, still nursing my gin and tonic.

He rubs at his eyes and slams a clenched fist down on the bar in frustration. The woman on the stool next to him turns with a look of concern etched on her face. I offer a smile to assure her that all is well.

I instinctively go to cover his hand with mine; a silent but staunch reminder that I am here for him. But just as our skin touches, I recoil, afraid that this crosses the invisible line between doing right by my client and helping a friend in need. I ignore the very real possibility that the simple action traverses even the most forgiving of boundaries.

But he catches my hand as I pull away and holds on to it as he looks at me. 'I'm sorry to have dragged you into this mess,' he says, offering the weakest of smiles. 'But I couldn't have done this without you.'

I attempt to make my hand my own again, but he

links his fingers through mine; an act so intimate that it feels as if he's undressing me. I try to convince myself that it's just a heartfelt gesture of gratitude, but as I survey the pair of us through an onlooker's gaze, say that of the woman next to us, for example, all I can see are two star-crossed lovers, revelling in the forbidden time they've managed to carve out for themselves.

I know that if I walked in on Leon and a woman in a hotel bar in such a compromising position, I'd be forced to accept that they were in an intimate relationship.

The sickening realization makes me yank my hand away and Jacob looks as if he's been given an electric shock.

'I should get going,' I say, standing up and taking my jacket off the back of the stool.

'I'm sorry,' he says. 'I didn't mean to make you feel uncomfortable.'

'You didn't,' I say nonchalantly. 'But I should be getting home as Leon's due back anytime now.' I don't know why I feel the need to lie.

'Please stay and finish your drink,' he says. 'I don't want to be on my own just yet.'

I chastise myself for allowing the moment to cloud my judgement. To forget that here in front of me is a broken man, who has been brave enough to leave his home and his job, because that's what it took to free himself from his abusive wife. He will *always* be looking over his shoulder, waiting for her to come and claim what she believes is rightfully hers. It's my fault for taking his need for reassurance as an inappropriate show of affection – not his. I can't help but wonder if it isn't also my fault that we've found ourselves sitting at this bar in the first place.

I smile and sit back down. 'So you'll stay here tonight?' I ask.

He nods miserably as he puts his empty glass onto the varnished mahogany of the bar top.

'Another?' asks the ever-attentive barman. I want to say no on Jacob's behalf, knowing that drowning his sorrows in the bottom of a whisky bottle is probably the last thing he should be doing. But he's a grown man who is in the pits of despair right now, not to mention in fear of his life, and the last thing he needs is another woman telling him what he can and can't do.

Jacob pushes his cut-glass tumbler towards the man in answer and, with his elbows on the bar, runs his hands through his hair and groans.

'It's going to be all right,' I say, careful to keep a physical distance. 'You'll get through this.'

He laughs sardonically. 'Unless my wife kills me first.'

I shiver, as if someone has walked over my grave.

'If you'd asked me as a twenty-one-year-old man whether I was ever going to be in this position – *allow* myself to be in this position – I would have laughed at you.'

'None of us know what life has got planned for us,' I say. 'We're all going in blind.'

He nods ruefully and his jaw clenches.

I don't want to ask the question, but I need to know what we're dealing with here.

'What do you think your wife is really capable of?' I chance.

'If she finds me?'

I nod, steeling myself for the answer I fear is to come.

'She'll kill me,' he says, without skipping a beat.

'So, don't you think it's time you went to the police?' I ask. 'Now that she's threatened you by saying she knows where you live.'

'Do you honestly think they'll take me seriously?' he asks. It's a rhetorical question. 'I'm six foot and fourteen stone. I don't look like someone who gets pushed around by their wife.'

'What does that person look like then?' I argue. 'Do you honestly think they'll not know that abused partners come in all shapes and sizes? That it's men like you who have to exert even more control because you know the physical power you can wield?'

He shakes his head. 'They'd laugh at me,' he says. 'It's a run-of-the mill domestic as far as they're concerned, and since when have they ever done anything to help victims of domestic abuse?'

'Things have changed,' I say. 'They're much more

aware of all the various guises domestic abuse comes in now and they take it pretty seriously.'

'If I was going to get them involved, I would have done it when the kids were younger and I was still there. There's no point doing it now that I've left.'

'But you're still in danger,' I say. 'She's still hounding you, still threatening you.'

'Can we not talk about her?' he says, sounding exasperated. 'For just a second?'

I look at him, wondering what else we'd talk about if not her. It's always been her; that's what he pays me for.

But he's not paying you now, is he? asks the voice in my head.

'What about you?' he asks, making anxious butterflies flutter in my chest. 'You know everything about me, there's no stone unturned, yet I know absolutely nothing about you, aside from that you're married to Leon. Tell me about you.'

My mouth dries up and my heartbeat quickens as the four words reverberate around my head. *Tell me about you.*

I remember going to interviews for various secretarial jobs when I left college, and all the time I was able to tell the prospective employer about the things I could do for them; my typing speed of seventy words per minute, the benefit of shorthand in a world which had rendered it obsolete, and my ability to work well within a team. I was able to wax lyrical. But the nail in the coffin would always be the excruciating pause that followed the question, *Tell me about yourself.*

You would have thought I'd have perfected a polished response over time. Been able to spin a yarn about my idyllic upbringing, living with my parents and little sister out on Long Island. Going to the local high school and excelling in Math and English. Wanting to be a professor of medicine because that's what my mother had always dreamt of being, and I so wanted to make her proud.

But that's where my story faltered because I knew what was coming. I'd start to stutter, trip over my well-rehearsed lines, knowing that I was lying by omitting to mention the single biggest event that had shaped my life up until that point.

Maybe if I'd told them that my father was in jail, serving a life sentence, I would have got the job. At least they'd know I was honest, if nothing else. But somehow, I hadn't quite got used to sharing that particular piece of information.

Nor was I able to tell them why he was inside because then I'd never regain my composure.

So instead I invented a persona that nothing of any consequence had ever happened to, and my default position of claiming to be uninteresting has served me well over the years. Until someone like Jacob comes along.

'There's not much to tell really,' I offer.

'Oh, come on,' he says. 'You're an American woman in London, for starters – well, as good as.'

'As opposed to an Englishman in New York?' I say smiling, referring to the song that Leon loves to have blaring when he makes us pancakes on a Sunday morning. Though thinking about it now, I can't remember the last time he did that.

'Exactly,' laughs Jacob, catching on to the reference. 'That doesn't happen by accident, surely.'

I shrug my shoulders, seemingly no better prepared with a story than I was twenty years ago.

'So, what brought you over here?' he pushes, bringing me perilously close to the edge of my comfort zone.

'Leon, mainly,' I say. 'I met him in New York seventeen years ago and when he came back to England, I came with him.'

'So you fell in love and left your old life behind?' Jacob probes.

'Something like that,' I say cagily.

'He's a lucky man,' he says.

I can tell by the lengthening of his consonants and the slur of his vowels that the whisky is beginning to turn him into someone he wouldn't normally be. I've spent my life actively avoiding people like him, so I'm not going to sit here and watch as the alcohol loosens his propriety, likely setting off a chain of events we're unable to come back from.

'I really should get going,' I say, stepping off my bar stool. 'He'll be wondering where I am.'

'Stay,' says Jacob, his mouth close to my ear.

Despite myself, my nerve endings catch fire, making my fingertips tingle. 'I . . . can't,' I say, unable to believe how difficult it is to refuse his request. 'I really can't.'

'Please,' he begs, his blue eyes boring into mine. 'Stay with me tonight.'

The way he says it and looks at me leaves no room for doubt. I cough as I struggle to compose myself, stalling for time.

'It wouldn't be a good idea,' I say, though I can't help but wonder what it would be like if I did. I imagine his fingers trailing down my cheek before he gently kisses my neck; his soft beard setting my skin alight.

The thought of showing him how sex is supposed to feel, rather than the torturous ordeal he's grown accustomed to, makes me giddy with delirium. I picture my hand on his as I gently guide him to where it needs to be. I can see the look on his face as he realizes for the first time how it feels to make love for the pure joy of it, without recrimination or punishment.

'Just for a little while,' he says, as his fingers intertwine with mine, sending a pulse of electricity through me. 'I just want to hold you.'

The hairs on the back of my neck stand on end and butterflies wait to take flight in my stomach at the first sign of me changing my mind. It used to feel like this with Leon, in the beginning, when we were still exploring each other. I'd wanted to bottle that spine-tingling sense of anticipation, desperate to cling on to it once the newness had worn off, knowing that the months and years that followed would invariably be filled with the void of what we once had.

When had that excitement drained from our relationship? When had we lost that spontaneity? Had it happened overnight? Leaving behind the depressing possibility that the only way we could relight a flame inside ourselves was by meeting someone new. Someone like Jacob.

'I'm married,' I say, as if it's the only reason I'm turning him down. Though now I think of it, I can't come up with another.

'I'm not asking you to do anything to jeopardize that,' he says. 'I just don't want to be alone right now.'

'Jacob, I—'

'I think I'm falling in love with you,' he blurts out, as if saying it faster will lessen the gravitas of his admission.

I look at him and a switch flips in my head, though I can't help but flinch that it's my reputation rather than my marriage that has made me see the light. I pull myself up, standing tall in the hope that he can see me for who I am, rather than the saviour he's made me out to be. 'Listen, I know that's how it might feel at this moment in time,' I say. 'But you're just out of an abusive relationship and you're looking for someone to make you feel safe again.'

'You do that,' he says. 'I can be myself with you.'

'But you'll feel that way with lots of people once you leave behind the scars of your marriage.'

He shakes his head.

'Believe me,' I say, taking his hand in mine. 'You're a good man, with so much to offer the right woman. But don't confuse our relationship for anything more than what it is. I'm your therapist who is helping you out in your time of need.' The words sound brutal on my tongue, but sometimes you have to be cruel to be kind.

'So all this time you've been leading me on to appease your ego?'

'What?' I say, aghast. 'Of course not. I—'

'The way you look at me, the things you say . . .'

'If I have ever given you cause to think there was more to this than a professional relationship, then I am truly sorry.'

He buries his head in his hands and laughs cynically. 'There's a name for women like you.'

'Don't,' I warn. 'That's not fair.'

'You've led me on and left me high and dry,' he says, getting up from his stool and pushing it back.

'Is everything OK here?' asks the barman, reading the palpable juxtaposition of our body language.

'Fine,' I say, tightly.

'Piss off then,' says Jacob, throwing a hand in the direction of the door.

'Jacob, please.'

'I don't need your pity,' he slurs. 'I don't need you to feel sorry for me.'

'I don't,' I say, desperate to stop the pendulum swinging between one extreme and another. 'I'm proud of you, there's a difference. I'm proud of everything you've achieved and everything I know you're still to achieve.'

'I thought you liked me,' he says.

'I do.' I dare to go towards him. 'But not like that, and in time you'll meet someone who you really care for and realize that whatever feelings you had for me were superficial.'

He looks at me sadly. 'But this feels different.'

'Anything will feel different after the relationship you've just come out of,' I say. 'But give yourself some time and space to be alone and work out what you want.' I smile at him cautiously.

'I'm sorry,' he says, falling back onto the stool and putting his head in his hands on the bar. 'I'm a little out of practice.'

'It's not a problem,' I say, as I shrug on my leather jacket.

'Can I still come and see you on Wednesday?'

'Of course, but I won't take your money if you're going to spend the hour imagining a relationship we don't have.'

'I've made a real fool of myself, haven't I?' he says.

'You've nothing to be embarrassed about. I'll see you on Wednesday.'

'Can I call you if I hear from Vanessa again?' he asks.

I go to say yes, but I shouldn't give him any more reason to think this is something that it isn't. 'If she contacts you and threatens you in any way, you need to call the police.'

He nods, but I can't help but wonder if I'll have cause to ring the police before he does.

6

My brain is still running over the day's events as I turn in through the gates of Tattenhall, the nerve endings sparking off each other as I weigh up how much danger both Jacob and I are realistically in. Him from the wife he has dared to leave. Me from the people I'd once called family.

I choose to push aside the added complication of what has just happened between us, knowing that if I acknowledge his misplaced perception of what we shared, I will also have to accept the role I've played in encouraging it.

I should never have gone. I should have left when he was two drinks in, knowing the effect whisky has on the brain. I should have known that the fourth was likely to have impaired his judgement. The man I've just left isn't the man Jacob is. Alcohol can turn you into someone you're not. Just look at my father.

Flames are flickering in the lanterns that hang from the flint pillars either side of the entrance and, as I drive onto the estate, with the gravel crunching under my tyres, I still can't get my head around the fact that we actually get to call this place home.

Both Leon and I had long been fascinated by the estate, so living deep within the grounds was a dream come true. And for the first month or two, it felt like the novelty would never wear off. Yet now, although we've never been so physically close to one another, it feels as if we've never been further apart.

I need to tell him about my father, but he's only ever known half the story and now is not the time to burden him with the rest.

The long driveway is eerily quiet, and the only light is coming from the crescent moon reflected in the glass-like water of the boating lake. I can't even begin to imagine how different it will feel in just a few days' time when the grounds will be teeming with thousands of people, who will all, no doubt, pretend to be Lord or Lady of the manor for the afternoon.

As the main house looms into view, its turrets shrouded in a soft light against the dark sky, I wonder what Earl Tatten is doing in there. With no family of his own, the silence amongst its fifty or so rooms, each more imposing than the last, must be deafening.

The word amongst the staff is that he only lives between two rooms in the attic, never coming down and rarely receiving visitors. Even Leon, who is employed directly by him, has only met him twice; once at the interview and again to discuss his intentions for the summer concert. Both of which were conducted in his surprisingly compact living room on the top floor.

By all accounts he's a very pleasant man, and Leon hazards a guess that his frugal lifestyle is more about keeping the running costs under control in the rest of the house than a weird, reclusive personality. Because owning and maintaining a stately home is a very expensive business, and the Earl is either fast running out of cash, or he's suddenly become aware of the commercial opportunities that he would do well to exploit. That's why he's opening up the grounds to the paying public for Tattenhall's first concert on Saturday, and that's why he has submitted architects' plans to convert the stables on the far side of the estate into five cottages which, with the renovation of the tennis courts and the old swimming pool, will make for an incredible holiday rental. Leon has been brought in to oversee all of this.

I'm consumed by a sudden burst of pride and instead of following the drive round to the right towards the cottage, I take the left-hand fork, going around the back of the main house. There, down in the dip, towards the far perimeter of the estate, is the metal structure that is being erected to stage the twenty-five-piece orchestra that'll be entertaining us on Saturday.

As I sit and watch the crew working under the floodlights, I feel terribly guilty, and wonder if I've given Leon the credit he deserves. He's had so much on his plate recently and there's no doubt that this event, if it's as successful as he hopes, will be the highlight of his career.

I should be working *with* him instead of against him,

and as I pull away and drive to the cottage, I promise both him and myself that as soon as this weekend is out of the way, I'll sit down and tell him everything.

I'm still thinking about how best to approach it, when I look up to see the dimmest of glows creeping out from around the closed curtains in our bedroom. I turn the engine off and sit unmoving with my heart in my mouth, knowing that I had neither drawn the curtains nor left a light on before leaving.

Whilst admittedly I went out in a rush, it had still been light outside, and I don't even think I'd gone upstairs. I look down to check I hadn't changed between work and making dinner. No, I'm still wearing black trousers and my Paul Smith cherry-print blouse, though my sling-back heels have been replaced with a pair of ballerina pumps. Were they upstairs or had they been lying by the front door on the hall floor? I'd bet everything I had on the latter, so why then is our bedroom light on?

I force myself to put one foot in front of the other, edging ever closer to the flint cottage with the blue front door. As much as I love this house, I suddenly wish I didn't live here. I consider calling Leon, just for reassurance, but since when did I become the woman who calls her husband to ask if he left a light on?

I check the side gate as if it's something I do every night, and I pretend not to look for unwelcome footprints on the black-and-white chequered porch tiles.

Nothing seems to be amiss, yet it still feels like I'm letting myself into someone else's house, silently turning the key in the lock so as not to disturb whoever's in here and then waiting, tense and rigid as I listen for movement. It occurs to me as I stand here on the parquet wooden floor whether it might be best to make as much noise as I can, giving anyone who might be in the house a chance to escape unchallenged. Because by the time I get to the top of the stairs, there's going to be nowhere else for them to go apart from through me, and I'm assuming neither of us want that.

I walk down the hallway into the kitchen and clunk and clatter my way around the room, opening and closing cupboards, banging saucepans against each other and rattling the cutlery drawer. I eye the carving knife and find myself wrapping my fingers around the handle without even realizing what I'm doing. This is ridiculous. I'm allowing a whole load of nothing to turn my normally calm mind into a chaotic frenzy of suspicion and fear.

Leaning against the countertop, where I can still see the bottom of the stairs, I force myself to take a deep breath and get some perspective. I know, if I think about it logically, that what feels like a personal vendetta right now is just as likely to be a series of tenuous coincidences and absentmindedness on my part. I wish I could convince myself that I'd imagined Aunt Meryl's phone call though.

The faintest creak comes from overhead and I instinctively look up to the ceiling, though what I'm expecting to see, I don't know. My eyes follow what sounds like footfall as the wooden joists bow and sag under the weight.

An image of the woman I now know as Vanessa comes into sharp focus. Because it's a lot easier to imagine that the intruder is her than my sister, who I last saw as a little girl in New York. But the glossy mane of golden hair I imagine Vanessa taking such care of when Jacob was under her control is now a dirty blonde, dishevelled mess. Her perfectly made-up eyes are now red-rimmed and circled by the dark shadows of sleepless nights. And her normally manicured and polished Rouge Noir fingernails have been gnawed to the quick in a fit of pique.

Having gotten to know her via her brow-beaten husband, I realize that Vanessa is not going to think for one minute that Jacob's leaving is anything to do with her. She's not the type to take the blame or accept responsibility for any part she may have played. This will all be Jacob's fault and, if she knows about me, mine, for encouraging him to stand up for himself and leave the woman who's made his life a misery for the past ten years.

Is that why she's here? I wonder. To take me to task for giving Jacob a lifeline? Or is she here because she knows I know where he is? I shudder to think what she might do to make me confess.

My breath catches in my throat as I hear very definite

footsteps coming down the stairs and I reach for the carving knife again. I don't know whether to hide and hope that she just lets herself out, or confront her and deal with the consequences – whatever they may be.

I opt for somewhere between the two and move to stand behind the fridge, with my closed fist raised to chest level, ready to pounce with the blade if I need to. My lungs feel like the air is being forced in and out of them through a tiny pinprick of a hole, and my heart hammers through my chest, its deafening beat reverberating in my head.

I remember this feeling from when I was a child and my father would count to a hundred out loud as my sister and I scurried around the house, frantically searching for somewhere to hide, bumping into each other and arguing over the best place to take cover. I'd invariably end up lying down in the cold cast-iron bath, desperately trying to quell the tightening in my chest and the pounding in my ears. Yet despite my discomfort, I'd still beg to do it again. Though I can't imagine I'll be looking to repeat this grown-up version of hide and seek anytime soon.

The footsteps are getting nearer and I suck my breath in as I feel someone's presence at the threshold to the kitchen. I push myself up against the fridge, desperately trying to make myself smaller and less visible.

'Naomi?' comes a voice, and I almost slide down to the floor with relief.

Leon.

He furrows his brow as he turns the corner to see me breathless and holding a knife at chest height.

'What the hell . . . ?' he starts.

'Oh, thank God,' I wheeze, the breaths I've been holding in all rushing to get out.

'What the hell's going on?' he asks, wavering on the spot, unsure whether to approach me or back away.

'I thought . . .' I gasp. 'I thought . . .'

'You thought *what*?' he says, stepping forward to gently prise the knife from my clutched fingers.

I backtrack over the day's events, berating myself for allowing my imagination to get the better of me. I don't know whether I feel more foolish or nervous at the prospect of having to explain my irrational behaviour to Leon.

'W-what are you even doing here?' I ask, stalling. 'I thought you weren't coming home until tomorrow.'

He eyes me warily. 'The traffic was good so I decided to come straight back.'

I can feel unexpected tears spring to my eyes and I go to him, burying my face into his neck. I don't know whether it's relief or panic.

As if sensing there's more going on, he holds me away from him and looks at me earnestly. 'Are you OK?'

I nod, willing my tears not to fall. 'It's just that I saw the light on and thought someone was in the house.'

'I didn't mean to frighten you, but you're not normally this jumpy.'

'I know,' I say, looking up at him. 'I just wasn't expecting you and . . .'

'It's OK,' he says. 'I should have phoned. Where have you been anyway?'

'I, erm . . .' My brain scrambles for a legitimate alibi, but I'm so much on the back foot that it can't work quickly enough. He knows me too well to be able to scam him. 'I, erm, I went out for a drive . . .'

Leon looks at his watch. 'It's almost ten o'clock at night,' he says, with a hint of suspicion.

'Y-yes,' I stutter, feeling like I'm under a microscope, being dissected in its spotlight. I resent him for making me feel this way, but then I realize I'm doing it to myself. All I have to do is tell the truth; after all, I haven't done anything wrong. But I already know that's not how Leon will see it, otherwise I would have already told him by now.

He's still looking at me with raised eyebrows, waiting for an answer that sounds more plausible than going for a drive on a whim.

'And then,' I go on, 'I popped into Shelley's for a cup of tea.' A beat passes as I wait, with a sickening feeling in my stomach, for Leon to call me out. He knows that I would never just turn up at my friend's front door on the other side of town unannounced. Especially given that I'd spent half an hour on the phone to her last night.

Yet he lets it go, and with it the expectation for me to elaborate any further.

'So the traffic was good?' I say unnecessarily.

He takes a mug out of the cupboard and I step aside as he comes towards the fridge for the milk.

'I don't suppose you want a tea, if you've just had one?' he questions, in such a way that it makes me feel as if he has an eye into my soul.

I shake my head numbly, even though I'd like nothing more, if only to settle my nerves.

'So, how's Shelley doing?' he asks, as he drains the teabag on the side of the cup and chucks it in the bin.

'Good,' I say, feeling as if my voice box is being squeezed. 'Busy with work, but all good.'

'So the dog hamper idea has taken off?' he asks, referring to the new business she mooted in passing a few months ago.

'Yes, it seems that every pet owner wants to treat their dog.'

He nods, but every fibre in my being feels as if he's testing me and knows full well that I'm lying. I guess that's what a guilty conscience does to you.

'We should get something set up with her and Dave,' he says. 'We haven't seen them since the choir competition.'

'Mmm.' I nod. 'That would be nice.'

'How is Dave?' he asks. 'Did you see him?'

'No. So did you get everything you needed?' I ask, desperate to change the subject.

He nods sombrely.

I go up to him and tuck myself under his arms. 'I love you,' I say, feeling a complicated mixture of relief and guilt. Relief that he's home and that I don't have to spend the night alone, and guilt that I've lied, and lied again, about something I should have been able to be honest about.

I kiss him to assuage both.

'This reeks of a guilty conscience,' he says, as if reading my mind. I pull back, saddened that I'm not able to kiss him without that being his first thought.

But he's right, isn't he? Still, I swallow the insult and nuzzle his neck, reaching for him through his trousers, though I can already feel his reticence.

'Have you done something you shouldn't have?' he asks, tilting himself ever so slightly away from me.

I stop, angry that I'd fooled myself into thinking that spontaneous love-making was what we needed. I'm even angrier when he lets me walk away.

'I'm going to do some work,' I say, letting myself out of the back door, knowing that I won't be able to sleep until I work out what Jacob's wife might know and where she got her information from.

Once I'm in the office, I put the lamps on and will Jacob's case file to fly from wherever it is and slot back into its rightful place in my filing cabinet by the time I get to it. I walk painfully slowly, as if giving it every last chance to do what I so want it to.

But no matter how hard I look, it's not here. *Shit.*

If Vanessa *has* managed to find him because my security is so lax, I'll never forgive myself.

I perch on the edge of my desk, reading through my notebook, though what I'm looking for I don't know. Defeated, I take my glasses off and rub at the bridge of my nose.

'Hey,' says a voice, making me jump out of my skin.

'Jeez, will you quit scaring me?' I say, as Leon's face emerges from the darkness into the light.

'What has got into you tonight?' he says.

'Nothing,' I say, waiting for my heart rate to subside. 'I thought you'd gone to bed.'

'I had, but then something came in on my phone and I had to get my laptop, which was on the dining table . . .'

I look at him, wondering where this is going.

'And then I found this and wondered if it was what you were looking for earlier.'

He holds out a folder and raises his eyebrows.

'Oh my god,' I say, snatching it from him. 'Where did you find this?' I check inside that it's what I think it is.

'It was on the dining table,' he says. 'In full view.'

'It couldn't have been, I had the whole place upside down.'

'Well, it was there, hiding in plain sight.'

'Thank God for that,' I say, almost to myself. If Jacob's wife hasn't got the information from me, there's a greater chance that she's just calling his bluff.

'So, can you come to bed now?' he asks, coming towards me.

Even in the low lighting, I can see that his eyes have changed. Gone is the coldness of just half an hour ago, having been replaced by the softness that made me fall in love with him.

Without saying a word, he pushes me back onto my desk, sending the pen tidy crashing to the floor. He unbuttons himself before lowering himself on top of me, planting soft feathery kisses on my neck.

'Turn the lights off,' I say, as he unbuttons my blouse.

'I want to look at you,' he says, reaching underneath me to unfasten my bra.

'But someone might see . . .' I lamely protest, already abandoning myself to the tingling sensation of his tongue.

'If there's anyone out there,' he says, daring to stop, to look at the inky blackness beyond the window. 'Then they can have a ringside seat.'

7

I should have slept soundly with Leon by my side, but my night was punctuated by nightmares that had me calling out in fear. The vivid intensity of how real they felt is already fading, but I can still remember my relief at seeing my father in a prison cell in my dreams, dispelling the rumour that he'd been released. I'd walked towards him, full of bravado and satisfaction that he would never see the light of day for what he'd done. But as I drew nearer, he'd put his head through the bars, looking like Jack Nicholson in *The Shining*, and prised them apart with his bare hands.

I'd turned and run – straight into my sister, who stood there with a demonic look on her face, blocking my escape. Her eyes were black, devoid of emotion, and as she parted her lips a swarm of wasps flew out of her mouth.

I'd woken myself up with a scream and vaguely remember a hand on my shoulder, gently reassuring me, though in my warped slumber I thought it was Jacob lying beside me.

Now, I instinctively reach out across the bed, willing Leon to be there, even if just to assuage the guilt and shame coursing through my veins, making me feel as if I've done something terribly wrong. But the sheets are empty and cold.

Blinking at the sun streaming brightly through the curtains, I rub the sleep from my eyes, as I try to remember who my first client is. But I can't even work out what day it is yet, let alone who's coming to see me. I'm normally so organized and always check what I'm doing the day before, just in case I need to prepare anything, but yesterday was . . . well . . . unexpected.

Despite trying to keep my mind devoid of thought, yesterday's problems run amok as the hot water from the shower falls onto my head. With each vying for attention, I can't help but lament how this time yesterday, I had so little to worry about. I was secure in the knowledge that my father was still behind bars, that my sister was no more aware of me than she ever was, and that Jacob saw me as nothing more than his psychotherapist.

As I frenziedly lather up my hair, alternating between feeling relieved that he and I hadn't crossed the line and regretting that I'd somehow allowed him to think that we might, I can't help but wonder how he's feeling this morning. Now that the whisky has worn off, I imagine he's woken up mortified, though the evening's events will be woefully misrepresented in his mind due to the convenience of memory loss designed to save us from ourselves.

I'd half expect the man I met, before the one who

downed four whiskies in quick succession, to call today to offer his apologies. Though if he doesn't do it this morning, he'll be too embarrassed by this afternoon as his fragmented flashbacks will have begun to piece together a bigger picture.

Perhaps I should call him, so that he doesn't have to worry about that on top of everything else.

By the time I get downstairs, I've resolved to do exactly that, not just to ease his awkwardness but to check he's actually OK, which should be my primary concern.

'Do you want a coffee?' asks Leon as I walk into the kitchen.

'Oh, I thought you'd already left,' I say, moving towards the dining table where my laptop is. After the fright of yesterday, I wasn't going to chance leaving it down in the office overnight.

'I just thought I'd give myself a moment's peace,' he says. 'Because I've got a feeling the next few days are going to be a bit full-on.'

'Where exactly was that file?' I ask, oblivious to what he's just said.

'Just on the table,' he says casually, as if it means nothing. I suppose it doesn't to him.

'But I looked here,' I exclaim. 'Again and again.'

'Well, it must have been there.'

'No,' I say resolutely. 'No, it wasn't. I looked high and low, especially on this table.'

'Well, that's where I found it,' he says. 'You must have been looking straight at it.'

I swing around to look at him. 'No, you must have had it,' I say, not sure whether my relief is enough to outweigh the frustration I feel that he didn't check his things properly yesterday, when I asked. It would have saved me a lot of time. And anxiety.

'I haven't been anywhere near that table since being back.' He comes towards me with a steaming mug of coffee and puts it down on a coaster. 'Whose is it anyway?' he says, taking his life into his own hands.

I close my eyes and grit my teeth. It's not his fault that the missing folder kickstarted a chain of events that had me thinking I was about to get killed.

'Erm, Jacob Mackenzie's,' I say blithely.

'Ah, the same fella that was here yesterday,' he says, making it sound as if my paranoia is all beginning to make sense.

'Mmm,' is all I can manage.

'I've been thinking,' says Leon. 'Maybe we *should* let him have the flat, if he still wants it, of course.'

A breath catches in my throat. It's as if he knows exactly what I've done and is playing some kind of tortuous cat and mouse game to see how far he has to push me to confess.

'Why the sudden change of heart?' I ask, trying to keep the air of suspicion from my voice.

'Well, I think you're right. The holiday rental market

isn't quite as predictable and it'll mean we have a guaranteed income, all the while helping out someone in need.'

My pulse quickens as I dare to hope that this might be my lifeline out of the sticky predicament I've got myself in.

'OK, great,' I say, as if it doesn't matter to me one way or another. 'I'll let him know and see what he says.'

'Are you able to call him?' he says. 'Or do you not have that kind of relationship?'

'He's actually coming to see me tomorrow, so I'll talk to him then.'

'Again?' exclaims Leon. 'Do you normally see him twice a week?'

'If that's what a client feels they need,' I say, keen to make it more generic, 'then yes.'

'Hey, why not?' he says, leaning in to give me a kiss. 'I suppose it's all money in the bank at the end of the day.'

'I'll see you tonight,' I say, eager to remove myself from the pressure cooker I feel I'm in.

I've not even opened my office door before my first client calls to say she's running ten minutes late. That means twenty, which will knock me off kilter for the rest of the day. Leon says the hour should start from their appointment time rather than when they finally manage to turn up, but I can't tap on my watch after forty minutes and say, 'Sorry, your time's up.' They'd often just be getting started. Though it still irks me, today more than normal, that my time is so carelessly disregarded.

As soon as I'm inside, I call Jacob's mobile, eager to catch him before his school day starts.

I keep a watchful eye on the house. Not that Leon would normally come down, but I wouldn't want him to overhear this particular conversation. It's not one I particularly want to have myself, but the ice needs to be broken and I'd rather just get it over with done with.

It rings four times before clicking into voicemail.

'Hi,' I start, feeling weirdly nervous. 'It's me . . . Naomi. Erm, listen, about last night, I'm sorry that it ended up like it did. I think the alcohol played a large part.'

I clench my fist and knock my forehead in frustration. That's not what I meant to say.

'Anyway,' I go on. 'I hope we can wipe the slate clean and put it all behind us. I'll see you tomorrow, but if you hear from Vanessa in the meantime, call me.' *Shit.* That's not what I meant to say either.

'So, I'll see you tomorrow then,' I say, repeating myself. I put the phone down before I make any more of a hash of it. That was a bad idea.

8

As expected, my appointments all over-run and it's gone six thirty by the time I lock up the office. I'm about to ask Leon if he fancies getting a takeaway, but he's already dishing up meatloaf. The one I'd started last night and hastily abandoned when Jacob called me in a panic. I can't remember where I got to before leaving – had I already put the eggs in? The sage?

I know, for sure, that I must have left an almighty mess behind me; there would have been breadcrumbs all over the worktop and ground mince coated in the gloopy slime of an egg white. I hadn't even noticed that it had all been put away when I got in last night. If I had, I would have realized a lot sooner that Leon was home and saved myself untold stress. Unless, of course, my over-active imagination would have had Vanessa putting the meatloaf in the oven and tidying the kitchen before she killed me.

'Well, this is nice,' I say, smiling, trying to deflect what I know is coming next. 'It's not quite my mom's, but it's not half bad.'

'You'd already done most of it,' he says, looking at me. I've walked straight into this one. 'Though it looked like a crime scene when I got in.'

I go to tell him that's too near the truth to be funny, but think better of it.

'So what was the rush to go out for a drive?' he says as he puts a loaded fork into his mouth.

I've suddenly lost my appetite, but refrain from pushing my plate away.

I wonder how he would react if I told him that I'd dropped everything to go and meet Jacob. I'd like to be able to tell him, and perhaps even laugh about the turn of events that had left me feeling horribly exposed yesterday.

'I'm probably not going to do myself any favours here,' I say, still undecided where I'm going with this.

Leon's face clouds over, as if he's got an inkling of what's coming, but is holding back until he's proven right. It tells me all I need to know. We don't need to have a row over something not worth rowing about.

'So . . .' I go on, racking my brain to come up with something feasible. 'So, I was halfway through preparing the meatloaf and I started thinking about Mom . . .' It's a cheap shot, but it's all that I've got right now.

Leon's expression changes to one of sympathy, making me feel even worse.

'It's the little things that take me back,' I say. 'Meatloaf Mondays were my favourite day of the week, before . . .'

Leon nods, negating the need for me to finish the sentence.

'Mom would pick me and Jennifer up from school

and we'd go to Arthur's store on the corner to get a candy bar.' I smile at the memory. 'Jen would shove hers in her mouth before Mom had even paid for it, but I was mature enough, at ten, to know that it needed to be savoured. So it took me until we were almost home, just to unwrap it.' I laugh as I picture myself, slowly peeling back the foil of that Hershey's bar like Charlie Bucket – half expecting a golden ticket to shine out of it.

Leon smiles tightly.

'And then I'd walk through the front door, smell that meatloaf in the oven and feel the house wrap itself around me. I was home and safe.' I resist the urge to add, 'Or so I thought.'

'So you just went out for some breathing space?' asks Leon.

I look at him, wondering what he's talking about.

'When you were in the middle of making the meatloaf,' he says, bringing me back to why I started this trip down memory lane.

'Exactly!' I say, thankful for the prompt.

Leon puts his knife and fork down and looks at me.

'Do you not think you're due a proper break?' he says.

'What makes you say that?' I ask.

'Because that filing cabinet of yours is definitely over-loaded,' he says, referring to the metaphorical system that I so often call my brain. Every now and again, the drawers get so full that I struggle to withhold the simplest piece of information, and when that happens, I need to take a break and declutter.

'You've not taken any time off for months,' he goes on. 'You seem super anxious, you're losing things, you're taking yourself back to your mum . . .'

'I *like* thinking about her,' I say defensively.

'Yes, I know – I didn't mean that you shouldn't, but when you start to do it more often and walk out like you did, it's often an indication of burnout.'

I wish I could tell him that actually wasn't the case yesterday. Or perhaps it was?

'You give so much of yourself to everyone else that there's rarely much left in the tank for you.'

'I'm doing OK,' I offer.

'But making yourself available to your clients twenty-four-seven isn't helping.'

He doesn't know the half of it.

'You go above and beyond,' he continues. 'You always have; it's what got you in trouble last time.'

I throw him a warning glance.

'But this is your own practice now,' he goes on. 'You have responsibilities. You can't go making rash decisions any more.'

'I get that it's hard for you to understand how it feels to have no one to talk to. You've got me, your parents, the football team, the lads down the pub. We all serve a purpose and without you even realizing, we help you navigate your daily life. But imagine not having that support network and struggling with your mental health? If I'm the only person they can talk to honestly, what am I supposed to say? *Sorry, but if you're feeling low and suicidal outside office hours, don't bother me?*'

'You know that's not what I mean,' he says, taking a sip of his beer. 'I'm just saying—'

The doorbell rings and we both freeze momentarily, looking at one another as if to say, 'Who's that going to be?'

'I'll get it,' says Leon, wiping his mouth on a napkin and standing up.

I watch him walk through to the hall and listen out for the intonation in his voice to give me a clue as to who it might be. It's not yet late enough to rule out a delivery, but I can't remember ordering anything. It's also not too late for one of the site team to be needing Leon, but his curt and clipped voice doesn't suggest either of those.

'Wait here,' I hear him say. 'I'll go and fetch her.'

It's someone for me? Who's being held at the door? So it's not Shelley or anyone else who'd automatically be invited in.

My breath quickens as I dare to imagine it being Jacob. Not that that in itself would be a problem. But by being dishonest about last night, I've potentially opened a whole can of worms. Even if it's Shelley, I'm aware of the myriad ways this could all go pear-shaped.

As Leon comes back into the dining room, with his mouth pulled tight and his nostrils flared, I know that whoever it is, he's not happy.

'Someone here to see you,' he says without giving anything more away.

I walk to the front door like a cat on a hot tin roof, trying to prepare both my expression and my brain for every eventuality. The irony that I might be about to create more suspicion than if I'd just come out and told the truth is not lost on me. I vow never to lie again, whilst crossing my fingers that my dishonesty isn't all about to blow up in my face.

'Anna!' I cry out, in genuine and relieved surprise.

'Hi,' she says, her eyes darting manically from side to side. 'I'm really sorry, I know I shouldn't be here – it's your free time – but I didn't know what else to do.'

'Why don't you come in?' I say, beckoning her in from the drive.

'No, I couldn't, it'd be too much of an imposition.'

'Come in,' I coax gently. 'It's fine.'

She stands in the hallway, nervously looking around and biting on her lip. I can't help but notice that her normally coiffed blonde bob looks dishevelled.

'Is everything OK?' I ask as calmly as I can.

Her face instantly crumples. 'I just can't go on like this any longer. We're destroying each other and I'm scared of what might happen if I stay. I have to get away. I have to get the children away – for all our sakes.'

I wonder how much of this Leon can hear, quickly followed by whether it really matters.

He can't fail to see that here is a woman who is desperately in need of help, *my* help. How can he begrudge the half-hour it's going to take to give it to her?

'Come through,' I say, turning to walk down the hall. 'I'll put the kettle on and we can talk about it.'

'I can't . . .' she says, still rooted to the spot.

'It's honestly fine,' I assure her, assuming she's worried about upsetting Leon.

'No, I can't . . . I can't pay you,' she says. 'For an extra session.'

I smile and walk back to her. 'This isn't a session,' I say quietly. 'This is a chat between friends.'

Her shoulders visibly relax and the corners of her mouth turn up ever so slightly.

I'd hoped that Leon would have made himself scarce, but he's back at the dining table, finishing his dinner and, unbeknown to Anna, making a point.

'This is Leon,' I say. 'Leon, this is Anna.' He doesn't even look up from his plate.

'We've met before,' says Anna, taking me by surprise.

'Oh,' I say, looking between them.

'He probably doesn't remember,' she says, as if he isn't here. 'I don't tend to leave much of an impression.'

Leon offers a tight smile and I will him to say something to prove her wrong, even if he makes it up, but his silence is deafening.

'So what's happened?' I ask, clicking on the kettle.

Her eyes dart nervously towards Leon.

'It's OK,' I say, reaching out to reassure her, but she recoils as if she's in pain.

'Anna, are you hurt?' I ask, my voice high-pitched. 'Has he hurt you?'

She averts her eyes, but she can't stop them from filling up.

'Oh God,' I say, going to her and wrapping my arms around her. I can feel her tears instantly soak through the thin cotton of my t-shirt and hold her even tighter.

'Where are the children?' I ask.

She looks at me, as if in a daze.

'The children?' I say again, trying to ward off the alarm bells that are ringing loudly in my ears. I study her carefully, suddenly concerned for her and her children's wellbeing. Her hands are trembling and she's looking at me wide-eyed.

'They're with friends.'

'So they're definitely somewhere safe?'

'Yes,' she says. 'I'll pick them up on my way home.'

'OK, we need to get you all out of there.'

'I can't go to a hostel,' she says, sobbing into my shoulder. 'But I've got nowhere else to go.'

'It's OK,' I say, rocking her as if she were a baby. 'We'll figure something out.'

As I look over the top of her head, I see Leon, his

outline blurred as if in portrait mode, shaking his head slowly from side to side. He can read me like a book.

'Could I use the bathroom, please?' she asks, attempting to wipe away the mascara shadows that circle her eyes.

'Sure, it's just up the stairs and straight ahead.'

She offers an awkward smile to Leon as she leaves the room, which I hope will assuage any incoming wrath.

'Don't even think about it,' he says, as soon as she's out of earshot.

'What?' I say, feigning ignorance.

'She's not staying here.'

'It hadn't even occurred to me,' I lie.

'I mean it,' he says, sounding as if he's berating a child.

'But what harm would a couple of days do? It will give her the space she needs and time to get herself back on her feet.'

Leon's shaking his head. 'You know nothing about her.'

I laugh scornfully. 'I know *everything* about her. There isn't another person in this world who knows more about her than I do. I know where she's from, what her upbringing was like . . .'

'Just because she comes from the same city as you doesn't give you the inside track on who she really is.'

I wasn't aware I'd told him she was a fellow New Yorker. He must be able to detect it from her elongated and high gliding vowels.

'I know her fears, her fantasies, the nightmare that wakes her up night after night,' I say, not sure whether I'm talking about Anna or myself.

'But she's not your problem,' he says.

'So what am I supposed to do? Just abandon her?'

Leon sighs heavily and I go to him, wrapping my arms around his neck and kissing his cheek.

'Oh, sorry,' says Anna, through a strangled cough.

Feeling self-conscious and not wishing to make her feel excluded, I pull away.

'I need to go and run a few checks,' says Leon, pushing his chair away from the dining table and standing up.

I watch as he walks down the hall and turns to give me a parting glare, silently warning me to do the right thing. But is that the right thing by Anna, or him?

'Nick and I used to be like you two,' she says wistfully. 'He wouldn't let me pass by without giving me a kiss or telling me how much he loved me. Our friends used to tell us to get a room. Now we can't even be in the same house as each other.'

I pull a chair out from the dining table and invite her to sit. 'Do you want to talk about what happened?' I ask, sitting down on the still-warm seat that Leon's just left.

Anna pulls out a tissue from her sleeve and blows her nose. 'He didn't come home last night, but it's something he does occasionally, just to let off some steam, so I wasn't particularly worried. But when he got in this afternoon, he was drunk.'

I shudder.

'He's not had a drink in over a year,' she says. 'Not since we lost Ben.'

'Right,' I say, knowing first-hand the difference alcohol can make to someone's personality.

'He's . . . he's never gone for me before,' she says, biting down on her lip and staring through the patio doors to the garden. 'But he was so drunk and so mad that he just couldn't help himself.'

My stomach lurches. I knew a man like that once. At weekends, when he was away from work and the lure of the bars in the city, he was the man my mother married, and the father Jennifer and I loved with all our hearts. But on weekdays, when he was unable to resist the temptation of 'just one more', he'd become completely unrecognizable.

Despite trying hard not to, I'm suddenly transported back to my parents' bedroom and the look on my mother's face when we heard my dad crash through the front door that day. We'd been lying there, her and me on the bed, talking about the boy who'd just asked me out. He was in ninth grade and I'd had a crush on him for ages, so when he asked me to the cinema that coming Saturday night, Mom and I were excitedly planning my outfit.

'Why don't you wear those denim overalls Aunt Meryl bought you for your birthday?'

'Mom,' I'd shrieked in faux exasperation. 'I'm thirteen, not nine.'

'Oh, but you look soooo cute in them,' she'd said, laughing as she tickled me.

'Yeah, if I was in the Mickey Mouse Club.'

'You used to *love* that show,' she'd said.

If the truth be known, I still did, but so too did Jennifer, whose being four years younger than me made it decidedly uncool to watch.

'Go on, do that Britney routine you used to do,' she'd said, nudging me.

'Mom, stop it,' I'd giggled, protesting and revelling in her attention all at the same time.

I used to love that hour before bed, when Jennifer was asleep and Dad was invariably propping up a bar somewhere in town. We'd watch an episode of *Friends* under a comforter in the living room or lie on her bed, talking about school – or on that particular night, boys.

'What about my denim skirt and that red top you bought me last week?' I'd said.

'Well, as long as it's warm enough,' she said, in typical motherly fashion. 'And what shoes are you going to wear?'

'We-ll,' I'd said, dragging the word out. 'You know we're the same size now . . .'

Her eyes had narrowed and she'd looked at me suspiciously. Like most young teenagers, I always thought I was able to outsmart my mother, naively assuming that she didn't have a clue what was going through my pubescent brain. But now I'm the age she was then, I can see that I clearly didn't give her enough credit.

'Yes,' she'd replied, warily.

'Well, I thought your sneakers would look super-cute with it.'

'Which ones?' she'd asked, knowing full well the pair I'd coveted ever since she'd bought them six months previously. The pair she was wearing right now.

I'd rolled my eyes and smiled.

'Oh, you mean *these* ones?' she'd said, laughing as she lifted her feet in the air.

'Can I?' I'd pleaded, crossing my fingers.

She'd wrapped her hands around mine and looked at me, her eyes a swirling pool of unconditional love.

'If you want them, you can have them,' she'd said.

'*Really?*' I'd squealed.

'Really,' she'd said, smiling.

I'd rolled into her, breathing in her unique scent of cucumber melon, warm dough and clean linen. The essence that always made me feel safe.

'Thank you,' I'd breathed excitedly into her ear.

'You can have anything you want, Naomi. Wherever you find yourself in life, whatever you want to do, if you put the work in, you can have whatever you want.'

I'd nodded into her chest.

'I mean it,' she'd said, holding me away to make sure I was listening. 'Don't end up like me.'

I didn't know whether she meant as a stay-at-home mom or a battered wife. 'I wish I'd listened to my parents,' she'd said. 'They did everything in their power to keep me in med school, knowing deep down that's what I wanted to do. But your dad came along in the first year and it was game over.'

I looked up at her. 'Did he tell you that you couldn't carry on?' I'd asked incredulously.

Her eyes shimmered with tears and melancholy. 'Not in so many words, but he was only visiting Virginia for a few months and I couldn't possibly imagine life without him.'

'So you moved to New York to be with him?'

She'd nodded. 'He promised that once we were settled, I could restart my training here.' A tear fell from the corner of her eye, instantly blotting the pillow. 'But that never happened.'

'Don't be sad, Mom,' I'd said, stroking her cheek.

'I'm fine, darling,' she sniffed. 'But I don't want you to be like me. I want you to be the person I never got to be. I want you to live with abandonment; travel, love, dance, eat good food . . .'

The front door had slammed shut and her eyes widened with fear.

'Close your eyes and pretend you're asleep,' she'd whispered.

I'd swallowed hard, my heart beating fast at the thought of what was to come.

'Don't *ever* let anyone tell you you can't do any of those things,' she'd said under her breath.

I'd blinked through my own tears and given a half-nod. 'Promise me.'

I'd nodded again, with vigour.

Her eyelids fluttered shut just before mine did, but I could already feel my father's presence in the room, like a whirring tornado about to strike.

She made the tiniest of whimpers as he lifted her off the bed by her hair, her eyes willing the cracks in mine to stay closed.

'You haven't got time to lie down,' he'd roared, dragging her towards the door. 'I haven't had my dinner yet.'

I'd wanted more than anything for her to fight back, to show him that he couldn't keep treating her that way, but there wasn't an ounce of resistance left in her. She gave in to him and let her body go limp as her shoulder hit the doorframe.

I've since heard from clients that it doesn't seem to hurt as much once you resign yourself to it. But I don't ever want anyone to feel that they have to accept abuse.

'It was just a push,' says Anna, bringing me back. 'Maybe I'm making more out of it than I need to.'

I lean into the table. '*Just* a push is more than enough,' I say. 'And next time, *just* a push turns into *just* a slap, and the time after that it's *just* a punch.'

She blows her nose into a tissue. 'The look in his eyes,' she says. 'I thought he was going to kill me.'

'So what do you want to do?' I ask.

'I've got a little bit of money put by,' she says. 'I've been saving some of the housekeeping that Nick gives me. It's not much, but it pays for you, and there's now enough for a security deposit and a month's rent. I can get a job as soon as I'm there.'

I recoil at the thought that the money she's saving to safeguard her future is being spent on me.

'OK,' I say, knowing that I won't ever charge her for my time again. 'So do you want me to try and find you somewhere?'

She nods. 'Could you? I mean, I don't know how to do anything like that because Nick's always been in charge. I wouldn't know where to start.'

'I can help you,' I say.

'But I don't want to put you in a position where you feel as if you don't have a choice. This is hardly within your remit, but I really don't know who else to ask. You're the only person I trust.'

'It's fine,' I say. 'I will always help my clients in whatever way I can.'

Her shoulders fall as she breathes out. 'So I'm not the first?' she asks.

I smile. 'And you won't be the last.'

'You've helped other clients find somewhere to live?'

I think of Jacob and immediately feel a tightening in my chest.

'One or two,' I say, brushing off my unease, knowing that it's obviously different with Anna.

'How much would I need for a couple of months' rent?' she asks.

'Well, it all depends on where you go,' I say. 'Anywhere around here is going to set you back at least fifteen hundred a month for something big enough for you and the children.'

She looks at me wide-eyed. 'I-I had no idea. I can't possibly afford that.'

'What about going into Canterbury? You'll be able to get more for your money there.'

'Maybe,' she says. 'But the children are so used to being close to the beach and I have to say that I feel a real affinity to the sea too.' She looks at me. 'I guess that comes with being a New Yorker. You never want to be too far away from the water.'

I smile. I hadn't ever thought of it like that before, but she may have a point, as I've never lived more than a mile or two from the shoreline. And there's no doubt that, for one reason or another, Leon and I were inextricably drawn here.

He was adamant he didn't want to return to his hometown of Manchester, so it was a case of closing our eyes and pointing to somewhere on the map; a bit like pinning the tail on the donkey, and Whitstable, luckily for us, was the donkey's ass.

'Although you were nearer than me back then,' Anna

goes on. 'You must have been on the beach all the time, living on Long Island?'

'We used to go to Jones Beach,' I say.

'With your family?' asks Anna.

I nod, as I remember Dad burying Jennifer and me up to our necks in the sand, and Mom laughing as we thrashed our way out and ran down the beach after him.

'That must have left you with such special memories,' she says.

'It was the only time my sister and I were allowed a Slush Puppie,' I say, smiling. 'Mum would beckon to us in the ocean and we'd race each other out of the water to the kiosk to see who could get the bluest tongue.'

Anna laughs. 'I remember them, weren't they called Blue Raspberry or something? Like, when have you ever seen a blue raspberry?'

'Exactly.'

'What did your family think of you coming over here?' she asks.

An involuntary tic pulsates in my jawline, giving away more than I want. 'Oh, you know what families are like,' I say nonchalantly. 'They don't want you to go, then forget about you as soon as you've left.' I force a laugh because I have no idea what my family think of me emigrating to another country. Because I no longer have a family. At least I didn't until yesterday.

9

There's a feeling of trepidation swirling around my stomach this morning, mimicked by the draining bath water as I pull the plug out. I watch transfixed as the undercurrent drags the soap suds down into a spinning whirlpool and imagine my insides snaking in the same way.

As soon as I get those first uncomfortable few minutes with Jacob under my belt, I know I'll be fine. But not knowing how he's going to play it has kept me up most of the night.

I've imagined every feasible scenario, from him coming in all guns blazing, accusing me of leading him on, to saying hello, sitting down on the couch and pretending it never happened. In an ideal world, I'd like somewhere in between.

We need to address what happened if I'm to continue seeing him, but it needs to be done in a calm and mature manner. It would have helped if he'd returned my call – even if he'd just left a message, as I'd have been able to gauge his tone and read the gaps between the words. But I've not heard from him and I'm beginning to panic that something has happened.

It's that thought I battle with all day as I sit at the dining room table, attempting to do some admin. Despite the sun shining through the window and Motown Gold on the radio, I still can't shake off the horrific image of Vanessa handcuffing Jacob to a bed and torturing him until he begs for mercy and promises that he'll go back to her.

I wonder how much he'll be able to take before he bows to her demands. Will he succumb at the first physical blow? Or will the months of therapy have taught him that he's so much stronger than he gives himself credit for?

With my fifth coffee of the day in hand, I take myself down to the office and watch the minutes tick ever closer to six p.m. Jacob's always on time, if not early, and he's got about thirty seconds until I start pacing the floor, wondering what to do if he doesn't show. I absently thumb my necklace as I check the garden path, believing that if I pretend everything's all right, everything will be all right.

But by ten past, the storm clouds are beginning to gather in my head, their ominous presence darkening any prospect of Jacob being alive, let alone feeling comfortable enough to come and see me.

I try to remain calm, forcing myself to acknowledge that he could be late for a variety of reasons, none of which involve Vanessa, or me. He might have forgotten (though he remembered the night before last). He might have had an unforeseen event happen at school. I go so far as imagining him being lumbered with detention duties or an unscheduled meeting with a concerned parent.

At half past, I call his mobile and it goes straight to answerphone. I wonder if my garbled message from yesterday is still lying unheard, banked up with those from everyone else wondering where he is.

I chastise myself for being over-dramatic; he's probably gone straight to the pub with his colleagues, drinking to his new-found freedom and having fun.

I smile, warming to the version I like best, but none of it accounts for the fact that a dangerous woman had threatened him the night before last, claiming to know where the safehouse he had tried so hard to make a home was.

At quarter to seven, unable to keep the worst-case scenario from whirring around and around in my head, I call the hotel I'd left him at.

'Royal Garden, how may I assist you?'

'Hello, could you put me through to Jacob Mackenzie's room, please?'

There's a deafening silence at the other end of the line. 'Hello?' I ask, checking I haven't been cut off.

'One moment, please,' says a voice that wouldn't sound out of place in an automated lift. 'I'm just trying to locate that for you.'

I chew the inside of my cheek as I wait.

'I can't seem to find a guest with that name,' she says eventually.

'Well, he's definitely staying with you,' I say, knowing that Jacob wouldn't risk going back to the apartment. 'He checked in the night before last.'

I wonder if saying he was one half of the couple having a heated moment in the bar might jog her memory. It would almost certainly have been talked about. The barman would have told the restaurant manager who would have told the concierge, who would have told housekeeping, each version being embellished with every mouth that spoke and every ear that heard, like an elaborate game of telephone.

I'd learnt pretty quickly from working in that very same hotel when I first came to the UK that that's how it works. As a receptionist, I knew who was stashing their complimentary toiletries, who had a drink problem, whose 'wife' was really a prostitute, and who'd left their vibrator behind.

'How are you spelling that?' asks the woman.

I sigh. 'M-A-C-K-E-N-Z-I-E.'

'Ah, that's where I'm going wrong,' she says, tapping noisily on a keyboard. 'I've dropped the A.'

'That'll be it,' I say, hoping she's right.

'Nope,' she says, a few seconds later. 'There's still no one coming up with that name, I'm afraid. Can I try another for you?'

I'm sure that's in the client services manual, but she'd

do well to tweak it in this instance, as looking up another guest entirely is of no use to either of us. I make a mental note to mention it to Andy when I next speak to him.

'No,' I say, more abruptly than I intended. 'Thank you.'

There's a sickening thud in my chest. Something doesn't feel right and with every passing minute, I'm becoming more and more convinced that Jacob's wife has got something to do with it.

I feel compelled to try harder to find him – call up his work, go around to the flat – but then I'm hit by the thought: what if he doesn't want to be found? What if he'd realized, after finally escaping his wife's abuse, that he was more miserable without her?

He'd certainly displayed classic symptoms of Stockholm Syndrome in our early sessions; showing empathy when she mistreated him, and defending her when I dared to suggest that their relationship was one of captor and captive.

Perhaps what we'd both initially perceived as a threat was actually her tracking him down to promise that things would be different from now on; that she'd get help and change, if only he came back to her. So maybe he did just that, because he believed she was telling the truth. And who am I to tell him he can't? Maybe Leon's right. I can't save everyone, especially those who don't want to be saved.

But if I knew deep down that Jacob didn't want to be rescued, why is that niggle at the back of my mind turning into an itch under my skin that I just can't scratch?

Am I honestly prepared to be the one person who knows the danger he's in – the one person he reached out to – and not do anything about it?

I'm in my car before I have a chance to question myself any further. I have to do what my conscience tells me, otherwise I'll never be able to sleep soundly again.

I call Jacob's mobile as I drive along the harbour road, the ringing on the car speaker drowning out the cacophony of seagulls and halyards as they clank against the masts of the fishing boats moored up for the night.

'Pick up, pick up,' I plead out loud.

It rings a couple of times, and I dare to hope that he'll answer and tell me that he's sorry but he's had a hell of a day at work and our appointment totally slipped his mind. That's how simple the explanation could be. That's how simple I desperately want it to be, but it goes to voicemail, again.

I pull up on the tree-lined avenue, just opposite the Victorian house where Leon and I own the flat. The flat I'm renting to Jacob without Leon's knowledge.

The front bay window, where the living room is, has curtains drawn, and my mind instantly conjures up the image of a rotting corpse being hidden from view behind them.

'For God's sake, get a grip Ni,' I remonstrate with myself out loud, remembering that we, too, used to close the curtains at this time of day, as the sun was so bright that we weren't able to see the TV.

My insides relax and I let out the deep breath that my clenched muscles had prevented me from releasing. I'd had no idea how uptight I'd been; though it's no surprise that my body is reacting to the stress my mind is under.

I take a moment, after unplugging my seat belt, to gather my thoughts. This is still going to be awkward, not least because of how it was left the other night, but because I'm knocking on his door at seven o'clock in the evening.

But awkwardness is a risk I'm going to have to take, as I can't possibly drive away without seeing him and knowing he's OK.

I clear my throat as I press the buzzer for Flat A. There's a click as if someone has answered the intercom and then nothing. I push the door, wondering if the noise was the door being let off the latch, but it's stuck fast. I wait a few seconds and try again. There's that click again.

'Jacob?' I say. 'Are you there?'

It sounds as if the line's open, that someone is there but not responding.

I call his mobile again and walk around to the front window, pressing my ear up against the glass. It's muffled, but there's no mistaking the persistent ringtone of an incoming call. He's definitely in there.

My finger presses down on the doorbell until it clicks again.

'I know you're in there,' I say into the speaker, lowering my voice as a passer-by looks my way. 'Look, I'm sorry about what happened the other night, but surely we've got to be a bit grown-up about this?'

Although it's a rhetorical question, I'd quite like a response. But there's nothing except a loud silence.

'Why don't you just open the door so we can talk?'

It occurs to me for the first time that this might not actually be a simple case of embarrassment and dented pride.

'Is she in there with you?' I ask, unable to stop myself from picturing him bound to a chair and gagged. 'You're going to need to come out,' I go on, sounding braver than I feel. 'Because I'm not leaving until I see you.'

'I don't think he's in,' comes a voice as the door finally opens. A weary-looking woman stands there with a baby on her hip, jiggling him up and down. 'But if you know where to find him, I'd appreciate you asking him to turn off the music that's blaring from the back room on repeat – it's keeping my baby awake.'

'Oh, right,' is all I'm able to offer, my head a fog of confusion, as I picture Vanessa conducting a *Reservoir Dogs*-style interrogation to 'Stuck in the Middle with You'.

'Would you mind if I come in?' I say to the woman. 'Just to make sure he's not here.'

'Be my guest,' she says, opening the door a little wider. 'If it goes on much longer, I'm going to have to call the landlord.'

'But I . . .' I say, confused, before remembering that Leon is the contact she's likely to have. I wonder what he'd make of a complaint of loud music from a flat he thinks is empty.

Once I'm in the hall I knock on the door, and when there's no movement from the other side I reach into my bag, feeling my way past the lip balm, hand sanitizer, receipts and tampons, for the keys on a Canterbury Cathedral fob.

My stomach lurches as I silently slide the Yale key into the lock, my head fast-tracking forwards to what I might find. Of all the broken pieces in this sorry state of affairs, it's the neighbour's reports of incessant loud music that's spooked me the most.

As soon as I push the door slightly ajar, I can hear Alanis Morissette blaring out from down the hall. Her bitter words resound in my head as I tiptoe ever closer to the source, forcing myself not to look anywhere but straight ahead, to where the music's coming from; Jacob's bedroom.

The door's closed and my heart is in my mouth as I grab hold of the handle, knowing this is my last chance to back out. But as much as I want to, how can I?

With trembling fingers, I turn the knob slowly, desperately trying to rid myself of the image of Jacob's lifeless body hanging from the ceiling. Would he have done that to himself, before she had the chance to? Or might she have set it up so that it looked like he couldn't live without her?

My chest heaves and I swallow the retch that pushes its way up my windpipe.

As soon as it's off the latch, I throw the door open, forcing myself to acknowledge that whatever's there, it isn't going to be any easier to deal with in slow motion.

The music is deafening, but besides Alanis reminding me of the mess I left when I went away, there's nothing to suggest that anything is amiss. The bed is neatly made, photos of Jacob's children stand proudly on the nightstand, and a suit in dry-cleaning cellophane hangs on the wardrobe door.

'Alexa, turn the music off!'

The sudden silence makes me want to cry, as all the pent-up nerves and emotion rush to flood out of me. But I sink my teeth into my lip in an effort to hold it together.

I call Jacob's mobile again and follow the sound to the front room, giving the bathroom and kitchen a cautionary glance as I pass by. There's a pan on the stove and a bowl of pasta beside it, abandoned halfway through, it seems. I go in, lift the pan up to check that the gas ring isn't on.

Jacob's phone has stopped ringing, so I call it again before following its trail once more. It leads me to his jacket, slung casually over the back of a dining chair. The flashing screen lights up the blue lining and I reach in to reject the call.

Where the hell is he?

I slide the screen up, in the unlikely event that it will give me access without a password, but it immediately asks for the four-digit code.

'Who goes anywhere without their phone these days?' I ask aloud.

It's then that I'm struck by the two fear-inducing options. The first being someone who doesn't want to be found. The second: that they already have been.

10

I'd set my alarm for six thirty, ready to try to call Jacob again first thing, but it turns out that I didn't need to be woken, as I never actually fell asleep.

I'd spent the night tossing and turning, going over everything Jacob had said and done in the lead-up to him disappearing off the radar. At one point, somewhere between four and five a.m., I'd tiptoed out of bed, careful not to wake Leon, and gone down to the garden office to retrieve Jacob's file.

Taking it to my desk, I'd put the lamp on and pored over every scribble and nuanced doodle in the hope that something jumped out at me; a clue as to where he might be and who with.

Looking back on the notes from our first session, I'd asked him to tell me about a time in his life when he had been at his happiest. I often use it as the pathway to open up someone's mind; to take them back to when they weren't bogged down by the troubling thoughts and negative energy that had made them book an appointment to see me.

He'd told me about a week he'd spent at the beach in Whitstable, with his wife and three boys.

'When was this?' I'd asked.

'Just over ten years ago,' he'd said. 'Before we bought a place here.'

'And what was so special about it that you're able to take yourself right back there, all this time later?'

'It was the children's summer holidays and we'd rented one of the fisherman's cottages on the beach,' he'd mused. 'The kids just loved being by the sea, and on that particular day we'd taken them out on a boat to see the seals at Horse Sands. Our youngest loved animals and his face was so full of wonderment as he watched them sunbathing on the sand bar.'

Jacob had lost himself for a moment and when he came back, his eyes were shimmering with tears.

'It was a magical day,' he'd gone on, pulling himself up. 'And when we got back to the cottage, the kids were in hysterics as I hosed them down by the back door, trying to get the sand and salt out of every crevice.'

He'd laughed heartily at the memory. 'Though no matter how much you wash them, you'll still be finding hidden grains a month later.'

I'd smiled, though was unable to relate to the trials and tribulations of parenthood.

'Anyway,' Jacob had said. 'Once they were all clean, I got a fire going on the beach and the little one snuggled up to me as I read him a story.'

'It sounds idyllic,' I'd said.

'It was,' he said. 'I couldn't imagine being happier. I

126

had everything I could possibly ask for; three beautiful sons, a gorgeous, loving wife who I loved more than anything, and a new job that I'd worked my whole career for.'

'So what changed?' I'd asked gently.

'Everything,' he'd said, looking out of the window. 'And we were never the same after that.'

I'd often circle back to what had happened to trigger a sequence of events that had turned his wife into an abusive sociopath and him a shadow of his former self. But I'd been unable to get him to return to that place.

It struck me, just as the sun was coming up, that despite Jacob being so open and honest about his marriage, he had actually been very scant on any identifiable details of who he really was.

So, feeling as if I have no other choice, by eight o'clock I'm in my office armed with the phone numbers of all the secondary schools in Canterbury. There's nothing to tell them apart, as all I know is that he teaches somewhere in town, so I work my way through the list alphabetically. It's sod's law that it's the last one that proves to be the most fruitful.

'Can I ask who's calling?' says the woman on the other end of the line, when I ask to speak to Jacob Mackenzie. Bingo!

'Yes, it's Naomi Chandler,' I say.

Now I'm at this point, knowing I'm about to speak to him, no matter what, I find myself not knowing what to say. I'm not angry about the other night; neither am I going to stand in judgement if he's decided that he's happier when he's with his wife. I only ever wanted to make him see that he had options.

As the phone is picked up and he says, 'Hello, Jacob Mackenzie speaking, how may I help you?' I realize I just want to know that he's all right.

'I'm so sorry to call you at work,' I say, exhaling the breath I feel like I've been holding in for forty-eight hours. 'But I just wanted to check that you're OK.'

'I'm perfectly fine,' he says, clearly bemused. 'Can I ask who's calling?'

'It's me, Naomi,' I say, unable to understand why he doesn't recognize my voice. But then I suppose I don't really recognize his either. It actually doesn't sound like him at all.

'Naomi?' he presses, as if needing something more to identify me.

'From Tattenhall,' I say, not wanting to divulge any sensitive information, because an unease is beginning to work its way across my chest.

'Ah, the estate in Whitstable,' he gushes. 'Is this about the concert on Saturday? I do hope there's not a problem, as my wife and I are very much looking forward to it.'

'Er no, no,' I stutter, sure that this isn't the man I think it is. 'Everything's fine, though I think I have the wrong number.'

'Oh,' he says, before laughing. 'I thought you were

going to tell me that the lead violinist had fallen ill and you needed me to stand in for them.'

I force a laugh. Now I'm really listening to his voice, there's no way this is the Jacob I know. The Jacob I need to find.

'I hope you enjoy the event,' I say, before putting the phone down.

I fall into the chair with my head in my hands, struggling to understand how I thought I knew Jacob so well just a couple of days ago.

Despite myself, I can't help but feel I've been duped in some way, but I can't for the life of me work out how or why. Had it all been about the apartment? An elaborate ruse to get in there, knowing I'd have the devil's own job of getting him out again? Had he invented his abusive wife? Created an entirely different life from the one he was actually living?

The sun's just beginning to filter through the lowered blinds and as I pull them up, I'm met with undulating meadows that roll as far as the eye can see. And for a moment, I allow myself to appreciate the view, revel in it even, as I have done every morning since moving here. Though today, for the first time, it is a little harder to garner gratitude for a new dawn when I'm not entirely sure what it will bring.

Desperate for a coffee to mask the bad taste Jacob's lies have left in my mouth, I head back up to the house.

I'm daydreaming, watching the swirling coffee granules

dissolve in my mug, when the doorbell rings. I check the time on the oven; it's not yet nine and I immediately panic that it's someone coming to get Leon because there's a problem on site.

Walking down the hall, I can see two shadowy figures on the other side of the stained-glass panels in the front door, their outlines aglow with the sun behind them. I pull my dressing gown tighter around me, in need of comforting reassurance.

'Naomi Chandler?' asks the woman, her attempt at a smile unable to belie the fact that they're obviously here on official business. Just their stance and weathered expressions tell me they're police officers.

I offer a stiff smile, but it's almost as if my face has forgotten how to be normal.

'Yes,' I croak. 'How can I help you?

'I'm Detective Inspector Robson,' she says. 'And this is Detective Sergeant Harris.'

They make a show of presenting their IDs but my brain is racing so far ahead that it could have been their library cards.

'We're investigating the disappearance of Michael Talbot,' says the man, looking like the classic English TV detective with his Barbour-esque jacket and navy chinos.

'Oh, I don't know if I can help you,' I say. 'Is he a local man?'

They look at each other. 'May we come in?' says the woman.

I go to stand aside but feel suddenly vulnerable, as if I'm inviting a pair of serial killers into the house. I'm almost too embarrassed to question their status. I wonder which is the lesser of two evils.

As if sensing my reticence, the woman offers up her ID again and I squint to read the small writing.

I lead them through to the front room and invite them to take a seat, but they say they'd prefer to stand.

'So,' I offer, when they're not forthcoming. 'How can I help?'

'As I said, we're looking into the disappearance of Michael Talbot,' says the man. 'Do you know him?'

My brow furrows. 'No,' I say more abruptly than I intended.

They give each other a conspiratorial glance again.

'Are you sure about that?'

I look between the two of them, getting the distinct impression that they know something I don't.

'So you're not in any kind of personal relationship with him then,' asks the woman, who I think is Robson, tilting her head to the side.

'Why . . .' I start, my tongue feeling like cotton wool. 'Why would you think that?' I wonder if I've misunderstood what she's trying to imply.

'Because we've been following some leads and your name has come up on more than one occasion.'

A heat creeps up from my toes, encompassing my whole body, inch by inch, until it reaches my ears.

'I-I'm sorry, I don't understand,' I manage. 'You must have the wrong person; I don't know a Michael Talbot.'

Robson gives an almost imperceptible nod to her colleague, who reaches into his inside pocket and pulls out a photo.

As I study the man, a burning hot liquid sets my chest alight. It's travelling with such ferocity that I throw a hand over my mouth to stop it ending up on the detectives' shiny shoes.

'So, you *do* know him?' says the man, almost smugly.

I don't look up, unable to tear myself away from the man in the photo. His laughing eyes crease his crow's feet and his gentle smile sends daggers through my heart.

'Th . . .' I go to speak, but can't form the words.

'Take your time, Mrs Chandler.'

'Th-that isn't Michael Talbot,' I stutter.

They look at each other with raised eyebrows.

'So, who is it then?'

My trembling hands can't keep the picture still. I wait for the face on it to change; to one I've never seen before. But the longer I wait, the sharper the image becomes, imprinting itself on my brain.

'Th-that's Jacob Mackenzie.'

If she wasn't so intuitive, so curious, then perhaps I could have told her my real name. But she'd only poke around and find out things she didn't want to know.

I'm not ready for that. Not yet.

I have to be patient, stick to the plan, because if she finds out who I really am, there'll be no coming back from it.

PART TWO

PART TWO

11

'So how do you know the man you know as Jacob Mackenzie?' asks Detective Inspector Robson.

I can't think straight and wonder if I shouldn't go and wake Leon up to translate my muddled thoughts into coherent words. But then again, perhaps it's best that he stays where he is. What would he make of what is being implied?

'H-he's a client,' I say. 'I'm a psychotherapist.'

'And why do you think his name is Jacob Mackenzie?' asks Robson.

I look at her blankly. 'Because that's what he *said* his name was,' I say, wondering what other reason there could be.

'And this is definitely the man you know as Jacob Mackenzie?' she asks, showing me the picture again.

I nod. 'So that's not his real name?'

The detective shakes her head. 'No, it appears not, and we're wondering why he would use an alias.'

'You and me both,' I say tartly.

'So your relationship with Mr Talbot . . .' says the officer. 'Was purely professional?'

'Of course!' I say, almost choking on my words. 'I don't know why you would think any differently.'

'It's just that we've managed to link him to a flat not too far away from here . . .'

My breath catches in my throat; I know what's coming.

'A flat that seems to be owned by you and your husband.'

I imagine Leon walking in right now. How would I possibly explain myself? To him, or the officers standing in front of me?

'Erm, yes,' I say, going over to the door and closing it.

The pair of them look at each other. 'Is your husband *here*?' asks Robson with raised eyebrows.

'Y-yes,' I stutter. 'He's upstairs sleeping.'

'Might he want to join us?' she asks.

'No, there's no need,' I say quickly. 'Jacob's a client who rented our apartment when he needed somewhere to stay.'

Detective Robson tilts her head to the side. 'So you *do* share more than a professional relationship?'

Tiny beads of sweat instantaneously spring to the surface of my skin, making me feel hot and uncomfortable.

'He needed help and I was in a position to give it to him,' I say. 'Though it was all within the realms of our working relationship.'

'Can you tell us why he was seeing you?' asks Harris. 'The problem you were treating him for.' The little man has an unpleasant smirk across his face that I feel like slapping off.

'I'm not in a position to breach client confidentiality,' I say tightly.

Robson sits down next to me. 'We believe Mr Talbot might be in danger, so it would be really helpful if you could tell us anything you know, so that we might be able to help him.'

I've watched scenes like this play out on TV and wonder if this is the point where I demand a lawyer.

'Am I being treated as a suspect?'

'Not at all,' she says. 'We're just trying to form a clearer picture of his life in the hope it will help us ensure that he doesn't come to any harm.'

I know what's happened to him, so how can I possibly keep that to myself if it's going to be the only way of finding him? In this instance, I deem it my right to waive Jacob's confidentiality in good faith, and, in this instance, I hope he'd agree with me.

'I specialize in domestic abuse,' I start. 'Many of my clients are trapped in relationships where they're being mentally or physically abused. Sometimes both.'

Robson nods. 'Is that why Mr Talbot started seeing you?'

I look at her through narrowed eyes, my faculties slowly returning.

'Jacob was being abused by his wife,' I say, leaving it there. I don't want to say any more than I need to.

139

They exchange a look of surprise. 'Emotionally, you mean?' says Harris.

I take a deep breath. 'Yes, and physically,' I say.

He almost laughs. 'Have you *seen* Mrs Talbot?'

Robson glares at him and turns to face me. Harris clears his throat awkwardly.

'He left because he was in fear of his life and I gave him a place to live while he sorted himself out.'

'And you weren't planning on living there with him?' steams in Harris, like a bull in a china shop.

'No!' I say resolutely.

'Have you been to the property since Mr Talbot moved in?' asks Robson.

My mouth dries up as I consider how much I should tell them. Do they need to know I was there last night? That I was so worried about his wellbeing that I went there, let myself in with the spare key and found his phone, yet no sign of him?

They'll want to know why I didn't call them then. I'm wondering that myself.

'No,' I lie, unsure of what I need to save most, myself or my marriage.

'In your professional capacity,' says Harris, 'do you honestly think Mr Talbot was justified in being in fear of his life?'

'What's your name again?' I bark, incensed by his attitude, both towards me and the man I know as Jacob.

'Er, Harris,' he stutters, suddenly not so cocky.

'Well, maybe you'd do well to revisit your training manual on domestic abuse,' I seethe. 'His wife was attacking him and threatening him on a daily basis.'

'I apologize for my colleague's glib and insensitive comment,' says Robson, seemingly genuinely.

I nod my reluctant acceptance. 'I think you should be speaking to his wife.'

'She's the one who's reported him missing,' says Robson.

I snort. 'He left her. That doesn't mean he's missing. They're two very different things.'

'Was she aware that her husband was seeing you?' asks Robson.

'I don't know,' I say, shaking my head, trying to fit the jigsaw pieces into place. 'He was so careful.'

They give each other a sideways glance. 'Careful?' says Robson.

I force myself to take a deep breath, to slow myself down, because every word I say seems to shine the light of suspicion on me even further.

'He went to great lengths to hide it from her,' I say, feeling a weight bearing down on my shoulders, making me feel like I'm being restrained. 'He quite literally went out of his way to get here, so that she couldn't follow him.'

'Do you know why she might have been following him?' Robson asks, her colleague seemingly on mute. That's probably the best place for him.

'Because she needed to know where he was,' I say. 'She needed to be in control and when she didn't feel as if she was, she'd go to extreme lengths to get him back under her command.'

'Did she ever threaten him?' asks Robson.

'Yes,' I say. 'She'd often tell him that if he ever left her, she would hunt him down and kill him.'

'So when was the last time you saw Mr Talbot?' asks Harris. 'When was his last appointment?'

I flinch, knowing that they're not one and the same thing. I take a moment to decide which version I should give them, knowing that the further down this rabbit hole I take myself, the harder it will be to get back out.

'His last appointment was on Monday,' I say.

'So, three days ago?' he asks unnecessarily.

I count the days myself; anything to give me more time to work out what the hell is going on here.

'Yes,' I say.

'And how did he seem to you? Any different to how he normally is? Did he talk about how he was feeling?'

'If you're asking me whether it's possible he might have harmed himself, then no, I don't think so. He was in a good place; happy to be in the flat and enjoying his new job.' My brain is going at a hundred miles an hour, desperately trying to filter the information that will help find Jacob, yet keep myself from being in any way implicated in his disappearance.

'Though he did call me later that evening,' I add, in an effort to emphasize the gravitas.

Robson's eyebrows shoot up. 'To say . . . ?'

My legs are twitching, as if they can feel the hot water I'm immersing myself in, as it slowly and painfully rises. I wonder if I shouldn't just put myself out of my misery and tell them everything, but I can picture Leon's face as he finds out that I met Jacob in a hotel and lied about it. And that I went to the flat last night, the flat that he thinks is empty.

'To say that his wife had found out where he was,' I say, naively believing that I've found some safe ground. This will give them the evidence they need to pursue her, because sitting here questioning me is wasting valuable time.

'And you haven't seen or heard from him since?' she asks.

I feel as if I'm being slowly injected with a noxious substance, numbly waiting for the effects to take hold. If I admit to seeing Jacob in the hotel, I'll be incriminating myself, not just to the police but to Leon as well. But if I don't come clean, I might hamper their efforts to find him.

'Mrs Chandler?' prompts Robson. 'So you haven't seen him since?'

I look her straight in the eyes. 'No,' I say, choosing my poison.

I only hope I don't choke on it.

12

I'm half a bottle of wine down by the time I hear Leon's key in the lock this evening. I'd thankfully been ensconced back in my office by the time he left for work this morning. But now I regret not telling him about my police visit then, because even with the wine softening the sharp edges, this is going to be difficult.

What am I supposed to say to him? Do I tell him exactly what I told the police, selfishly disregarding the role I played in the lead-up to Jacob's disappearance? Or do I tell him the truth? Because despite myself, I can't help but feel I'm going to need him on side.

As I peer around the kitchen door and see who's walking down the hall, I fear the decision's already been made for me.

'Look who I found loitering around,' says Leon, with a big smile on his face.

'Shelley!' I exclaim.

'Well, I wouldn't exactly call it loitering,' she says, laughing. 'It was more of a slow saunter past in the hope that you'd offer me a coffee.'

'We can do better than that,' says Leon, eyeing up the half-empty bottle of wine on the kitchen counter.

I stand there, poleaxed, as Shelley's Irish terrier jumps up at me, her demands for attention ignored.

'Sorry,' says Shelley. 'You look like this is the last thing you need.'

'No,' I mumble. 'It's fine. It's lovely to see you. What are you doing over this way?'

'Well, I just thought we'd have a nose at the preparations for Saturday,' she says. 'It's incredible to see the place transformed into a venue. The stage, the lighting – even the portaloos . . . it's like a mini-Glastonbury. You've done a great job, Leon.'

'Well, let's see how great it is when two thousand people need the toilet,' he says, laughing.

'I was also hoping to have a look at the old stables,' she says. 'But it's all fenced off.'

'We had to make it out of bounds,' says Leon. 'Just in case a member of the public wandered over there from the concert.'

'Right,' says Shelley, nodding. 'Though they'd have to be going out of their way.'

'True, but we couldn't take any chances. Not on health and safety. Don't forget – as well as the old stables, which are in very real danger of collapsing, there's also a disused swimming pool over there, which is full of dirty water. God knows what's lurking under the surface, and if someone happened to trip and fall, we wouldn't find them until we start the renovation works.' He laughs awkwardly.

'Well, that was what I was trying to get a bit more of a feel for,' says Shelley, looking a little embarrassed. 'This is strictly between us, as my fellow Parish Councillors won't thank me for it, but it looks like we'll be objecting to the planning permission Tattenhall has applied for.'

'On what grounds?' says Leon, instantly agitated.

Shelley sighs. 'The chairman thinks there's enough of a holiday rental market within the town already; so not only will it bring more tourists in, but it will likely take the business away from a local, who needs all the bookings they can get.'

'It's five cottages,' says Leon. 'Buried so deep in the estate that they won't even know they're there.'

'Hey, don't shoot the messenger,' says Shelley, holding her hands up. 'I'm on your side. It's just typical nimbyism and I'll be reporting back favourably.'

'Maybe I should invite the residents to come and see for themselves how little it will affect them,' says Leon.

'That might not be a bad shout,' says Shelley, sipping on her wine. 'When might you be able to do that?'

Leon rubs at his forehead; as if he hasn't got enough to do. 'As soon as the concert's over with, I'll get the place cleaned up a bit and put a post up on Nextdoor – see if anyone has any questions or wants to come and have a look.'

Shelley nods. 'That'll definitely help.'

Leon grimaces, but I can't tell if it's at her or me.

Though any doubt is quashed when he says, 'So how's your day been, darling?'

I didn't think it could get much worse, but now I'm not so sure.

'Actually I won't,' I say, as he goes to pour me a refill. 'I've got a bit of a headache.' I hope that Shelley might take the hint.

'You do look a bit heavy-eyed,' is all she says.

My heart sinks as I wonder how long I've got to stand here and pretend everything is normal.

'So, how have you been?' Shelley asks, looking directly at me. It doesn't sound like a question you'd ask someone you'd seen a couple of days ago.

'Not bad,' I bat back quickly, before she has a chance to add, *I haven't seen you in ages.* 'Not much has changed since the last time I saw you.' I chuckle so that Leon thinks I'm making a joke. This is already exhausting.

'So what's been going on with you?' asks Leon, when I neglect to.

'Well, the kitchen is *finally* finished,' she says. 'And the living room and hall have been redecorated.'

'Great,' says Leon. 'Are you happy with it?'

I feel as if I'm on mute, unable to join this conversation for fear of saying something incriminating.

'Yeah, the decorators did a really good job,' says Shelley.

Leon nods appreciatively. 'It might be worth getting them to look at the flat,' he says. 'Were *you* impressed?'

'Yes, might be a good idea,' I say, ignoring the last question so clearly directed at me.

'You ought to come around and have a look,' says Shelley.

I want to pretend she's talking to Leon, but beads of sweat instantly collect on my upper lip when I realize she's talking to me.

'Oh,' says Leon.

Everything stalls, as if I'm watching the scene in front of me unfold in slow-motion. Leon's mouth opens, and I want to rush towards him and cover it to stop him from saying anything more. His lips move and a low-pitched sound buffers around my head, like a lagging tape recorder.

'Didn't you see it the other night?' he asks, tilting his head to the side.

My eyes dart from him to Shelley, desperately trying to gauge how much attention she's paying and whether I can stop the scales from tipping precariously against me.

She raises her eyebrows questioningly and I widen my eyes to silently plead with her not to push this any further. But how can I alert her and answer Leon with a single look?

'I-I . . . don't think you've seen it,' she says, knowing full well I haven't.

'I thought you were round there the other night,' says Leon. A rhetorical question he expects an answer to.

Shelley looks at me with a furrowed brow, waiting for me to take the lead. A flush of heat engulfs me as I try to work out how to navigate my way around this, though as the pair of them stand there looking at me, it seems my only option is to steamroll my way straight through the middle of it.

'Well, I didn't actually go in,' I offer, unable to meet Shelley's inquisitive gaze which I can feel burning into me. 'So I didn't get the chance to see it.'

'But I thought you said you had a cup of tea,' presses Leon.

My head spins as I try to unwind myself from this web of deceit I've spun. How can a tiny lie have spiralled so out of control? Been turned into something that could have devastating consequences, not just for me, but for everyone? Perhaps if I'd been honest with Leon in the first place, I would have felt better equipped to tell the police what I know, so that they have all the facts at their disposal.

'I brought her one out,' says Shelley, in a sudden rush. She says it so quickly that as I turn to look at her, it's clear to see she has no idea how to follow it up.

'Yes,' I say. 'They were still working in the house and she didn't want me to see it until it was finished.'

Shelley laughs awkwardly. 'So I made her stand in the porch,' she says, warming to the theme. 'And brought the tea to her.'

We look at each other and I can see the cloud of confusion in her eyes; hurt, even, that I'd use her as an alibi for something that didn't happen.

13

I barely sleep a wink again that night.

It's preposterous, I know, but I can't shake off the gut-wrenching possibility that my father is somehow involved. If I'm honest with myself, he's always involved, because as much as I try to pretend that I've never given him a second's thought, I live with what he did every day of my life. He's why I veer between being helplessly needy and fiercely independent. He's why I have no friends who know me well enough to know that I love dancing to old Britney Spears songs, too scared to get close enough to anyone for them to find out. He's why I made the difficult decision not to have children, so terrified that someone would take them away from me, tearing my heart out. And he's why I do the job I do; in the hope that I can save just one person from the same fate as my mother.

A notification pings on my phone and I wearily lift my head up to look at it; an email from Wendy at Gulliver's Travels. If they're trying to tempt me with a too-good-to-miss offer, they've picked the wrong day. I go to swipe it off the screen, but notice that the subject heading reads: *Your upcoming flight to New York (JFK)*. I frown.

I click on it, waiting for the spam to reel me in, but it's a personalized itinerary for a trip I don't remember booking. I do a quick scan and see that the flight I'm supposedly taking is tomorrow. Something's not right.

Slipping my robe off the hook on the back of the bedroom door, I pad downstairs, grateful that Leon has already gone to work, as I don't need him asking me questions I don't want to answer. That's all he seems to do lately. That's all everyone seems to do.

'Morning, can I speak to Wendy, please?' I say, nestling my mobile awkwardly between my ear and shoulder whilst I fill the kettle. Coffee's going to be solely responsible for getting me through today.

'This is Wendy speaking,' says the cheery woman.

'I wonder if you can help me,' I say, careful to keep my cards close to my chest in case it's a scam. 'I've just received an email from you this morning, confirming a flight for tomorrow.'

'O-kay.'

I force a laugh. 'It's just that I haven't actually booked anything with you. Or anyone else for that matter.'

'Oh,' says Wendy. 'That's odd.'

I imagine her sitting in a cubicle in an illicit call centre looking for the 'what to say when they tell you they haven't booked anything', section on a laminated card.

'Can you give me your name, please, and I'll look into it?'

I give her my name and the flight booking reference, and hear her tapping away on a keyboard.

'OK, so you're on a Virgin Atlantic flight tomorrow from Heathrow to JFK departing at 16.35,' says Wendy.

'Yes, I know what it says, but it's not something I've booked.'

'So, are you looking to cancel the booking?' she asks.

Ah, there it is. I silently count how long it's going to take for her to ask for my bank details to process a refund.

'Well, yes,' I say, stating the obvious.

'OK, no problem, let me just organize that for you now,' she says, tapping away. 'I can credit the original payment method, but there will be a cancellation fee.' I have to hand it to her; she's very good.

'Thanks,' I say blithely.

'Will Mr Michael Talbot be looking to cancel his seat as well?'

My breath catches in my throat, obstructing my airways.

'I-I'm s-sorry?' I stutter, sure that I've heard her wrong.

'Mr Talbot is down to travel with you on the same booking,' she repeats with crystal clarity. 'Will you be wanting to cancel his seat as well?'

I throw the phone down onto the kitchen worktop and watch it spin, hanging on to the granite to stop myself from spinning with it.

What the . . . ?

'Hello, Mrs Chandler . . . ?' calls out Wendy. 'Are you still there?'

I numbly stab at the end call button, but she's still talking. 'Hello? Hello?'

What the hell is going on?

I can't help but think of my father, my sister, Jacob's wife; their faces warped caricatures of the people I imagine them to be as they goad me. Who knew I had so many enemies?

Boiling water splashes onto my hand as I carelessly tip the contents of the kettle into my mug. I cry out, more in panic than pain.

What if Jacob is a completely fictionalized character? A puppet created and controlled by a master manipulator? He could have been told what to say, how to behave, what to do to reel me in. Vanessa probably doesn't even exist, a made-up cast member in this debauched pantomime designed to bring me down.

The rising sun streams through the kitchen window, its bright rays falling like daggers onto the tiled floor. A prism of seven colours dances on my bare foot as I step in and out of the shadows.

My mother used to say that we should always try to be a rainbow in someone else's grey cloud, the brightness when their world is dark; the overarching bridge for them to get to the other side. It's what she always strove to be, instilling in me that everyone deserves to have colour in their lives.

154

I'd thought *I* was the colour in Jacob's life; selflessly laying myself down for him to cross. But perhaps I'm just a narcissist who feeds my own need for gratification with other people's insecurities. Even as I'm thinking it, I know it's not true, but I don't know what to believe any more.

There's a movement down the end of the garden, and I freeze, mug in hand, my breathing shallow as I try to focus on what it is. The branches of an imposing oak tree overhang the front of my office, creating moving swathes of darkness and light as they sway in the breeze. And the low sun is blindingly bright, obscuring my vision, but there is definitely a figure there.

I rush to my laptop on the dining table and check my schedule for the day to see that my first client is Melanie Langley at nine.

I inwardly groan. The last thing I feel like doing right now is propping somebody else up when all around me it seems that my good intentions are being exploited. But my dread is immediately replaced with guilt. It's not all around me; it's one person and it's not anyone else's fault that my trust has been so poorly misplaced.

I check the time on the corner of the screen and again on my watch, wondering why Melanie is an hour early. Or, more likely, how my ravaged brain has got the time wrong.

I hate being late for my clients. I don't want them to be knocking on a door that's not going to be opened.

Or spend even a minute waiting for someone who they think doesn't value their time. It all erodes their fragile spirit; yet another person has let them down. And I don't want that person to be me.

I gather up the files on the table and tuck my laptop under my arm.

'I'm so sorry,' I call down the garden to the figure shrouded in shade. I rummage for an excuse, but it's not as if I can get away with 'the traffic was terrible' or 'I missed the train'. So instead, I'm honest and say, 'I completely lost track of time.'

A woman who looks a lot like Anna steps out from the shadows, which completely confuses my already discombobulated brain.

'Oh,' I say, as I wait for her to morph into Melanie Langley.

'I'm sorry, I just needed to see you before your first client,' she says.

'Is everything OK?' I ask, conscious that I've not yet got around to finding her somewhere to live.

Her eyes instantly fill with tears.

'What is it? What's wrong?'

'Can I come in, for just a minute?' she says.

'Of course,' I say, fumbling with my keys to try to open the door.

'Here, let me help you,' she says.

As she reaches out to take the folders and laptop from under my arm, I see a vivid red welt on her wrist.

She catches me looking and quickly rearranges herself, pulling down the sleeve of her jacket.

'What's happened?' I ask.

She doesn't say anything as she follows me into the office.

'Anna?'

She puts my things on the desk and takes a moment before turning around – I guess in an effort to compose herself. But she doesn't need to put on a brave face for me.

'Anna?' I ask again, going to her and putting a hand on her shoulder.

As soon as she feels my touch, her shoulder caves in, as if it has been waiting for an excuse to.

'What is it?' I ask, my voice thick with empathy.

She automatically turns into me, her body racked with deep sobs. 'I-I can't . . .' she whimpers. 'I just can't do this . . .'

'It's OK,' I say, wrapping my arms around her. 'It's going to be OK.'

'No, no, it's not,' she cries. 'Nick went for one of the children last night.'

'Oh my god,' I say, holding her away from me. 'What happened?'

'It's my fault,' she says. 'I should have expected it. He's been acting so strangely recently and it's all been building up to today.'

'Today?'

She nods. 'It's the anniversary. It's a year today that we lost Ben.'

'Oh Anna, I'm so, so sorry.'

She falls heavily onto the couch. 'I understand how hard the last few days have been; waking up to the sickening reality that after today, we can no longer say, "This time last year, Ben was alive."'

I nod, knowing first-hand what a devastating milestone that is. It suddenly feels that the person you love and miss more than life itself is so much further away than they were before.

'But I never dreamt he would take it out on the children,' she says. 'Doing what he did to me the other night was shock enough . . . but the children?' She shakes her head. 'I can't have that. I *won't* have that.'

I sit next to her and place a reassuring hand on her knee. Every part of my training told me to keep a distance from my clients, both literally and metaphorically, but it goes against human nature to see someone this distressed and not reach out a hand to comfort them.

'You and the children can stay here whilst we figure out a game plan,' I say.

'I couldn't . . .' she chokes. 'I—'

'It's OK,' I say.

'I don't want to cause a problem between you and your husband,' she says, her eyes searching mine.

'Why would you think that?' I ask, hoping that she can't see through my veneer.

'He didn't seem very happy that I was here the other night,' she says. 'And the last thing I want to do is make things difficult for you.'

'It's absolutely fine,' I say. 'He was probably just distracted because he's got a lot going on.'

She tries to smile, but it doesn't reach her eyes. 'Could I . . . could I get a glass of water?' she asks, her voice hoarse.

I look around for the jug I always bring down with me, but remember I was caught on the hop, so didn't get around to it.

'I'll go and get you one,' I say, starting to stand up before thinking better of it. I really don't want to leave her on her own.

'It's fine,' she says, as if reading my mind. 'I'll be OK.'

I spend the time it takes me to walk up the path back to the house to practise what I'm going to say to Leon. But then I wonder if it might be the distraction we need, *I* need, to hold off the freight train that's railroading my life right now.

'Hello,' he shouts down the phone, when I call him from the kitchen whilst waiting for the tap to run cold.

'Hi, it's me, I know you're busy, but I just wanted to give you the heads up that Anna, the woman you met the other night, is going to stay with us for a few days – with her children.'

There's a loaded silence at the end of the line and I'm

secretly hoping that he's too busy to care. But who am I trying to kid?

'Is this a joke?' he barks.

I close my eyes and try to calm myself. I don't want another row. 'It's not going to make much difference to you,' I say. 'You'll be working all weekend.'

'Yes, exactly! And in the rare moment I'll get to myself, I'd like to be able to come back to my house, for a few minutes away from all the madness.'

'I promise you won't even know they're here,' I offer.

'When are you going to stop with this one-woman crusade to save the world?'

'That's not fair,' I say. 'I've only ever wanted to help people.'

'What, by setting up some halfway house where all of life's waifs and strays can come and go as they please?'

'No, if you'll just—'

'I tell you what,' he says, and I know another barb is coming. 'Why don't you put *her* in the flat as well?'

My blood runs cold.

'We can turn it into a commune for battered husbands and wives, or would you prefer to keep it for just you and lover boy?'

'Leon . . .' I start, though I have no idea how to say what needs to be said.

'Do what you like,' he snaps. 'I've got work to do.'

The line goes dead and I take a few minutes before

going back down to the office, jug in hand and a fixed smile on my face.

'Thanks,' says Anna, as she sits back down on the couch and pours herself a glass of water.

'Leon says it's absolutely fine,' I say with a reassuring smile. 'We've got two spare rooms, so there's plenty of space for you and the children.'

'Thank you,' she says. 'It's just until I get myself sorted out.' She snorts derisorily. 'If you'd have told me that I'd ever be in this position, that Nick would ever turn violent . . .'

'None of us know what turn of events our lives are going to take,' I say. 'Even the strongest relationships can do a complete one-eighty.'

'I would never have thought he was capable of . . . of bringing the children into this dark world he inhabits, especially after everything with Ben.'

I place a hand over hers in a show of solidarity. 'There's certainly a line that has to be drawn and that's normally when the children are directly impacted.'

She nods her head sagely. 'D'you know, there was a case in New York when I was a teenager, of a wife – the mother of a couple of kids, if I remember rightly – who was stabbed to death by her husband.'

I almost stop breathing. I'm trying to fix my focus on Anna's mouth which is still moving, but millions of tiny white dots are floating in front of my eyes, making me feel dizzy.

I must have imagined it. She couldn't have said what I think she said, yet her words are resounding in my head as if they're coming from a megaphone.

'You were probably too young to remember,' she's saying, through the wall of cotton wool that my defence mechanism is quickly attempting to build. 'But I vividly remember this horrific case and asking myself why that woman didn't get out when she had the chance. To save herself. To save her children.'

I suck in air that seems to be in short supply and Anna looks at me with a concerned expression.

'Are you OK?' she asks.

A sudden flash of the courtroom dazzles me and I'm back in the witness box, being interrogated by my father's lawyer.

'So that night, when your mom was dragged from the bed you were both lying on, what did you do?' he'd asked.

'I-I waited a while,' I'd stuttered. 'And when she started screaming, I ran into the kitchen.'

'And when you got there, you saw your mom with a knife in her hand,' said the lawyer, circling the courtroom floor as if he were performing in a high-brow play off Broadway.

My mouth had instantaneously dried up. I went to speak, but nothing came out, like when you're trapped in a nightmare and want to scream but there's no sound.

'Could you please speak up?' the lawyer had pushed,

in an effort to intimidate me even more than I already was.

I cleared my throat. 'N-no, she didn't have the knife.'

The lawyer had looked momentarily perplexed, as if I was playing some kind of a joke on him.

'OK,' he'd said patronizingly, as if he'd decided to play along. 'So where was the knife when you walked in?'

'I don't know,' I said. 'I think it was on the side.'

'You don't know,' he repeated, as if he hadn't heard the second half of the sentence.

'It was on the side,' I said more concisely, leaning into the microphone.

'And where was your mother?'

I looked at my father, sitting there in his best three-piece suit, the one he saved for church on the odd occasion he went to repent his sins.

'She was bent over,' I said. 'He had her by the hair and was kneeing her in her stomach.'

'OK, so she picked up the knife to stop him from hurting her any further?' said the lawyer, putting words in my mouth.

'No,' I said, not wanting to say what happened next, but knowing that I had to. '*I* picked up the knife.'

The lawyer had looked from me to my father and back again.

'He was hurting my mom and wouldn't stop,' I said. 'I was screaming at him, telling him to stop, but he wouldn't listen – he just kept on hitting her and kicking her again and again. So I picked up the knife and asked him to stop one more time.'

The lawyer's eyes had shot up to the brass plaque impregnated into the panelled wooden wall behind the judge, as if he were silently praying for patience.

'But didn't your mother say, "I'm going to kill you." Meaning that she was intending to kill your father.'

I'd looked at my father, who was surreptitiously nodding his head.

'Your honour, the defence is leading the witness,' said the prosecution, standing up.

'Rephrase the question,' said the judge, a woman with short grey hair, whose face completely changed depending on who she was looking at.

'So what happened next?' the lawyer asked me.

I wasn't quite sure. It had flashed in front of my eyes so many times, but it was at such speed that I couldn't make sense of it. I'd tried to slow it all down, but it was still chaotic.

'I . . . I . . .'

'Just take your time,' he'd said, but the angst on his face suggested he meant the opposite.

'I . . . I stabbed him with it,' I said, as quiet as a mouse.

'She's lying!' my father yelled, gesticulating as he leapt up.

The judge slammed her hammer down on the desk.

'You will refrain from speaking out unless asked to do so.'

I'd sat on my shaking hands, watching my father shrug off the security guard who was standing by his side.

The lawyer returned to where my father was seated and whispered something in his ear.

Dad's mouth was pulled tight and he glared at me as he nodded in response.

'Naomi. May I call you Naomi?' asked the smug man, as he returned to stand in front of the witness box.

I didn't want him to call me anything. I wanted to go home.

'What has happened to your mother – to your family – is something no young girl should ever have to go through.'

The threat of tears pulled at my throat.

'But I'm sure that you don't need me to remind you that if your father wasn't protecting himself against your mother, he can no longer cite self-defence for the crime he has committed.'

I'd nodded, fully aware of what I was doing, if not entirely sure what it would mean for me. But I didn't care – as long as he got what he deserved.

He'd looked at me before going on. 'So you understand that there is a much higher chance that he will go to prison for a very long time. He'll be away from you, away from your younger sister. Who will be there to take care of you? You have to be honest about what happened, so that we can get your dad back home and start rebuilding your family.'

'Your honour, the defence is leading the witness,' stated the prosecution again.

'Do you have a question?' the judge had asked.

The lawyer had looked at me through narrowed eyes. 'So I'd like to ask you again,' he said, pausing for effect. '*Who* stabbed your father?'

I'd leant into the microphone, aware that the deadly silent courtroom was holding its breath. 'I did,' I said, as clearly and succinctly as I could. 'I stabbed him.'

14

I feel sick, as if I've been kicked in the stomach. I can't shake off the feeling that everybody is out to get me and I'm a flailing ship without a port in the storm. I need to steady myself, so that I don't sink beneath the rising waters that are perilously close to taking me under.

I knew that my father's trial was a big deal in New York at the time, but I could never have imagined that it would follow me to England almost thirty years later; that there were people in the world who were affected by it back then and were still able to recall a life I've tried so hard to forget.

Unable to help myself, I ease up the lid of my laptop and sit with fingertips poised over the keyboard. I've never thought to do this, but it suddenly occurs to me that even those who weren't aware of the case at the time only have to put a few keywords into Google to find out all about it.

I type in 'Man kills wife 1995 New York' and hover over Enter, asking myself if I really want to do this. I swallow hard, hit the button and close my eyes, not knowing what is waiting for me when I open them.

Eventually working up the courage, I squint and am

immediately sucker-punched by an image of two little girls: me, holding an ice cream, smiling self-consciously into the camera lens, and my sister, with her trusty pink bunny rabbit beside her and half her ice cream smeared around her face.

Tears immediately spring to my eyes and I let out an anguished whimper. I remember this being taken at the Richmond County Fair, just a year or so before our family was torn apart. Dad had won the watermelon eating contest, which had made me ridiculously proud, and we'd celebrated with all the candy we could stomach. I can still feel the wholeness I'd felt that day; the contentment of being with Mom and Dad, safe from the outside world. Who knew we needed protection from someone within our own home?

I look at Jennifer's chubby little face, her eyes alight with wonder at everything going on around her, and I hate my father even more for taking that away from her. Somehow, I forged my way through the debris he left in his wake, carving out a life I felt I deserved. But Jennifer wasn't so lucky. She got lost in the mire and it pains me every day that I wasn't able to pull her out. Though as she looks back at me from the screen, I can almost see her mouthing the words, *You didn't try hard enough*.

I slam the lid down and cry out into the silence of the house, in a desperate attempt to rid myself of the thought that my own sister could be masterminding a plot to bring me down. Would she go to such lengths? Does she really blame me for everything our father put us through?

There's only one person who can calm my over-active imagination, but as I pull my denim jacket on with the intention of going to see Leon, I'm reminded of his vicious words on the phone when I told him about Anna. On top of everything else, just when I need him most, it seems that my anchor is rapidly drifting away.

As I head over to the main house, I use the short walk to clear my lungs and my head of all the toxic thoughts relentlessly attacking it.

'Hey, Naomi,' says Tristan, as I approach the security lodge. 'How you doing?'

'I'm good thanks, any idea where Leon is?' I ask, sweeping my eyes across the bank of monitors on the desk.

'Mmm, there's a lot of activity today,' he says, seeing me looking. 'Everyone's getting ready for tomorrow.'

I smile.

'It doesn't make my job very easy,' he goes on. 'There's been people here all through the night. How am I to know whether they're supposed to be on site or not?'

'I guess you just need to stand down security between now and the concert,' I say. 'Otherwise you'll get an alert every two minutes.'

'That's what Leon said,' says Tristan. 'I've turned off

most of the cameras and I'm just getting rid of all the footage from last night.'

I watch as he blocks out a thirty-minute frame of time with his mouse and presses delete, before repeating the process again. 'I'll be here all day,' he says, rolling his eyes.

'So no sign of Leon anywhere?' I ask again.

'He was over by the stage the last time I saw him,' says Tristan.

'Thanks, I'll try him there.'

I follow the gravel drive away from the main house, walking down through the copse before it opens onto the sprawling lawns of the concert site. There are people everywhere, carrying out tasks like a colony of worker ants, each with a specific job to complete.

Music is being intermittently blasted through the sound system and there is a palpable sense of anticipation, a mixture of excitement and tangible stress, but perhaps the latter is just emitting from Leon. He's over by a speaker that's almost as big as he is, gesticulating wildly to the group of men in front of him.

I take my time to approach, knowing that seeing me is most likely going to create even more tension in Leon's already taut shoulders.

I'm proved right when his lips pull into a grimace, as if he has a bad taste in his mouth.

'OK, I'll come back and see how you're getting on in an hour's time,' he says, walking away from the men and towards me.

'How's it all going?' I ask earnestly; my attempt at an olive branch.

'We're getting there,' he says. 'Slowly but surely.'

'It's looking great.'

'What's up?' he says, walking away with purpose. I guess he's expecting me to follow him.

'I don't want to be arguing and fighting all the time,' I say. 'We've both got a lot on our plates and we should be supporting each other, not going out of our way to make things difficult.'

'You're doing that all by yourself,' he says spitefully.

'Look, I know that sometimes I frustrate you, especially where my work and clients are concerned, but I'm only ever trying to do my best by them. It shouldn't come between us. They're two very separate things.'

'Except you continue to blur the lines,' he says, striding so fast that I have to walk-run to keep up with him.

'OK, so I admit that I might not always act in as professional a manner as you'd like, but it's never done to hurt or upset you.'

He stops stock-still and turns to face me. 'Isn't it?' he asks.

'Of course not,' I say, half laughing.

'Well, if that was the case, you'd tell me exactly what's going on at the flat then,' he says.

My mouth dries up and I swallow the regret that I haven't been honest with him. About the flat, about Jacob, about the police . . .

'Leon, I—'

'I'm not going to do this now,' he says dismissively. 'I've got enough to deal with.'

The strain of everything he's trying to juggle is evident by his furrowed brow and wide eyes. He looks like a rabbit caught in headlights and I wonder for the first time whether he's taken on too much. Not helped by me.

'Is there anything I can do?' I ask. 'If you just point me in the right direction . . .'

He shakes his head. 'Haven't we got house guests this afternoon?'

'Yes, but not until early evening. Anna's gone shopping to get the bits she and the children need, to save her from going back to the house.'

His jaw spasms. 'And we're supposed to continue this charade of everything being fine between us all the time she's here, are we?'

'It's just a couple of days,' I say. 'Let's get the weekend over and done with, and then we can sit down when we're less stressed and talk everything through.'

He nods tightly and goes to walk away, but I grab his hand, forcing him to turn back and look at me.

'I *do* love you,' I say, as tears instantly spring to my eyes.

'I love you too,' he says, though it sounds as if he's got a gun to his head.

As I begin to walk back in the direction of the cottage,

there's a tap on the microphone that booms around the site.

'Testing, testing,' comes a voice, so close that the speakers screech.

I can't help but flinch at the unwelcome sound penetrating my fragile eardrums.

I instinctively turn to see a man standing on the stage, looking as if he's living out all his teenage fantasies.

'He-llo Tattenhall!' he yells, before smiling as if imagining a raucous response. 'I'd like to pretend that I'm about to launch into "Smells Like Teen Spirit", but unfortunately all I have to offer is a credit card I've just found over there.' He points to the area of long grass that runs into the coppice I'm walking towards. 'So if you or someone you know is called ... Michael Talbot—'

My ears shut off any sound. My feet stop moving. He couldn't have said what I thought he said. But as I shake my head, trying to banish the fragments of doubt, the man on stage only serves to compound them.

'So no takers?' he booms. 'Well, OK then, but if the elusive Michael Talbot doesn't claim it soon, I'll be heading to the pub with it after work and the drinks are on me.'

I force myself forwards, struggling to stay upright as I stumble through the undergrowth. My lungs can't work quickly enough as I suck in the air I need to stop myself from keeling over. I can't help but feel as if I'm an unwitting guest at a murder mystery party, trying to figure out the macabre clues that are being left like pieces of cheese; every single one of them luring me towards the spring-loaded, cast-iron jaws of a mousetrap.

15

I don't remember the route I took home, but my senses are returned to sharp clarity by the dark blue Ford sitting on the drive.

'Ah, Mrs Chandler,' says the policewoman from yesterday as she appears from around the side of the cottage. I immediately feel as if I've been caught out and my cheeks flush.

'Detective Inspector Robson,' she says, flashing her ID. 'And you remember my colleague, Detective Sergeant Harris. May we come in?'

'What's this about?' I ask, as I put the key into the front door.

'Some new information has come to light about Michael Talbot that I hope you might be able to help us with.'

Does she know about the credit card? Might she have overheard the announcement on the tannoy?

'I've told you all I know,' I say, as my mouth instantly dries up.

'Not on this matter, you haven't,' says Robson.

She's trying her best to keep the accusatory tone from her voice, but suspicion and distrust drip from every syllable. My chest tightens as I push the door open, knowing that her doubt in my story is validated.

'So, how can I help you?' I ask, as the three of us stand in the living room. They won't be staying long enough to warrant offering them a seat.

'We found Mr Talbot's phone in his flat,' says Harris.

I wonder if I should comment on how odd that is. That no one goes anywhere without their phone these days. Otherwise, it looks as if I already know that Jacob has.

'He wouldn't have left without his phone, surely?' I say, looking between them. 'Not if he'd gone willingly.'

'It's of some concern,' says Robson. 'But it *has* meant that we've been able to access all of Mr Talbot's recent activity.'

'Great,' I say feebly. 'Hopefully we'll get some answers.'

They look at each other before Harris takes a phone out of his inside pocket and swipes it open.

'Mr Talbot made a call to you on the night of the twenty-first of June. I assume that was when he told you that his wife had found out where he was.'

'Yes,' I say, feeling hot around the back of my neck. I lift my hair and pull it over my shoulder in an attempt to cool myself down.

'There are then six further calls from you and a text message asking him to call you.'

'I-I was worried. I just wanted to know that he was OK.'

176

'But not worried enough to call us?' asks Harris.

I snort. 'No disrespect, but you drag your heels when it's an emergency, so I didn't think a threat against a man from his wife was going to see you come out with a blue light.'

'You also left a voicemail,' says Robson, ignoring the slight.

Harris taps the screen a few times and holds the phone up on speaker mode.

'Hi, it's me . . . Naomi. Erm, listen, about last night, I'm sorry that it ended up like it did. I think the alcohol played a large part. Anyway, I hope we can wipe the slate clean and put it all behind us. I'll see you tomorrow, but if you hear from Vanessa in the meantime, call me.'

I want the ground to open up and swallow me.

'So this was a message you left on Michael's voicemail on Tuesday morning,' says Robson, looking at me through narrowed eyes. 'Do you want to explain what you were referring to?'

I think about denying it's me, but I say my name. I think about saying that the message was meant for someone else, but I mention Vanessa. I think about telling the truth, but that will get me in a whole heap of trouble. So I opt for something in between and cross my fingers.

'When Jacob called me, he'd clearly had a lot to drink,' I say, not yet knowing where I'm going with this. I pause, playing for time. 'He asked if he could come to the office, but it was late, so I said no.'

They're both looking at me, waiting for me to elaborate.

'He was insistent, but I stood firm and told him that if he had a problem, he should call the police.' That's not too far from the truth.

'But the next day, you'd had a change of heart?' asks Robson.

'I'd thought about it and wanted him to know that I'd not taken offence to anything he said the night before and if he did hear anything further from his wife, then it was OK to call me.'

I'm looking between them, hoping that I've let them know he needs help, but without entangling myself and confusing the issue.

'It's his wife you need to talk to,' I say. 'She's the one who will know where he is.'

Robson nods thoughtfully, though there's nothing but suspicion in her eyes.

'And you're still maintaining that you have never been in an improper relationship with Mr Talbot.'

'Absolutely,' I say adamantly.

She gives a nod to her colleague.

'You said that you hadn't been to Mr Talbot's flat since he moved in.'

I nod, swallowing the lump in my throat. 'Th-that's right.'

Harris turns the phone towards me and clicks on an app too quickly for me to see what it is. But suddenly, my face is on the screen, screwed up and pinched as I stare out of it.

I'm so shocked that I jump back, as if scared of my own reflection. My brain spurts and splutters as it hotwires itself to make sense of what it's seeing. I hope that by the time my eye sends the pixels to the part that puts them all together, the picture will have changed. But as I look at the phone, waiting, it's still me, looking like a deranged woman, staring out of it.

'Jacob? Are you there? I know you're in there,' comes a voice that sounds a lot like my own. 'Look, I'm sorry about what happened the other night, but surely we've got to be a bit grown-up about this? Why don't you just open the door so we can talk?'

I don't want to look at the screen, but I have to, to know it's me. My features are contorted, not helped by the curvature of the lens. 'Is she in there with you?' I hiss. 'You're going to need to come out, because I'm not leaving until I see you.'

Detective Harris taps a button and the torment stops, but I know it's only going to be a matter of seconds before it starts again. What the hell have I done?

'So, this footage is from a doorbell camera at the property that Mr Talbot rents from you,' says Robson.

'I didn't know he'd installed a camera,' I say, making myself sound even more guilty. I shove my hands into my pockets and look down at the floor. It's taking all of my concentration not to collapse in a heap.

'This was the night before last,' Robson goes on, ignoring the thumping of my heart that she must surely be able to hear. 'Yet, you said—'

'I did go around there,' I blurt out, unable to stop my conscience from telling the truth. But how can I possibly lie about this? 'I was worried about him when he didn't turn up for our appointment, so I went round there to check he was OK.'

'This was because he said his wife had threatened him?'

'Yes.'

'Yet from this footage, it seems that you were the one threatening him,' says Robson.

I run a shaky hand through my hair and pace up and down, unable to believe how my good deed has turned into me being accused of . . . of what?

'Why did you tell us you hadn't been round there?'

'B-because . . .' I stutter. 'I hadn't told my husband that Jacob, I mean Michael, was living in the flat.'

'Why not?' asks Robson, her interest piqued.

'It's just a bone of contention between us. He thinks I do too much for my clients, get more involved than I should. But the flat was sitting there empty and Jacob – Michael – needed somewhere to go. It was a matter of urgency, so I told him to go there. I just haven't got round to telling Leon yet.'

'Would you mind coming down to the station with us?' says Harris, putting the phone into his back pocket.

I almost expect him to bring out a pair of handcuffs in its place.

'Am I under arrest?'

'No, but we do need to take your fingerprints and a statement from you, and it would be easier if this were done at the station.'

'I need to leave a note for my husband,' I say.

Robson nods and I walk into the kitchen on legs that don't feel like my own.

Out of sight, I pick up the chalk pen and look at the chalkboard on the wall, where we normally write the shopping list, wondering how I'm supposed to leave a message of such magnitude next to eggs, bananas and teabags.

I imagine Leon's shock and confusion as he struggles to understand how the wife who'd just told him she loves him is now being questioned about the disappearance of a man it looks like she was stalking. And he thought putting Anna up for a couple of nights was a problem.

Shit, Anna! She could be back any minute and I'm not going to be here. I finger the chalk pen in my hand, trying to suppress the tears and panic that are welling up inside me.

Just popped out, I write. *Should be home in time for dinner, but there's mince in the fridge if I'm not.*

'Ready?' asks Robson, eyeing me up and down suspiciously, as if I might be concealing something from the cutlery drawer.

I nod, and as I follow them out, I surreptitiously pop a key under the doormat in the porch, in the hope that Anna will look there when she gets no answer.

16

The police station in Canterbury is a twenty-minute journey in a mercifully unmarked car. It's so nondescript that I'm not surprised I haven't noticed it before. It's like the ones you see on BBC cop dramas; a three-storey, Sixties-built building that looks like a block of flats rather than a place of authority.

I'm shown to a windowless room and asked if I want a hot drink. I decline, but they still leave me on my own for five minutes. I wonder which of the walls is a secret two-way mirror.

'So as I explained, this is just a formality at this stage,' says Robson, coming back in. 'But we'll be recording you whilst we take your statement.'

I nod, wishing I knew my rights.

They both sit down opposite me and introduce themselves for the purposes of the tape.

'So you've told us that you visited Mr Talbot's flat on the evening of the twenty-third of June.'

I nod.

'Would you mind answering the question?' says Detective Robson, tilting her head in the direction of the tape recorder.

'Yes,' I say loudly.

'Because you were worried about his wellbeing, but he wasn't in.'

'He didn't answer the door, no.'

I squirm as they play the incriminating doorbell footage again.

'What did you mean when you said, "Is she in there with you? You're going to need to come out, because I'm not leaving until I see you"?'

I sigh. 'I thought Jacob's wife might be in there, holding him against his will.'

'Michael's, you mean?'

I nod before remembering the rules. 'Right.'

'Because she'd allegedly threatened him on the phone?'

'Not allegedly, no. She called him to say she knew where he was and implied that she was going to come for him.'

I look from one officer to another. 'Can I just ask whether you're holding her to account in this matter?'

They both look at me blankly.

'She's the one you need to be talking to,' I cry. 'I'm in no doubt that she would follow through on her threat.'

'We're not at liberty to—'

'For God's sake!' I've lost the patience I've tried so hard to hold on to. 'He lived in fear of her and now he's disappeared, you're wasting your time on *me*.' I fall back in my chair, forcing myself to breathe and calm down. 'I have no reason to wish him any harm. He was my client, nothing more.'

Detective Harris pushes a print-out of an email across the desk to me, the tips of his fingers resting on it territorially.

'We have now managed to access Mr Talbot's emails and there are a number of messages between the pair of you.'

I squint, more at the false accusation than the piece of paper itself. I can't ever remember an email exchange between us. I can't see any reason why I'd even have his email address, as all our conversations were either on the phone or by text.

'I'm sorry, what's this?'

'It's an email exchange, apparently between you and Mr Talbot,' says Detective Robson.

Harris releases the piece of paper from his grip and my brow furrows as I pick it up and start reading.

Darling Michael,

I know you didn't mean what you said last night.

You've probably woken up this morning regretting it, but I just want you to know that I still love you, more than ever, and NOTHING you say will ever make me love you less.

Call me when you can.

Love always,

Naomi x

I look up at the two detectives staring at me. 'What *is* this?' I ask, hoping to God that all the irrational thoughts flying around my head are about to be squashed.

'Well, it seems that it's an email from you to Mr Talbot,' says Detective Harris.

My lungs feel like they're being squeezed. I hold on to the sides of the table to steady myself.

'Where did you get this from?' My voice is just a rasp.

'From Mr Talbot's emails on his phone,' says Harris.

'But I didn't write this,' I say.

'There's more,' says Robson, laying out sheet after sheet of paper on the table in front of me. 'This one is of particular interest as it was sent the night before his wife reported him missing.'

I look at the typed words as they swim in front of my eyes.

Dear Michael,

I know you said that it's over between us, but you can't just shut me out like this and pretend it never happened. I put everything on the line for you and I will not be tossed aside just as soon as you've had your fun and are ready to go back to your wife.

I love you and I know you love me too – we are made for each other and I will not allow you

to throw away what we have. If I can't have you,
no one will.
  Naomi x

My blood turns ice-cold as I read the words I don't
recognize.

'Can you explain what you meant by, "If I can't have
you, no one will"?' asks Robson.

'I can't believe you think I'd write something like this,'
I choke. 'I'm a happily married woman, with a professional
reputation I guard fiercely. Yes, I may overstep the line
sometimes, but not in this way. And as I've told you a
hundred times, I don't even know a Michael Talbot. The
man you're talking about is Jacob Mackenzie to me. Why
would I have a folder in my office with his name on?
Why would he be listed in my phone as Jacob Mackenzie?'

'To hide your true relationship with him from your
husband?' offers Harris. 'You've already said that your
husband didn't know he was living in the flat you own,
so I'm guessing he also doesn't know that you went
round there the night before last. Why wouldn't you tell
him if there was nothing to hide?'

'I've told you,' I say impatiently. 'Because he already
thinks I get too involved with my clients.' Every word
I utter feels like I'm sinking further and further into
quicksand.

I pick up a print-out of an email and look at the
sender's address: naomi5634hgt@hotmail.com.

'Anyone could have set this up,' I say, forcing a laugh, though nothing about this is funny.

The two police officers give each other a sideways glance.

'We're looking at all lines of inquiry at the moment,' says Robson.

I want to tell them to look into one they couldn't possibly have imagined. The recently released prisoner 491032-056 and his rehabilitated daughter who might well be leading this entire operation from a condo on Long Island. They might even be doing it from right here in Whitstable.

I shudder at the thought. Had they seen me? Followed me? Had my sister stood so close that she was able to smell my perfume? I wouldn't have known, I'm sure of that.

That blonde-haired, blue-eyed girl in the Google image is now a woman who haunts me. I try to kid myself that I would recognize her if I saw her now; that I'd have an innate sense of her being my own flesh and blood. But in reality she's a stranger, with a complex hatred for the sister who she believes abandoned her.

'So unless there's anything else you'd like to tell us,' says Robson, bringing me back into the room, 'you're free to leave.'

I scrape my chair back and stand up, desperate to get out from underneath her unswerving scrutiny.

We lock eyes and hers tell me everything I need to know.

She's adamant that I'm a jilted lover, that I've abducted Jacob, or Michael, or whoever he is, and am either holding him somewhere against his will, or have already done away with him.

She thinks that it's only going to be a matter of time before I slip up and reveal my secret. But I haven't got time on my side. The only way I'm going to get myself out of this is to find Jacob, and find him now.

17

I rush out of the police station, desperate for fresh air, and gulp it down.

I'm only a few miles from home, but standing on that roadside, I may as well be in another country. Everything feels so surreal, as if I'm frozen in time whilst everyone else rushes around me, utterly oblivious to the precipice I'm precariously balanced on.

It's as if I'm just waiting for someone to push me off, but without knowing which direction they're going to come from, it's impossible to shore myself up. I feel horribly vulnerable and exposed from every angle and would rather get it over with; for whoever is doing this to do their worst, so that I can open my eyes again. It's the waiting, the not knowing when and how, that's stopping me from breathing.

I have to take back control of this situation and wonder if I shouldn't just turn around, go back into the police station and tell them everything. Although I've done absolutely nothing wrong, there's still so much more I haven't told them, and I fear it's those untruths that I'm going to spend the rest of my life running from if something really has happened to Jacob.

Or I could just start eliminating myself from their inquiries, but to be able to do that, the evidence needs to match the narrative.

My head pounds as I walk to the train station, the facts and theories tugging and pulling it in every direction, making me feel like I'm living somebody else's life. I wish I was.

I try to pretend I'm on my old commute back to Whitstable and, as the train passes through the North Downs, I briefly lose myself in the banality of normal life.

The young man opposite, with bulbous headphones over his beanie hat, is playing out a drumbeat on his legs in time to the music. From his denim waistcoat over a black t-shirt, I'd hazard a guess he's listening to something like the Red Hot Chili Peppers. He's probably doing a history degree at Canterbury University, with a bar job on the side to supplement his marijuana habit.

He catches me looking and I move my attention to the girl two seats down from him. She's tap-tap-tapping on her phone, her thumbs moving faster than I'd think possible, smiling at whatever she's reading. She laughs out loud, before self-consciously looking around the carriage, as if surprised to find herself in the real world and not the one she's created on the screen.

She's rushing home to watch the new series of *Love Island*, whilst her boyfriend's in the next room playing *Call of Duty* against a stranger in Australia.

Having made my stereotypical judgements, I pull myself up, wondering what a passing stranger would think my life looked like right now. Dressed in calf-length printed trousers and a white shirt, I probably seem like your average office worker.

My ring finger will give my enviable status away, telling them I'm in a secure relationship that's meant to last a lifetime. I'm old enough to warrant perhaps three children, who are all currently being fed wholemeal pasta with an organic tomato sauce by their grandmother.

An unexpected barrage of tears rushes to my eyes, but I don't know if they're for the nan my mother will never be, or the fact that my world is so far removed from the one I'm portraying. An onlooker would never guess, as I twist my wedding band, that I'm about to go into battle to save my marriage. No one would know that the denim jacket draped so casually over my arm had to be taken off when I perspired under a police officer's questioning. And I'd give a thousand pounds to anyone on this train who thinks I'm a prime suspect in a man's disappearance.

As I squirm under the invisible microscope, an overwhelming heat envelops me. Pinpricks of sweat spring to my fingertips, as every pore on my body feels like it's being suffocated. My legs are like red-hot pokers, burning from the inside out, and my ribs feel charred from the furnace that's emanating from my core. I have to get off; I have to get some air.

If the train wasn't coming into Faversham, I'd pull the emergency stop lever, such is the panic collecting in every fibre of my being. I gasp as I fall through the opening doors, stumbling onto the platform, no longer caring who sees me or what they think. I drag myself over to a bench, collapsing onto it, fighting for breath.

I can't go home to Leon in this state; I need to think. I need to have a plan of action. I just need to sit him down and start from the beginning; explain why I haven't told him about the flat, tell him that I couldn't admit to meeting Jacob in the hotel . . .

The hotel. *Shit*.

Without even making a conscious decision to do it, I'm racing down the stairs and through the underpass to the other side of the tracks. I hear the slow rumble of an approaching train and take the stairs two at a time, reaching the top just as it thunders onto the platform.

'The train approaching platform three is to Dover Priory,' sounds the announcer. 'Calling at Selling, Canterbury East . . .' I don't listen any more; I've heard all that I need to hear.

I don't know if Andy, my former boss, is even working a shift at the hotel right now, but I've got to take this chance. It might be the only one I get.

Once I get back to Canterbury I want to run up the ramp towards the hotel, but I can't risk drawing attention to myself so I speed-walk instead. The lobby is surprisingly quiet, caught in the lull between guests having gotten in from their day's expeditions and going back out again for dinner. I force myself to walk slowly over to the reception desk.

'Hi, is Andy on duty?' I ask.

Everyone knows who he is; he doesn't need a surname.

'Andy Kerridge?' asks the receptionist, disproving my point. She must be new.

I smile and nod. 'Please.'

'I certainly saw him earlier,' she says. 'Let me see if he's still here.'

'Thank you,' I say, tapping my fingers on the marble countertop.

'Who shall I say is looking for him?' she asks, covering the mouthpiece of the phone with her hand.

I hesitate, suddenly conscious of leaving a trail that witnesses will be able to attest to later. This is ridiculous. I'm a victim, not a suspect.

'Can you just tell him it's Naomi.'

She looks at me waiting for more, clearly worried that it won't be enough. I offer her a tight smile to let her know it is.

I loiter around the potted palm trees, trying to blend in so no one will remember me if asked. Though my cover is blown when Andy strides across the polished stone floor with his arms aloft, shouting, 'Darling!'

I fall into his open embrace and kiss him on each cheek.

'I haven't seen you in ages,' he says. 'How are you?'

'I'm good,' I lie. 'How are things with you?'

'Well, Lance is driving me *insane*,' he says. 'But when isn't he?'

I smile, remembering the warm rapport he shares with his boyfriend, even though he likes to pretend he doesn't.

'Listen, I wonder if you could help me out?'

'Of course,' he says. 'Anything for my favourite former employee turned superstar psychotherapist.'

'It's actually a bit sensitive,' I say, leading him gently by the elbow out of earshot of anyone else.

'In-triguing,' he muses with a widening of the eyes. 'Tell me more.'

'Well, a few days ago, one of my clients came here, was supposed to check in, but hasn't been seen since.'

'Oh no!' says Andy.

'I know he was here,' I say, wondering how much I should share. 'Because I met him in the bar to make sure he was OK.' I'm in it now.

Andy nods thoughtfully. I give him a few seconds to hopefully come up with the suggestion before I have to spell it out.

'So you left him in the bar and he was fine?'

I nod. 'I could just really do with knowing where he went afterwards.'

'We'll look on the CCTV,' he announces.

'Could we?' I ask gratefully. 'Does it cover the lobby?'

He nods excitedly, thrilled by the opportunity to play Columbo. 'It covers the bar as well.'

My heart lurches, wondering what angle it captures, knowing that it could make all the difference in portraying what happened between Jacob and me as either an unrequited advance or the spark of sexual chemistry.

'Come this way,' he says, beckoning me over to the *Staff Only* door I used to go through at the start of my shift.

Not much has changed in the labyrinth of corridors beyond it, aside from the lilac uniforms the housekeeping team are bustling past in. They were blue in my day.

As we turn the corner to where a bank of monitors used to be tucked into a cubby under the stairs, I'm reminded of Ian, the security guard who worked here at the same time as me. He was Canadian and we forged a friendship over the fact that neither of us had visited the other's country, even though we were neighbours.

I'd spent many a lunch hour hunched under these stairs, eating a limp sandwich whilst alternating between studying for my licensing exams and playing the 'business or pleasure?' game with the guests. Ian and I would bet on whether a couple were here for work or play, going by their body language and how they greeted one another. It never ceased to amaze me how often a furtive peck on the cheek in the lobby was a prelude to them taking it in turns to ascend to a room on the upper floors. Ian would almost always win the wager, but then he'd seen more secret liaisons than I'd had hot dinners.

I can't help but wonder how much he would have put on Jacob and me the other night.

'Do you know the date?' asks Andy, his fingers poised over the keyboard.

'June twenty-first,' I say.

'And approximate time?'

I wish I could pinpoint the moment I'd left and Jacob was still there, but I can't even remember when I got here.

'It would have been around 9.30 p.m.,' I say.

Andy sits down and inputs the date and time into the system, which doesn't look too dissimilar to the one Ian used to operate. He clicks the mouse, turning the lobby into a time-lapse video, sending guests scurrying in and out of the shot. As the timer in the corner approaches 21.27 he clicks again and the recording returns to real time.

'OK, so why don't we take a look at the entrance first,' he says. 'See what time he left, if indeed he did.' I can't help but wince at his foreboding words. 'You said he was supposed to check in?'

I nod. 'But I called reception the following day and they had no record of him.' It's only as I say it out loud that it occurs to me I was asking for the wrong man. 'Actually . . .' I muse. 'Could you check again for me, under another name?'

Andy nods and pulls a notebook out of the top pocket of his suit jacket.

'Can you try Michael Talbot?' I say.

'I'll go and check now,' he says. 'Are you OK to stay here for a minute? I'll leave this running, so you can keep an eye on it.'

I could kiss him. 'Yes, of course,' I say, sitting down on the wheeled chair and pulling myself in towards the desk.

As soon as his back is turned, I click onto the live image of the bar in the top right corner of the screen and repeat what I've just seen him do, rolling the tape back ninety-six hours, to a time when my life was so much simpler.

It takes me a couple of minutes to find us, but as soon as I do, I almost wish I hadn't.

Without sound, we look like any other couple walking into a bar for a hard-earned drink after a long day. I hadn't realized it at the time, but my hand is on his arm, no doubt trying to reassure him that everything will be all right, but without context it looks like an intimate gesture between two people who are more than comfortable with each other.

I look up, knowing I haven't got long before Andy gets back. I double up on the speed, watching Jacob down four whiskies in quick succession, and press play at the moment I had gone to stand up.

I watch, mortified, as the 'will they, won't they' moment plays out on screen. If I didn't know the outcome, I'd definitely put money on us heading to a hotel room beyond the security cameras.

The flash of intensity from Jacob, as he accused me of leading him on, only adds to the apparent sexual tension.

There's no way I can let the police see this; not least because of what it looks like, but because I haven't even told them I was here. Though now Andy knows I was. *Shit.*

I pick up the phone on the desk and dial reception.

'Hello, this is room 328,' I say. 'I want a member of the managerial team up here right now. I've been waiting for my room service to be cleared for over half an hour.'

'I apologize, madam,' says the receptionist, making me feel wretched. 'I'll get that sorted for you immediately.'

'I want to see the manager,' I say.

'Of course, I'll send him up straight away.'

The damning video is stuck on freeze-frame, Jacob's hand interlocked with mine. It's just a moment, like all those frozen moments we pore over online, when we're convinced we're witnessing a new celebrity coupling. Though if we were to press play, it would be a man chivalrously holding a door open for a woman he's never met before as they arrive separately to an event, caught in the lens of a desperate photographer.

That's all this is, I say to myself as I look at the screen. *Just a moment.* But I'm not the one who needs to be persuaded.

Keeping an eye on the corridor where housekeeping

and room service are bustling past with trolleys laden with both food and dirty laundry, I drag the moving image back to where Jacob and I enter the bar, willing myself to recall what Ian used to do every three months when the footage was no longer needed.

I frantically stab at the delete button on the keyboard, but the image is still goading me from the screen. Suddenly I remember Tristan in the Tattenhall security lodge, blocking out great swathes of time with his cursor, eradicating the events of the previous twenty-four hours. It takes a couple of tries, but I eventually manage to double-click the mouse to highlight the time period that compromises my future and am offered an option to *delete the selected frame*. My hand shakes as the cursor hovers over *Yes*.

I tell myself I have no choice. That it is far too incriminating for an innocent person like me to risk leaving. But then I fast-forward to the police dramatically storming the hotel after a tip-off that the missing man, whose photo will be all over the news by then, was here shortly before he disappeared. They'll demand to see the CCTV, find that it's been wiped, speak to Andy, who'll have to admit to me being here and show them the hard drive back-up . . .

Stop! I scream at myself, my internal monologue threatening to spontaneously combust. This can't get any worse than it already is. And what I need to do now is absolve myself of any involvement.

I look up to the heavens and ask Mom for forgiveness as I hit *Yes*, hoping she'll understand my need to turn this investigation back onto the real guilty party, whoever that may be.

With all trace of myself now erased from the scene, I carry on watching the video as Jacob orders another whisky before answering a call on his mobile. He seems scared as he listens to whatever the caller is saying, looking around covertly as if frightened of what he might see.

I follow his gaze, but as his eyes fleetingly pass over the man at the other end of the bar, mine are rooted to the spot.

It can't be. It just can't be. I zoom in on the man's face, the image becoming grainier the closer I get, but there's no denying the blue checked shirt I'd laundered just this morning.

Numb, I watch the barman who'd served me just moments before put down a tumbler that Leon picks up and knocks back in one. What the hell was he doing there, and how had I not seen him? Had he been there all along or had he only come in once he'd seen me leave? I wince as I imagine what he might have heard . . . what he might have seen.

My heart is pounding as I watch him watching Jacob. His face is almost unrecognizable from that of the husband I know and love. His jaw is set and his fixed eyes are empty and dark, seemingly devoid of anything other than hate and intent.

Struggling for breath and with fingers that feel anaesthetized, I fumble for the mouse and will myself to remember what I've just done. I can't let anyone see this, but my brain just won't cooperate with my hands.

I cut and chop whole frames of time, indiscriminately hacking at whatever's there, desperate to erase all trace of anything that may incriminate me, and now, more importantly, Leon. If the police get wind of him and me being here on the night Jacob disappeared, the spotlight of suspicion will rest firmly on us both; the only distinction being that I *know* I've not done anything wrong. The sickening swirl in the pit of my stomach tells me that I can't say the same for Leon.

18

'Hi, I'm home,' I call out as I step into the hallway, desperately trying to sound as normal as I possibly can. But he knows me well enough to hear the falter in my voice; he may even be able to see the horrific images playing out in my head. Because try as I might, I'm unable to stop the rolling film of him bludgeoning Jacob to death.

I brace myself against the hall wall, biding my time, waiting for some kind of divine intervention to tell me how best to approach this.

When I walk into the kitchen, Leon's standing there barefoot, tending the pot on the stove. 'You OK?' he asks, when I go straight to the fridge for wine. He looks like the same man, sounds like the same man, but everything's different.

'We need to talk,' I say, going to the cupboard to get a wine glass. 'Do you want one?'

He stops stirring and looks at me, no doubt trying to gauge the seriousness of what I'm about to say.

'Do I need one?' he asks.

I take out two cut-glass goblets – a wedding gift from Leon's parents – and start to pour the already open bottle of Sauvignon Blanc.

'Can you come and sit down?'

'Mmm, sounds ominous. Should I turn the pan down?'

I want to tell him to turn it off altogether as I can't imagine either of us are going to have much of an appetite after this.

I nod and lead the way into the living room.

'So . . . ?' he asks.

'You remember my client, Jacob Mackenzie?' My stomach lurches as he shrugs his shoulders nonchalantly.

'What about him?' he asks.

I swallow, wishing I could stop this conversation. 'Well, he's gone missing.'

There's the tiniest intake of breath, but an onlooker would miss it. Tears teeter in my eyes as I wonder how far I'm going to have to push him to elicit a reaction.

'And the police seem to think that I've got something to do with it.'

'You've spoken to the *police*?'

'Yes, and they . . .' I start, unable to look at him. 'They seem to think that we've been having an affair.'

He takes a deep breath, puts his hands on his hips, and fixes me with a glare so intense that it makes my skin prickle.

'And have you?' he asks, his voice icy.

'Of course not!'

The loaded silence permeates the air, its weight sitting heavily on my chest, as I wonder who's going to be brave enough to speak next.

'So why is he living in our flat then?' he rasps, barely audible.

'How did you know?' I ask, whilst wanting to close my ears off to the answer.

He sighs. 'I went round there a few days ago. Imagine my surprise when I let myself in to find someone else's belongings filling the place.'

'I'm sorry,' I gasp. 'I wanted to tell you, I *should* have told you, but I just couldn't find the right time.'

'So, what's been going on?' he asks, his eyes boring into mine.

'Nothing,' I cry. 'Absolutely nothing.'

He walks away from me with his hands on his head.

'Have you . . . have you done something?' I ask, feeling braver now that he has his back to me.

He spins around. 'Like what?' he asks, his tone accusatory.

'Leon, we need to be honest with each other,' I say, going towards him. 'If we don't figure this out, work through this together, then we're going to be in a whole heap of trouble.'

He shrugs his shoulders.

'I saw you,' I say, swallowing hard. 'At the Royal Garden hotel.'

His eyes widen and he starts pacing the living room floor.

'What have you done?' I plead. 'You need to tell me.'

'I haven't done anything.'

'You went to the flat. You saw us at the hotel. His credit card was found on site *here*.' My voice is getting hoarser with every accusation. I imagine it's the stone-cold fear setting in.

'Credit card?' he exclaims. 'What credit card?'

'The one that guy announced over the microphone.'

Leon rummages in his pocket with a confused expression on his face. 'This is . . . Michael Talbot's credit card,' he says, looking at the thin piece of plastic in his hands.

I step away, knowing that being this close to a crucial piece of evidence will only incriminate me even more than I already am.

'That's his real name,' I cry. 'Apparently his real name is Michael Talbot.'

'So how the hell . . . ?' He shakes his head. 'I mean, what is his credit card doing here, at Tattenhall?'

I search his face for any sign of him knowing more than he's letting on, but there's only utter confusion etched there.

'I honestly don't know,' I say.

'So this is the guy you were in the hotel with,' he asks, holding the credit card in the air.

I nod.

'So why did you tell me you were at Shelley's?' he snaps, as if suddenly remembering why this all started.

'Why didn't *you* tell me you'd seen me?' I bite back.

'I didn't know how to,' he says, his shoulders slumping.

'I thought you were having an affair with him and was still working out what to do about it.'

'Why would you even think I'd do something like that?'

'Because he's living in our flat,' he barks. 'Though for some reason, you didn't see the need to tell me. And then you're in a hotel together . . .'

'We weren't in a hotel together,' I sigh. 'We were in a hotel bar.'

'Looking all cosy,' he says, bitterness still lingering in his voice.

'How did you even know I was there?' I ask.

'I followed you,' he says.

'But you were supposed to be in Birmingham . . .' I start, before it dawns on me. 'Did you even *go* to Birmingham?'

He looks at the floor sheepishly.

'So there wasn't an issue with the lanterns?'

He shakes his head. 'I knew he was in the flat, I saw the way you were together in the house that morning, and I wanted to see what would happen if I wasn't here. And as I suspected, you went straight to the hotel the minute my back was turned.'

'He called me in a panic,' I say. 'He told me his wife had found out where he was and he needed my help.'

'From what I could see, he looked like he wanted more than your help.'

'What did you see?' I ask, imagining it through his eyes. Though the eye of the CCTV was bad enough.

'He looked like a puppy dog,' he says, grimacing. 'Drooling and pawing at you.'

'He was drunk,' I offer in Jacob's defence. 'And he had confused our professional relationship with being something more. But we've got a bigger problem than that.'

Leon looks at me with raised eyebrows.

'The police have emails,' I say.

'What kind of emails?' asks Leon, his voice thick with suspicion.

'They say they're from me to him, but they're not. I've never sent him an email, nor has he ever sent me one. They're supposedly me proclaiming my love for him.'

The way Leon looks at me sends shivers down my spine.

'And threatening him when he doesn't reciprocate,' I almost whisper.

An involuntary spasm pulsates in his jaw and he locks eyes with me.

'What the fuck is going on here, Naomi?'

'I honestly don't know,' I cry. 'I think someone's setting me up.'

'Why would someone set you up?' he asks, his voice high-pitched. 'Who would want to do that?'

You, my father, my sister, Jacob's wife, I want to say, as I imagine them all circling above me like vultures waiting to pick the meat off my bones.

The very thought that the man I love more than

anyone in the world might be capable of stabbing me in the back and twisting the knife to such a degree devastates me. It's as if my heart is being ripped out of me by the very hand I trust the most.

I shudder, unable to comprehend what he might have done to Jacob, even though it would be the last thing I could possibly imagine him doing. But didn't I think the same about my father?

'OK,' he says when I offer no response. 'So the police have got nothing other than a bunch of fake emails, and anyone could have set those up to look like they were from you.'

He says it as if it's as easy as that, and I can't believe that we haven't yet had the hardest part of this conversation.

I swallow hard. 'They have doorbell footage as well.'

He looks at me, unblinking.

'I went round there the other night, when I was worried about him.'

'So you've visited him at the flat?' he asks incredulously, fixing me with a steely glare. 'And you wonder why I don't trust you.'

A sharp breath catches in my throat as the slight's jagged edges make themselves felt.

There's a distant ringing of a phone and I follow it to my bag on the back of the dining chair. It stops in the time it takes me to find it, but as I look at the screen, I see two missed calls from Anna.

'Oh my god, Anna!' I exclaim. 'Has she been here? Have you seen her?'

Leon looks at me in disbelief. 'Do you not think we've got far bigger problems to deal with?'

'But she was supposed to be here,' I say, making my way to the front door and lifting up the corner of the mat I'd thrown the key under when I left with the police officers. It's gone.

My phone rings again, and I rush back into the living room and snatch it up from the dining table.

'Don't answer it,' says Leon sharply.

'But Anna might be in trouble!'

'I swear to God, Naomi, if you pick that up—'

'Just give me a second,' I say holding one finger up. 'Let me just make sure she's OK.'

He throws his hands up in the air and I turn my back on him.

'Hello?' I breathe down the line. 'Anna, are you OK?'

'No,' is all she says.

'Where are you? Why aren't you here?'

'I'm done,' is all she says. 'I can't do this any more.'

'Anna, where are you?' I ask, at pains to keep my tone soft and calm.

'I'm at the beach,' she says, and I can hear the faintest slur in her voice.

'Is someone with you?'

She laughs. 'I've got gin and a whole bottle of Prozac for company.'

I can't disguise my sharp intake of breath. 'Anna, listen, you need to tell me where you are.'

I grab my keys from the dining table and throw my bag over my shoulder. Leon stands open-mouthed as I brush past him on my way to the door.

'Stay on the line,' I say, fumbling to open the car. 'I'm coming to get you, but I'm going to need a little help.'

'It's too late for that,' she mumbles. 'I'm past helping.'

'Anna, you need to tell me exactly where you are,' I say, trying desperately hard not to let her hear my growing sense of hysteria.

'I'm with Ben,' she says.

'Anna, please, just listen to me . . .'

The line goes dead and I suck in my rising panic.

With Ben? I rack my brain as to what she might mean. Then I remember her telling me how they'd bought a beach hut in Tankerton and painted it yellow, Ben's favourite colour, in tribute to him.

Despite continuously trying to call her back whilst I make the five-minute journey along the coastal road, my mind runs amok with what I'm going to find when I get there.

I park, and half walk, half run down the slope towards the beach, where four rows of brightly coloured huts merge together like a pick 'n' mix selection. Pink candy stripes and baby blue panels jar against my impending sense of doom as I race along the promenade, towards the only yellow one I can see.

A woman, sitting with her dog on the front veranda of number forty-one, looks up and gives me a friendly smile as I pass. If she'd seen anything that had given her cause for concern, surely she wouldn't be sitting there watching the world go by, would she?

My heart thumps in my chest as I come to a stop outside number forty-nine.

I turn the handle and peer into the darkness.

'Anna?' I say huskily as I step inside, leaving the door behind me open, to throw light into the ten-by-ten cabin. There's nobody here, but as my eyes adjust I can see a single candle burning on a shelf, illuminating a row of framed photos lined up around it.

Every picture shows the same smiling little boy, with white-blond hair and dancing eyes. I recognize Anna in one where a sleeping baby is lying on her chest and she's staring into the camera lens, with a look of utter contentment radiating from deep within.

A blond lock of hair lies on the desk next to a painting of what looks like a sunflower field, created out of tiny yellow and green handprints. The paper is stiff and crunchy as I lightly pass my fingertips over the palm shapes.

How could so much pain and suffering be cast on one family?

There's an agonized wail from outside, and I race out of the hut and onto the shingled beach where Anna is standing against the sunset with her arms aloft.

She moves towards the water's edge as I run to reach her, and the tide rolls over our shoes as I grab her tightly around the waist from behind.

'Please,' I say, gently pulling her back into me. 'Let's talk.'

She turns to look at me and her face is so twisted that at first, it seems like she might lash out. But she melts into my arms and for a moment, we're lost in the sound of the waves.

'What have you taken?' I ask.

'I . . . I . . .' she says, shaking her head.

'Anna!' I shout, in a bid to rouse her from her stupor. 'What have you taken?'

'N-nothing,' she says. 'I haven't taken anything.'

The breath I've been holding in escapes from my lungs like a missile, and I flounder as I guide her back across the pebbles. 'Come inside,' I say, not knowing whether the shrine to her son will help or hinder her.

She falls down on the daybed and instinctively picks up the blue blanket square beside her, poking her fore-finger through one of its silk loops.

'Ben would go to bed with this every night,' she says, holding it against her cheek and inhaling its scent. 'He would slip his finger through like this and rub the material with his thumb to send him off to sleep.'

Her wistful smile suddenly disappears and her mouth pulls into a thin, tight line as she looks at her watch. 'This time last year he was still alive,' she says, her voice cracking as the enormity of the milestone hits her. 'If I'd known then what I know now, I would have spent the next few hours loving him, smelling him . . .'

I sit down beside her and put an arm around her back. 'You've never told me what actually happened on that day.'

She shakes her head and bites down on her lip.

'Do you want to talk about it now?' I ask. 'Might we be able to honour Ben in the way he deserves?'

She rubs at the loop, which I can now see is worn, attached by the thinnest of threads. I imagine Ben wasn't the only one who slept with it every night.

'It was here,' she says, her face crumpling as she looks around. 'This is where he died.'

Tears immediately spring to my eyes as I imagine the little boy in the photos running around on the beach, fetching water in his bucket and making sandcastles with his devoted family. How could something so tragic have happened in this beautiful place?

'I held him in my arms, begging him to open his eyes,' she cries. 'I honestly believed that if I prayed enough, he'd come back to me, but his little body had been through so much . . .'

A guttural sob ricochets around the wooden walls.

'I'm so sorry,' I say, pulling her into me. 'I can't imagine . . .'

'I should have been able to save him,' she croaks, her eyes searching mine. 'My only job as his mother was to keep him safe and make sure no harm ever came to him, so how . . . how could I have let it happen?'

'You mustn't blame yourself,' I offer.

'Well, who else is there?' she screams, turning on me; her face twisted and her lips pulled back to reveal her gums. 'I should have trusted my instincts. I should have known not to listen to Nick; he was drunk – why would I have taken him at his word? Who in their right mind, would take the say-so of an alcoholic over the safety of their innocent child?'

I shake my head, at a loss for what to say.

'I'll never be able to forgive him,' she says, jumping up off the bed. 'And I'll never be able to forgive myself.'

She rushes out onto the veranda, down the wooden steps and across the pebbled beach, sinking to her knees at the water's edge.

Running to her, I fall onto the stones and pull her into me. 'It's OK,' I soothe. 'It's OK.'

'I need to be with Ben,' she sobs, falling into me. 'If I could just be with him, everything would be all right. '

"Listen to me,' I say, holding her at arm's length, where I can look her in the eye. 'You still have two beautiful children who need you.'

'But Ben needs me,' she cries.

'You'll be with him in the fullness of time – he will always be waiting for you – but right now, you have to love and nurture those who are here. You are their world and, believe you me, they will never recover from losing you at such a young age.'

She looks at me as if she's hearing me for the first time. 'You sound as if you're speaking from experience.'

I nod. 'I can't imagine what you must be going through, but please, I'm begging you, don't put your children through it as well. They've been through enough already.'

She pulls herself up. 'You're right, I couldn't possibly leave them with him. Look what happens when he's in charge.'

'You've both been through the worst trauma imaginable,' I say softly. 'But there's nothing to gain from blaming one another. It'll destroy you.'

She chews on the inside of her cheek, deep in thought.

'Where are the children?' I ask.

'The children?' she questions, looking at me blankly, sending a sudden rush of panic through me.

'Yes, where are they?'

'Oh, they're with my parents for the night,' she says. 'I thought it would be easier that way . . .'

I daren't ask her to elaborate.

'OK, so why don't we go and pick them up and go back to mine? It'll give you some breathing space to think about your next move.'

She shakes her head vehemently. 'No, they're happy where they are.'

'OK, so why don't *you* come back then? We can talk and see how you feel in the morning.'

'And Leon will be OK with that, will he?'

Shit, Leon.

'Of course,' I lie, though I can't help but think Anna might be the distraction we both need right now. He just doesn't know it yet.

'D'you know what?' she says, pulling her cardigan tighter around her as she looks out to sea. 'I'm going to go home and talk to Nick.'

My brow furrows. 'Are you sure that's a good idea? Today of all days?'

She turns to look at me. 'I can't go on like this. I can't keep running away from what happened. I'm tired of living in the shadows.'

'I understand that, but I really don't think you should go and see Nick right now, not when you're feeling like you are . . .'

'But perhaps I need to tell him how I'm feeling,' she moots. 'Because bottling everything up is clearly not doing either of us any favours. He's lashing out and I'm walking around like a zombie. Both of us have lost the ability to communicate.'

'I really don't think I should let you go off on your own.'

'I'll be fine,' she says, putting a hand over mine. 'I'm sorry I scared you, but as ever, you really have helped me see things a little clearer.'

'Anna, I—'

'I'm OK,' she says, locking eyes with me. 'I promise.'

I only hope she's telling the truth.

19

'Naomi! Naomi!' my sister screams from somewhere far away. I run to where the sound is coming from, but just as I see her standing at the end of a long corridor, dressed in her white nightie and holding her pink bunny rabbit, a door slams shut in my face.

My eyes snap open, desperately searching the darkness for proof that that didn't really just happen. I force my breath under control and roll onto my back, waiting for the ornate ceiling rose above our bed to emerge from the shadows.

There's a noise, much like the slamming door in my dream, but further away and fainter. My ears prick up like a dog's on guard, waiting to hear it again. I'm trying to still the *thump thump thump* of my heart, as it competes with the underwater noise that is rushing around in my ears.

I need to separate reality from the nightmare, but my thoughts and terrors are all metamorphosing into the same thing.

It's the tiniest of sounds, but one I know so well; the slow, unavoidable creak of the third stair from the bottom, as it bows under the weight of even the lightest foot.

I throw a hand over to Leon's side of the mattress, hoping to find his sleeping body, rising and falling with his silent breath. But the bed is empty and the sheets are cold. I sit up, trying to force my brain to track back to last night. Had I dreamt that Jacob had gone missing? Had Anna really threatened to kill herself? Had Leon and I resolved our row? A heap of thoughts crowd my brain and I tick them off one by one. *No, yes, no.*

Leon had been asleep when I came home – at least he'd pretended to be – so as I come to, the knowledge that we've still got to iron out our problems instantly gnaws away at me.

Knowing I won't be able to go back to sleep until he's in bed beside me, I pull on his t-shirt, which is balled up on his pillow. If I'd thought about how strange that was – Leon always sleeps in his t-shirt – I would have perhaps known that all was not well. But the benefit of hindsight is a wonderful thing.

There's a noise again.

I tiptoe to the bedroom door and stare out into the darkness of the landing, listening for a clue as to where he is and what he's doing. There's nothing but silence.

I peer over the banister to the hall below, hoping to see a glow of a light creeping up from the kitchen where he must be making a cup of tea, but the house is cloaked in shadows.

An unfathomable sense of unease wraps itself around me as I gingerly put a foot onto the landing. Feeling like I'm walking through a minefield, I stand and wait before doing it again.

I'm three steps down and on the mezzanine when I hear faint voices coming from downstairs. Now I'm here, I can see a white glow trickling through the crack in the kitchen door, and my insides uncoil as I realize that Leon must be watching late night television.

I take the rest of the stairs more confidently, relying on the creak from the third tread from the bottom to alert him to my presence.

'Hey,' I croak, as I push the door open, my voice rusty from sleep.

I fully expect him to be standing there, munching on cereal in the light of the TV, but the room is empty.

'Leon?' I call out, walking around the island and into the open-plan dining room.

It's there that I see it. My laptop open on the table, playing a scene from an X-rated film. I can't help but wince at the sound effects, but moreover I cringe with embarrassment at having caught Leon in the throes of whatever it was he was doing.

Yet as I get closer, the blurry faces of the 'porn stars' come into focus and I double over as the sucker punch winds me. The moans become clearer, the voices become more distinguishable, the act too unbearable to watch.

It can't be – it just can't be.

'Leon!' I scream, my angst echoing in the stillness of the house.

I slam the top down, shutting the noise off but sending the room into complete darkness.

'Fuck!' I yell, stubbing my toe as I fumble for the light switch. 'Leon!'

I rush through the ground floor of the house, turning every light on as I go. I take the stairs two at a time and flounder for my phone on the bedside table. I check the spare rooms and the bathroom, but Leon's nowhere to be seen.

'Pick up your fucking phone,' I shout, as I call his number and it rings into voicemail. I immediately try again and he answers.

'Where *are* you?' I yell, as I almost lose my footing coming back down the stairs.

'I'm not going to do this now,' he says.

'You're *what*?' I say, my voice high-pitched, unable to believe what I'm hearing.

'I'm not going to do this now,' he repeats.

'Where *are* you?'

'I'm on site,' he says, bluntly.

'But it's the middle of the night.'

'I can't stay with you,' he says.

My brain is so discombobulated that I can't even begin to process what he's saying.

'Have you *seen* it?' I ask.

There's silence at the other end of the line.

'Have you *seen* it?' I cry, my throat closing in around the words.

'Yes,' he says, calmly. 'Were you hoping I hadn't?'

'I'm hoping you can tell me why the hell you thought it was OK to film us having sex and then post it to my computer.'

'What?' he exclaims, making a good attempt to sound surprised.

I fall heavily onto the dining chair, knowing that that mortifying video is lurking on the underside of my laptop, waiting to be played again.

How could he possibly think this is OK? Even without everything else that's going on, he knows more than anyone that I'm an immensely private person who would find this excruciating.

I suddenly feel so desperately alone and vulnerable, magnified by the knowledge that the one person who could make me feel secure again has just invaded my privacy in the most unimaginable way.

'The video you left running on my laptop,' I say, impatiently.

'What are you even talking about?' he asks, sounding exasperated. 'I don't know anything about a video.'

'You must do!' I shriek, struggling to hold it together. 'How else would it have ended up on my laptop? How else would it have been *filmed*?'

'You're not making any sense,' he says.

'There is a video on my laptop – of you and me – having sex,' I say in clipped syllables.

'Of you and me?' he repeats.

'Yes!' I snap.

There's a long silence. 'And it's definitely us?'

His doubt is so convincing that I feel forced to open my laptop and have another look.

The video has freeze-framed with my face contorting in ecstasy whilst Leon's head is buried between my breasts, both of us naked. I can't bear to press play.

'Oh God, it's so awful,' I cry, dropping my head into my hands.

'Is it us?' asks Leon, still keeping up the pretence that he knows nothing about it.

'Yes,' I choke.

'Well, where? When?'

'How often are you in the habit of videoing us making love without my consent?'

'Never,' he says. 'I would never do that to you.'

I press play, shutting my ears off to the animalistic noises we're both making.

'Oh my god, we're in my office,' I say, turning the sound to mute. 'It was the other night, when you—'

'Jesus,' he exclaims. 'Has someone *spied* on us?'

'I-I don't know.'

'Has it been sent to you?' he asks, his voice thick with trepidation.

Hot bile shoots up into my chest as the possibility, and what it means, worms its way into my psyche.

'As in blackmail?' I say out loud.

'Well, I don't know,' he says. 'I can't see any other reason for doing it otherwise.'

'But how would somebody have got this in the first place?' I ask. 'And why would they try to use it against me?'

'I don't know,' he says wearily. 'Perhaps it's the same person you meant to send the text to.'

'Text? What text?'

He sighs, breathing heavily down the phone. 'I don't know what's going on here, but I think it's best if we take some time out.'

'What?' I say, almost laughing. 'You want us to take a break?'

'I don't know what I want, but I can't be with you while all this is going on.'

'So just when I need you most, you do a midnight flit?' I say, unable to believe what I'm hearing.

'It doesn't sound like it's me you're in need of.'

'OK, this is crazy,' I shriek. 'You're being completely insane.'

'Naomi, you sent *me* the text,' he says. 'Instead of him.'

'What fucking text?' I yell, losing my patience with this ridiculous conversation.

'Hang on,' he says. The fan noise that made him sound as if he was in a wind tunnel suddenly disappears.

His voice comes back on the line.

'"Hi, it's me",' he says. '"I haven't told Leon yet, but

I will, I promise. Just give me a couple more days and we'll be together. Love you more than you'll ever know. N."' He adds, '"Kiss kiss",' with such vitriol that I can't possibly relate him to being the man I've loved for seventeen years.

I try to speak but my tongue feels too big for my mouth.

'So, that's it?' he barks. 'You've got nothing to say.'

'Do you honestly believe that I wrote that text?' I croak.

'Well, it all seems to add up, doesn't it? You're just biding your time, playing some kind of weird game with me, waiting for the right moment when you can be together.'

'I can't believe you'd even think I was capable of that,' I gasp. 'What the hell has happened to us?'

'I think we need some space,' he says, dismissing me.

The line goes dead and I'm left looking at my phone in disbelief. I'd gone to bed last night daring to believe that when we woke up, we'd work *together* to get to the bottom of whatever's going on. Now, I'm alone. And I can't even be sure whether or not, despite his protestations, Leon is somehow involved.

I go to my emails to see if the video has been sent as an unwelcome attachment. There's nothing showing in my inbox and I'm consumed with relief as I check my sent items, pathetically grateful that it hasn't been sent to everyone in my contacts. Though the very next second, I'm faced with the unnerving reality that whoever's behind this has been in my home and downloaded it onto my laptop.

I think back to when Leon had interrupted me in the office, which he rarely ever does, and seduced me into making love. He didn't have to work too hard to persuade me, but I can't remember the last time we'd had sex outside the bedroom.

I'm sure I'd asked him to turn the lights off and he made the lewd comment that if someone wanted a ringside seat, then let them have one.

A gut-wrenching nausea coils around my insides as his methods of manipulation play out in my head.

But how had he filmed it? I surely would have noticed if he'd been holding his phone.

I force myself to press play again and watch through my fingers as Leon drives himself into me, with his hands either side of my hips. His fingers dig deep into my flesh as he quickens his pace, and as much as I almost want to spot his phone, because it's suddenly the better option, it's nowhere to be seen.

The thought that he had someone else watching us and filming it *for* him not only horrifies me but fills my head with so many questions that I don't even know where to begin.

I'm about to turn the tap on, to pour myself a glass of water, when I hear the unmistakable creak of the third step on the stairs again. The video had distracted me so much I'd almost forgotten what had awoken me in the first place. My muscles tense, my body too frightened to move from where it's pinned against the sink. I swallow the metallic tang in my mouth.

'Hello?' I say, into the eerie silence that used to be my safe place. Not any more.

I back myself slowly towards the French doors, checking, with my hands behind me, that they're locked. I can't turn my back on the room, as I feel sure that the danger is inside the house.

'Is anybody here?' I ask, hoping to God I don't get an answer.

I inch over to the knife block on the island and grab the largest handle. My hand is shaking as I hold it out in front of me, my eyes darting into every dark corner, my heart jumping as the shadows play tricks on me.

My feet feel as if they're encased in concrete with every step I try to make as my body fights against what my brain is telling it to do. I can't help but be reminded of all the horror movies I've watched where I've shouted at the screen, 'Don't go upstairs,' to which Leon always responds, 'But the director's told her to.' We'd laugh and I'd appreciate the released tension, but there's no one here to shout 'cut' now, is there?

With my back to the wall, I rise up the treads of the staircase, taking care to avoid the third from the bottom. As I reach the top, a door creaks and I almost fall back down. Clinging on to the banister, I swallow the ball of fear lodged in my throat.

I look at the bathroom door at the end of the corridor off the mezzanine, fully expecting it to suddenly swing open. I almost wish it would – to put me out of my misery.

There's a draught as I edge closer towards it, a cold stream of air that chills the intense heat raging through my body. Holding the knife out at arm's length, I kick the door open with my foot and make a noise that doesn't sound like it's come from me.

Switching the light on, I catch my breath, forcing myself to focus, even though all I want to do is squeeze my eyes tightly shut. The closed shower curtain sways gently in the breeze coming through the open window, and as much as I'm relieved that it explains a lot, I still can't relax until I'm sure that nobody is hiding in the bath behind it.

I count to three in my head, or it might have been aloud, and pull it brusquely backwards. The metal rings screech on the pole, jangling the very few nerve endings I have left.

It's empty.

Is it me? Am I allowing paranoia to poison my mind and alter my senses? Am I hearing things that don't exist? Seeing things that aren't there? My faculties are so compromised that I feel as if I could conjure up anything if it matched the narrative that everyone else is convinced is my life.

I look at myself in the bathroom mirror, alarmed by

the hollowed-out version staring back at me. I could collapse in a heap, giving in to whoever has set out to destroy me, or I could fight back, safe in the knowledge that I've not done anything wrong, aside from holding out on a few home truths. I pull myself up, standing taller and holding my head high, revelling in the inner strength such a simple gesture can spawn. I need to focus on the things that implicate me in a crime I didn't commit and discard the psychological attempt to bring me down. It's time to sort the wheat from the chaff.

By the time I've crossed the landing to our bedroom, I've already forgiven myself for thinking that someone had been in the house and am convinced that everything that has happened up to now can surely be explained. Nobody is out to get me; it's all just a catalogue of coincidences. I almost believe it until I see my sister's pink bunny rabbit lying on my pillow.

20

I don't even attempt to go back to bed – how can I when I know someone has tainted the very place where I sleep?

Instead, I make myself a hot chocolate and sit at the dining table with my laptop, wondering who has violated my home by placing Jennifer's stuffed toy on my pillow. It wasn't there before; it wasn't even in the same room, as I always keep it in a box in the wardrobe where my mom's clothes are. But it's the intention behind it that bothers me the most; that whoever did it knows its significance and specifically chose it to cause the greatest impact.

The thought of Jennifer herself being involved clamps itself around my throat as I question what she'd be trying to prove. I know her motive; I can feel her bitter resentment at being 'abandoned' as keenly now as I did all those years ago, but does she really think she's going to scare me into confessing something I had no control over?

And what of Jacob? It's not impossible to believe that my alleged involvement in his disappearance is connected with the break-in at my home.

In spite of all the conspiracy theories as to who might be doing this to me, I know the only way I'm going to get myself out of it is by finding the man called Michael Talbot. And right now, whichever way I look at it, his wife is my first port of call.

I type 'Michael Talbot' into Google and the page is immediately flooded with the same stock image of a man with piercing blue eyes, a soft smile and a trimmed beard. His disappearance has only been reported in local newspapers, it seems, the incident not deemed serious enough just yet to run in the nationals.

But the *Kentish Gazette* has mentioned him in a two-by-one column and I guess the others will follow just as soon as they get a whiff of the backstory that accompanies it.

POLICE NAME ALLEGED MISTRESS AS LOVER'S KILLER is the headline I visualize across the front pages, as Jacob's body is found washed up on the pebbled beach of Whitstable.

The papers would have a field day with that golden nugget alone, though it will only be a matter of time before it becomes *KILLER'S DAUGHTER TURNS KILLER HERSELF*, once an unscrupulous journalist sniffs out the real story.

I imagine the various articles and essays written by people like me; psychologists who will look to boost their profile by stating that killers are born with the killer gene. And red-top hacks will be dispatched to

New York to track down the father who I inherited it from.

I subscribe and pay for an electoral registry service that lists two Michael Talbots in the district council of Canterbury. It's a starting point and I scribble the addresses down on the pad next to me, eager to start unravelling the dichotomy that's become my life.

As soon as it's a respectable enough hour, I ashamedly call the one client I have today and tell them I'm not feeling well and wouldn't want them to catch it. It seems the more I lie, the easier it becomes.

Not wanting to stand out, I dress in a beige A-line skirt and white blouse, and throw a string of amber beads around my neck. With my hair pulled loosely back into a clip and oversized sunglasses on, I look like every other well-off Londoner who's bought a holiday home in Whitstable in the five years since it's become the place to be.

In the car, on my way to the first address on my list, I call Anna, just to check she's OK, but it immediately goes to voicemail. I wonder where she is and what she's doing.

I hope that she and Nick somehow managed to find some middle ground last night because I fear that if they couldn't do it then, of all nights, then they probably never would. But my gut tells me they would have collided with each other head-on, clearly unable to traverse the most painful of reminders by themselves, let alone together.

I can't take the chance of Anna feeling even more desperate than she was yesterday, so as soon as I'm done here, I'll have to track her down and make sure she's OK.

I park in Canterbury town centre and take a shortcut through the cathedral grounds. I'm reminded of the last time I was here. It was a couple of months ago, and Leon and I were with Shelley's husband Dave to watch her compete in a choir competition. I'd gone to the bar to get us all a beer when, turning round with a plastic pint glass in each hand, I had bumped, quite literally, into Jacob.

'Naomi!' he'd exclaimed, clearly as shocked as I was.

I'd looked around furtively, searching both the people close to us and his face for a prompt on how best to deal with this situation.

'My wife's inside,' he said, answering my predicament. 'She's in one of the choirs.'

'Oh, right,' I said. 'Well, I wish her luck.'

He'd looked at me oddly, almost as if he was expecting something more, but I wasn't keen on my bumping into his wife, any more than I imagine he was.

'Good to see you,' I said, moving away.

'Erm, yeah, I'll see you on Monday,' he said after me.

I'd spent the rest of the concert feeling like I was being watched; though whether by him or his wife, I couldn't be sure. He'd have no reason to tell her I was there – by rights she wouldn't have known I even existed – yet I still felt I was in the disadvantaged position of someone knowing exactly where I was, training their eyes on me, whilst I only had a sea of a thousand faces to focus on. A bit like how I feel now.

When I get to King Street, I wonder how to approach this. Do I ask for Mr or Mrs Talbot? If a woman answers the door, should I assume that it's Vanessa? If it's her that's setting me up, she's sure to recognize me as she's already gone to extreme lengths to find out everything there is to know about me. But if someone else is involved in this, Vanessa may just be a pawn in the game, being moved and placed to wherever she needs to be, ready for my capture.

Even though I must have walked down this road before, it's the first time I really take in the houses, which stand cheek to jowl with their neighbours, their front doors opening directly onto the pavement.

Number twenty-one is halfway down on the right-hand side, adorned with red geraniums standing erect in painted window boxes. It looks like a friendly house, as if nice people live there; not people who would frame someone else for a crime they didn't commit.

I press the antique gold bell and wait breathlessly, not knowing whether the door is going to be opened by a stranger – or someone I know.

'Hello?' says a woman with long brown curls that look like they've just been coiffed at an expensive salon. 'Can I help you?' If she recognizes me, she doesn't show it.

She looks about the same age as me but could well be ten years older, judging by her taut, wrinkle-free brow and feline features.

I clear my throat to speak. 'Erm, hello, my name's Naomi Chandler,' I say, watching her carefully. Her expression doesn't change, though I don't know whether it's because it can't or because the name means nothing to her.

'I'm looking for Michael Talbot,' I press on. 'Does he live here?'

She smiles sweetly and holds the door open. 'Yes, he's expecting you, do come in.'

I'm taken aback and find myself floundering on the doorstep, wondering what my next move is. What if this woman *is* the one who has embarked on an elaborate plan to frame me? She must have thought all her Christmases had come at once when she saw me at the door, and now I'm about to walk straight into her trap. I imagine her husband in a soundproofed room in the basement, with just a few inches of concrete between us, and know that I have to go in to make absolutely sure that he isn't. It's only as I step over the threshold that I wonder if I might be about to join him.

I almost expect the woman to push me to the ground as soon as she shuts the door behind me, but she directs me into the 'drawing room on the left' and tells me Michael will be down shortly.

All my senses are on high alert, looking and listening

for anything out of the ordinary. I scan the console tables for photos, but the room is too elegant for anything personal to be on show. Instead, the floor-to-ceiling bookcases are filled with tomes I can't pronounce, let alone recognize, and the two overstuffed sofas facing each other don't look like they've been sat on in years.

There's mumbled talking from upstairs, but I can't quite hear what's being said, or more importantly a voice that I recognize.

What am I going to do if Michael, who I know as Jacob, walks through that door? I'm filled with panic that I may be breaching his confidence, consumed by the thought that I've got this all wrong. Were the police really looking for him? Was I honestly the prime suspect in his disappearance? It sounds so preposterous that in that moment, I wonder if I've made it all up.

As I hear a male voice getting nearer, I'm unable to separate fact from fiction in my head.

'Hello, sorry to keep you,' says a distinguished-looking gentleman who I don't recognize. 'Michael Talbot, pleased to meet you.'

A rush of relief floods through me as he shakes my hand and offers me a seat on one of the high cushions.

'Erm,' I say, not having anticipated how to handle this eventuality.

'May I start off by saying that I love the work that you do,' he says, smiling kindly. 'And my wife and I are very keen to get involved.'

I'm not sure that I could feel any more wretched than I do now. 'I'm sorry,' I say, because it's all that I have to offer. 'I think there's been a misunderstanding.'

'Oh?' he says, taken aback. 'But I thought—'

I throw my bag over my shoulder and bolt for the front door, leaving him no doubt open-mouthed in my wake. I only feel mildly appeased by the young woman walking down the street towards me with a Young People Matter brochure tucked under her arm. I sincerely hope she's who Michael was really expecting.

21

As soon as I'm back in the safety of my car, I look at my phone to see that the same number has called me three times in quick succession and left a message. I'm shaking as I hold the phone to my ear to hear Detective Robson's voice booming from my voicemail.

'Hello, Mrs Chandler, there have been some new developments in the case and we're outside your house now. Could you please give me a call as soon as you get this?'

The thought of her being at the house when I'm not there sends me into a blind panic, even though I've got nothing to hide; even less now that Leon knows what they know. Yet it still feels as if I'm a mouse with a cat clawing at my tail, holding me still before releasing me again.

I go faster than I should on the A290, spurred on by the Foo Fighters at high volume and my dark thoughts. As I pull into the gates of Tattenhall, I doubt the police will still be there, but as the cottage comes into view I see Robson leaning against her car in the driveway. The look on her face, when she sees me approach, is one of smug superiority.

'Naomi Chandler,' she says, as I open my car door. 'We have a warrant to search your property.'

'I'm sorry?' I say, my brain scrambling to understand what she's saying. 'What do you mean?'

'We have a warrant to search your property in connection with the disappearance of Michael Talbot.'

I feel like I'm stuck in a low-budget police drama and I almost want to laugh.

'What are you honestly expecting to find?' I ask.

'Our investigation is ongoing,' says Robson, studying me carefully. 'But we have reason to believe that serious harm has come to Mr Talbot.'

'And you think you're going to find evidence that I've got something to do with that?'

'I don't know, Mrs Chandler. Will we?' She cocks one eyebrow.

'You're wasting your time,' I say in answer.

'Well, I'll be the judge of that,' she says, moving me aside at my own front door.

I numbly fall back onto the porch, wishing I could melt into the wall, as two, three, four plainclothes officers make their way into the house, the last giving me an apologetic tight smile.

I swallow my pride, forcing myself to believe that the truth will out. If I don't, I may as well ask them to handcuff me now because they seem pretty set on me knowing more than I'm letting on. They wouldn't be wrong though, would they? It takes all my willpower not to bang my head against the wall. How could I have been so stupid? Why didn't I just tell them the truth in the very beginning? It had seemed insurmountable then, but not half as much as it does now.

I walk in, looking at the home I love being ransacked by strangers. It doesn't feel any different from how I'd imagine it would feel if they were burglars looking for valuables. It's just that the valuables the police are hoping to find don't exist.

'Is this the only computer in the property?' calls out Robson, from the dining room.

'My husband Leon has his own system set up in the spare bedroom,' I say wearily.

'And where is Mr Chandler right now?' asks Robson.

'At work,' I say, hoping that suffices, because I really do not want to be answering questions about his whereabouts and the current state of our marriage.

I pull myself up, swallowing down the threat of tears as I wonder how we've all but fallen apart in such a short space of time.

But then I wonder if I should really be that surprised. It was always going to happen at some point; in fact, my subconscious has probably spent the seventeen years since we first met waiting for it.

If I'm honest with myself, it's what I've done with every relationship I've ever had. Certainly before Leon, I would almost go out of my way to destroy it before it had the chance to destroy me. That way, I felt I had some control over the way people treated me, but in reality, it was my defence mechanism kicking in.

It's still a great surprise to me that Leon had somehow slipped through the net, especially when he'd come so close to being caught up in it. Because despite his concerted efforts to woo me in the reading room of the New York Public Library with the promise of coffee and bagels, he wasn't quite so convincing when I'd spotted him in Central Park with his arm around another woman.

We weren't dating, but the man I'd shared my thesis woes with had certainly not shared the fact that he was with someone else. I'd avoided the library for weeks after that, unable to bear the thought of him waxing lyrical about how pretty my eyes were or asking when I was going to let him take me out.

But the very first day I went back, he was there waiting for me, and despite not wanting to admit it, knowing it weakened every barrier I'd put up around myself, I'd really missed him.

I didn't let him off the hook easily though; he had to work hard to convince me that whatever he had with the other woman was definitely over. But once I was sure I could trust him, we were inseparable – living in each other's pockets, until he'd stopped me in the street outside my apartment, and with the snow falling down around us, had taken hold of my hands and put them on his chest.

'I have something to tell you,' he'd said.

I'd looked at him, unable to believe that I could ever love someone so much, when he said, 'I have to go back to England.'

I'd pulled my hands away as if they'd been scalded with a hot poker.

'They won't renew my visa,' he said, his eyes burrowing into mine.

'But I thought your company was sorting that,' I'd managed, as conflicting thoughts and snippets of conversations buffeted around my head.

'They tried, but . . .'

I remember being blinded by the sudden realization that of course it was never going to last. Nothing ever did if I was stupid enough to love it.

'Go then,' I said, pushing him away in an immature fit of pique. 'If that's what you want.'

'I want you to come with me,' he'd said, as I reached my front door.

'I can't,' was my instinctive reaction.

Yet I was thinking, *Why not?* even before he said it himself.

I had nothing to keep me in New York; I was waiting tables whilst trying to get my psychology degree, I had no family aside from Aunt Meryl, and I spent my days avoiding the sights and smells that took me back to a time before my life changed forever.

What did I have to lose by going to England?
Everything, it seems.

'We'll be needing to speak to your husband at some point,' says Robson now when we reach the box room, where Leon's monitor sits on the desk.

'About his computer?' I say, my mouth dry.

'About your whereabouts on the nights of the twenty-first and twenty-third of June,' she says dourly.

'I told you where I was on the twenty-third,' I say.

'No, Mrs Chandler, *we* told *you* where you were that evening. Remember?'

I clench my fists at my side in frustration.

'What is it your husband does?' she asks.

'He works here on the estate,' I say. I don't want to give them anything more than they need.

'So he works from home?' she says, taking in the architects' plans for the old stables that are pinned up on the walls.

'In a sense,' I say.

'So I imagine you're able to keep quite close tabs on each other?'

I have no idea where she's going with this or what she's trying to allude to, but it's making my skin itch. 'We both have demanding jobs and lead fairly independent lives,' I say, looking straight at her.

'Where would he have been on the night of the twenty-first of June?'

I shrug my shoulders far too quickly. 'I have no idea.'

She rubs at her forehead as if she's trying to massage a migraine away.

'It was only a few nights ago,' she says.

I picture Leon and me in the same hotel bar, only minutes apart, both of us within feet of a man who went missing that night.

'As you'll appreciate, Mrs Chandler, I'm having real trouble here.'

'Because you think I'm lying?' I ask, boldly.

'Well, you can't blame me, can you?' she says. 'You have a habit of holding out on me.'

'I've told you why I wasn't honest about going around to Jacob's – I mean Michael's – flat.'

She nods.

'And what about when you met Mr Talbot at the Royal Garden hotel in Canterbury?'

A heat starts in my toes and creeps up my legs. All the while my ears are trying to rid themselves of the rush of blood that makes me feel as if I'm drowning. My lips feel like they're forming the words I want to say, but no sound is coming out.

'I . . .' I start, my tongue suddenly feeling too big for my mouth. I have no idea what to say that can get me out of the very big mess I'm in. How can she possibly know about the hotel?

She leans in towards me, as if she's hard of hearing and I'm whispering.

'I don't know what you're talking about,' I manage.

'We have a report from a member of the public who believes they saw Mr Talbot at the hotel on the night he disappeared.'

I shrug my shoulders nonchalantly.

'I don't know what that's got to do with me,' I say.

'Apparently he was with a woman who matches your description,' she says, raising her eyebrows questioningly.

I snort. 'What – of average height with long brown hair? That just about covers half of the female population.'

Robson narrows her eyes. 'Perhaps, but I'm hoping that what she was wearing might narrow it down.'

The heat returns to envelop me as I force myself to remember what I had on. An involuntary twitch pulses in my cheek as Robson looks to her notebook.

'Apparently, the witness remembers Mr Talbot being in the bar with a woman who had on a rather distinctive blouse,' she says. 'It was red in colour, possibly depicting a fruit of some kind, though the witness can't be sure.'

It's taking all my effort to keep my expression nonplussed, even though I know the exact garment she's talking about.

'Does that sound familiar to you at all?' she asks, looking at me.

I shake my head, believing I'm safer on mute, but I'm screaming on the inside, the cacophony threatening to drown out all reason and show me for who I really am.

'Well, we'll soon see,' she says smugly.

'Ma'am, you might want to take a look at this,' an officer calls out.

My heart stops as Robson raises her eyebrows, as if offering me the chance to tell her what they might have found before she gets there.

I pull my mouth into a tight line, giving nothing away, but the words reverberate around and around in my head. *Tell the truth. Continue lying. Tell the truth. Continue lying.* The roar of the conundrum of how best to get myself out of this is deafening. The constant questions, should have dones, meant to haves, circle furiously, getting louder with every revolution.

I watch numbly as an officer hands her what looks like a mobile phone in a bag marked 'Evidence'.

'Is this yours?' she asks, showing me a black Nokia through the clear plastic. Its big buttons glare back at me and I force myself to think where it might have come from. If it was found in the 'man drawer' in the kitchen, where everything from dead batteries, takeaway menus from restaurants that have closed down and keys that we no longer own the locks to lives, then it could be a model harking back to our pre-iPhone days. But I can't help but notice that it looks relatively modern and new.

'I'm not sure,' I say. 'Where was it found?'

Robson looks at her officer.

'In the bathroom cupboard under the sink, ma'am,' he says, as if I'm not here. 'Concealed on a hidden shelf.'

'Concealed?' I blurt out, half laughing. 'Are you kidding me?'

As ever, Robson's expression is taut with seriousness, looking at me as if I have no idea of the shit I'm in. A *concealed phone*? Oh, I know the shit I'm in. I'm knee-deep in an intricately woven web of lies and deceit. Somebody is very definitely out to get me, and I need to find out who, before I'm spun up so tightly that I'll never be able to get out.

'I've never seen it before,' I say.

'So you have no idea how it came to be in your bathroom cabinet?'

I shake my head. 'Though I thought someone was in the house last night,' I offer.

I want to tell her that I *know* someone was in the house last night, but until I'm sure it wasn't my own husband playing some kind of fucked-up mind game with me, I'll play my cards close to my chest. This said, my record thus far of not being honest with the police has not been working out so well.

Robson looks at me, her interest piqued, though I'm sure I can detect a whiff of scepticism. 'Did you report it?' she asks, knowing full well I didn't.

'Well, like I say, I couldn't be sure. I was sure of it at the time, but you know how things can spook you.'

'So, are you saying you think someone put this there?' she asks incredulously.

'Well, I know I didn't, so it's the only possible

explanation,' I say. 'Although you seem convinced other-wise, I'm not the type of person to have illicit liaisons with my clients and pay-as-you-go phones hidden in my home.'

'How do you know it's a pay-as-you-go?' she asks.

I sigh. 'I don't, it's just a figure of speech.'

'And the illicit liaison?' she asks.

I feel like I'm a sitting duck waiting to be put out of its misery. 'I'm just saying that despite what you might think, I'm not in the habit of meeting my clients outside work.'

'Not even in the Royal Garden hotel?' she asks, raising her eyebrows questioningly.

'No,' I say adamantly.

'Well, let's hope the CCTV backs that up.'

22

Although the police left the house looking largely as they found it, I still feel violated, as if they've sullied everything they've touched. It's felt most staunchly in the spare bedroom, and fresh tears spring to my eyes as I trail my hands along the sleeves of my mother's dresses. I imagine them rifling through her belongings in their misguided efforts to find something that proves that I'm the person they think I am.

The cuffs of her blouses lost the scent of her favourite perfume many years ago, but when I really need to, I can convince myself I can still smell it. It immediately transports me back to happier times and I watch the four of us, as if through the shuttering lens of an old cine camera, being a normal family.

I can see us at the movies, where my father and Jen would sit behind me and Mom, throwing their popcorn over our heads to try and get it in our bucket. We'd be in hysterics until the usher came over to tell us we were ruining the cinematic experience for everyone else.

'Sorry, miss,' my father would say in a little boy's voice, sending us all into gales of laughter again.

But then, abruptly, the picture in my head goes from

glorious technicolour to grainy black and white, as the light and joy is replaced by darkness and fear. My father's twisted face suddenly comes into view, his once soft eyes have turned into black pools, and his disarming smile has been replaced by gnarled lips pulled back, baring his teeth.

I'd ask Mom what had happened to turn him into the monster he became, but she would always try to defend him.

'He's got a lot going on right now,' she'd say, as she knelt beside my bed and wrapped my hands in hers. 'He just needs a little space to work things out and then he'll be the dad you remember.'

'Does he not love us any more?' I'd asked.

'Of course he does, pumpkin. He will always love you, no matter what. You're his girls – nothing will ever change that.'

'But I don't like it when he hurts you,' I'd say, lifting her long brown hair up from around her neck where, despite her attempts to conceal it with foundation, I would still see the yellowing bruise blotting her skin.

'He doesn't mean to,' she'd said. 'When he has a drink, he gets angry – with himself more than anyone else – and he just doesn't know what to do with all that pent-up frustration.'

She'd lean in to kiss my forehead and the heady aroma of Elizabeth Arden's Sunflowers perfume would permeate my nostrils as I fell asleep. It was the scent of safety;

the promise that no matter how insecure I might feel some days, she would always be there to lift and protect me. Except she wasn't. One year later, she was gone and the fragrance slowly faded after her.

'Why did you have to go?' I ask aloud, falling onto the bed with my head in my hands.

I used to expect her to answer with a bolt of lightning and a crash of thunder, but I've come to realize that she relays her messages in more subtle ways. It could be in a dream, where I can see her so vividly that I wake up crying, only to look at the bedside clock and see that it's 3.22: her birthday. Or I'll notice that a picture has been moved ever so slightly, or the robin that graces our garden sometimes will sit on the table outside the dining room window and just peer in.

None of which offer any definitive answers to the questions I've often posed, but it means that she's around, and until now I've always believed that she wouldn't let anything bad happen to me.

So how come I find myself here?

'Who's doing this, Mom?' I ask out loud.

I look to her clothes hanging in the wardrobe, and almost expect them to come to life, to morph into living objects, like the Disney film *The Sorcerer's Apprentice*, and go about pulling me up, brushing me down and telling me how to get through this.

I imagine her red-starred sneakers, the ones I'd coveted so much when I was a young girl, flying off the bottom shelf to show me the way forward. I rise from the bed. *Where are her red-starred sneakers?*

An overwhelming panic fills my chest as I scurry around in the bottom of the wardrobe, sure that they're here somewhere. They've got to be.

They were the last thing she wore. She'd breathed her last breath in them, and not being able to see them sends me into a whole new world of pain.

I run into our bedroom and rummage through the cupboards, already knowing they're not in there. Why would I move them? Why would I need to?

It's then that it hits me. The police must have taken them when they searched the house. I hadn't seen everything they'd seized and to look at the house now, you'd be hard pushed to know they'd even been here, but I guess the missing parts of me are only going to be realized over the coming days. But why would they take my mom's shoes? Unless they thought they were mine.

I try to shake off the unsettling feeling that they're currently being analysed in a lab somewhere and instead focus on it being a sign from Mom. This is her way of telling me that they're going to do everything they can to pin this on me, but that she's going to do everything in her power to get me out of it.

Pick yourself up and dust yourself down, I can hear her say. *The only way you're going to get yourself out of this is to keep pushing to find out who's doing this to you.*

I can't help but acknowledge that every finger points to Leon. From him being at the hotel to the phone being found in the bathroom, there's not a more likely suspect, but why would he do this to me? Even if he'd done something terrible to Jacob in a jealous rage because he genuinely thought we were having an affair, would he really go to such lengths to make it look like it was me?

If he's killed someone, he's capable of anything, I say to myself, answering my own question.

I need him to tell me that I've got this all wrong; that he wouldn't dream of doing what I'm accusing him of.

'I can't talk right now,' he says curtly when he picks up the phone, doing nothing to allay my fears.

'Well, you don't have a choice,' I say.

'Just give me a minute,' he says. I think he's talking to me until I hear a woman's voice saying, 'OK.'

A spider moves across the floor towards me and I wonder if it's coming to claim its prey.

'What is it?' he asks, a few seconds later. 'I'm right in the middle of something.'

I briefly allow my suspicious thoughts to wonder what exactly he's up to, but pull myself back.

'The police have been here with a search warrant,' I say, leaving it there, waiting for a reaction.

There's a loaded silence at the other end of the line.

'And?' he says, finally.

'Is that all you've got to say?'

'I don't know what you want me to say any more.'

'That you're there for me,' I snap. 'That no matter what the police keep throwing at me, you've got my back.'

'I've got enough to deal with, without this,' he says, selfishly.

'You make it sound as if this is *my* problem – that you've got nothing to do with it.'

'Isn't that so?' he says bluntly.

'They know Jacob was at the Royal Garden hotel,' I say, betting he hasn't got an answer for this one.

I can hear his breathing change. 'How?'

'Apparently someone recognized him being there and reported it. The police are on their way there now to look at the CCTV.'

'Shit!' he says.

I should tell him that I'm hoping I've deleted all trace of him, but I don't want to let him off the hook just yet.

'They'll see me walking in,' he says, without any regard for me. I wonder if that's because he knows that I'm innocent. But he can only truly know that if he knows *he's* guilty.

'I need you to tell me what happened,' I say. 'I don't know what to think any more. Every passing second brings another piece of evidence against me and the only person who could possibly be behind it is . . .' I can't bring myself to finish the sentence.

'Is me?' he says, almost inaudibly.

'Well, yes, but I don't know why. I mean, even if you thought Jacob and I were having an affair and you'd done something, would you really go out of your way to blame it on me?'

'Do you honestly think I'm capable of doing something like that?' he chokes.

'I just don't fucking know any more,' I say, truthfully.

'Naomi, we were making love just a few nights ago.'

'And look how that turned out,' I cry.

'What is *that* supposed to mean?' he asks.

'A video of it ends up on my computer,' I shrill. 'And I can't help but wonder why you'd reject my advances in the kitchen and then half an hour later have a change of heart and come down to the office in the garden to seduce me. Did you need that time to arrange for whoever it was to film us?'

He exhales heavily, sending a whistling down the line.

'Well, *did* you?' I shout.

'I'd just come from seeing you in a hotel bar with another man,' he sighs, sounding at the end of his tether. 'Knowing that you'd barefaced lied about it. Is it any wonder that I was reluctant to make love to you?'

'So what happened in that half-hour to change your mind?' I ask, pressing for an answer that gives me just the flimsiest of reasons to believe him.

'What *happened*,' he says, 'was that I decided that no matter what, I loved you and wasn't prepared to lose you.'

A crack runs down the length of my heart.

'Though if the police see the CCTV from the hotel, I think that's already sealed our fate.'

'I've deleted it,' I almost cry out, hoping that by saying it quickly it will not incriminate me.

'You've what?' he rasps.

'I went to the hotel, spoke to Andy and deleted everything with you or me in it.'

'Jesus,' he exhales. 'Why would you think that was a good idea?'

'Because I'm innocent, and I knew if they saw me and Jacob in the bar, it would give them everything they need to charge me. But what I didn't expect to see was you. What was I supposed to do, leave you on it and feed you to the lions?'

'But even if you've been successful, there's going to be chunks of time missing on the videos and when the police ask Andy why, he's going to tell them it was you.'

'He might not,' I say, though I already know that whilst he may be a good friend, he's too career-minded to say anything other than the truth if asked. He'll know that I was left alone with the CCTV for long enough to destroy the evidence. He'll assume I'm guilty. I would.

'I don't know if we're going to be able to get ourselves out of this,' says Leon. 'But if we can, the only way we're going to do it is by sticking together.'

23

I wish I could believe him, but as much as it pains me, I still don't know if I can trust him, so until I'm sure that I can, I have to do what I've got to do on my own.

'Oh,' says Shelley, when she opens her front door to me ten minutes later.

'Hey,' I say. 'Have you got a minute?' I look at her, pleading for leniency.

'Naomi, I—' she starts, showing no sign of inviting me in. I wouldn't rush either, if she'd used me as an alibi for something she clearly didn't do.

'Please,' I beg.

She hesitates a split second before standing aside and beckoning me in.

'Tea?' she offers, though it's obvious that every fibre in her being wants me to say no.

I nod. 'Thank you.'

'Is everything set for this afternoon?' she asks, filling the kettle under the tap.

'I think so.'

'I guess it's been a real strain on Leon,' she moots.

'It's definitely taken its toll,' I say, feeling like I might cry. 'But I'm sure everything will calm down once the concert's out of the way.' If only that were true.

'So, do you want to talk about the elephant in the room,' she says.

I swallow. 'I'm sorry for putting you in that position the other night.'

'I was surprised, to say the least,' she says, looking at me disapprovingly. 'I like Leon and I don't want to be your alibi if you're doing something you shouldn't be doing.'

'No,' I say, shaking my head. 'It's not like that.'

'Well, what's going on then?'

I sigh. 'It's a very long story and not something that I gave a second's thought to at the time, but . . .'

She looks at me with raised eyebrows, waiting for me to go on.

'But if I'd known that telling a tiny white lie would lead to this . . .' I shrug my shoulders, looking around hopelessly. 'Then I would never . . .'

Despite trying desperately hard not to, I can't stop my eyes filling up with tears, and Shelley comes and puts her arm around me.

'What on earth's happened?' she asks.

'I can't go into it because I don't want you to be in any way involved, but you have to trust me that I've done nothing wrong.'

'You're scaring me,' she says, wide-eyed.

'It's going to be fine,' I say. 'But I need your help.'

'O-kay,' she says, hesitantly.

'Is there a woman in your choir called Vanessa Talbot?'

She looks beyond confused, her eyes silently questioning me. 'It could be Ness,' she says. 'But I don't know her surname.'

'Do you know anything about her?' I ask. 'Is she married? Does she have children?'

She looks away, almost embarrassed. 'I only know she's married because there's been talk of her having an affair.'

My chest tightens. 'Recently?' I ask.

Shelley nods. 'A couple of months ago,' she says. 'And as you can imagine, it caused quite the scandal. In fact, I haven't seen her since.'

'Do you happen to have her phone number?' I ask.

'I really don't know her that well,' she says, thinking. 'Though we are all on a WhatsApp group.'

She reaches for her phone on the worktop. 'Are you able to tell me why you need to get in touch with her?'

I pull a face. 'I promise I'll explain, but right now, I just need to find her.'

'Oh my god, do you think something's happened?' I watch as Shelley's brow becomes more and more furrowed as she scrolls through her screen. 'The last time she put anything on the chat was over a month ago.'

'If you can let me have her number, I'll check she's OK.'

She reads it out and I add 'Ness' to my contacts, feeling a little more in control, now that I might be closing in on whoever's doing this to me.

I'm about to put my phone back in my bag when an unknown number shows up on the screen. I hesitate, not knowing whether I want to have a conversation with whoever it might be right now, but then I wonder if it might be Anna calling from another phone and I immediately feel the need to pick up.

'Hello.' There's nothing but silence at the other end. 'Hello . . . ?' I say again.

'Naomi?' comes a quiet voice. 'Is that you?'

It sounds a lot like Anna, but something's not quite right.

'Yes, who's this?'

'It's me,' the woman says in a hushed voice. 'Jennifer.'

The air rushes out of me and I collapse onto the floor as the shock sends adrenaline through my body, rendering my legs useless.

'Jen?' I croak.

'Yes,' she says. 'I'm sorry, I didn't mean to just call you out of the blue, but I've been to see Aunt Meryl and I knew if I left my number with her, you'd never call me. I don't blame you, not after last time.'

'I . . . I can't believe it.'

'Look, we don't have to do this now,' she says. 'I just wanted to say hi and let you know that I'm in the UK.'

'You're here?' I gasp. 'Where?'

'London,' she says. 'You don't have to make a decision right here and now, you can take my number and think about it, but I'd really like to see you.'

My head is spinning. I've dreamt about this moment for so long, but now it's finally happening I don't know if it's what I want. So much happened back then. So much has happened since – not least in the last couple of days alone – that I don't feel able to trust anyone.

'I'm different now,' she says, as if sensing my reticence. 'But I completely understand if it's not something you want to do.'

'I just . . . I just need some time,' I say.

'Of course,' she says. 'It's a shock, I get that. But will you at least take my number?'

I sign to Shelley for a pen and paper, and write down the number Jennifer gives me with a trembling hand.

'How . . . how long have you been here?' I ask, as my faculties slowly return and my suspicions set in.

'Just a few days,' she says.

A chill runs through me as I imagine her spending that time sitting in her hotel room, plotting my demise.

'How long do you intend on staying?' I ask.

'As long as it takes,' she says, unnerving me.

'Like I said, I need time,' I say, suddenly desperate to get her off the line.

'I understand, take as long as you need.'

I sit and stare at the phone long after I've hung up, lost in the past and breathless at its impact on my future.

24

The second address on my list is just a couple of miles away in Herne Bay, and as I drive there from Shelley's, I decide to bite the bullet and call the number I have for Ness. As it rings, I wonder if I'm about to speak to the stranger who is wreaking havoc on my life.

'Hello?' she answers, her voice sounding so unlike the monster Jacob had portrayed her to be.

'Hi,' I say, allowing for the possibility that they might not be the same person. 'It's Vanessa, isn't it?'

'Yes,' she says, hesitantly. 'Who's this?'

'I'm really sorry to bother you,' I say, ignoring her question. 'But I'm trying to reach Michael. I keep trying his mobile, but he's not answering.'

There's a loaded silence at the other end.

'Is he with you, as I'd really like to talk to him.'

'Who *is* this?' she asks again.

'My name's Naomi,' I say, waiting before going on.

'*Chandler?*' she asks, her voice high-pitched.

'Yes, has he mentioned me?'

'You've got a fucking nerve,' she hisses, sounding much more like the woman I imagined.

'I'm sorry, I—'

'Where is he?' she screeches. 'What have you done to him?'

I don't know what I expected, but this isn't it.

'The police are on to you. They know what you've done.'

'Now, listen—' I start, before she cuts me off again.

'We were happy until you came along,' she yells. 'We were finally getting back to how we used to be, but what chance did we have once you decided to get your claws into him?'

A strangled sob comes down the line.

'I only ever tried to help him,' I say. 'Help *you*.'

'*Help me?*' she says, with a cynical laugh. 'What, by having an affair with my husband?'

'Wait,' I say. 'Whatever you think has been going on . . . you're wrong. We have only ever had a professional relationship.'

'So why has he left me to live in *your* flat? Why were you in a hotel with him on the night he went missing?'

'Look,' I say, my panic rising. 'He was a client, nothing more. I was only ever trying to help him.'

'He didn't need your kind of help. He may have had a few anger problems, but we were working through them. It was as much my fault as it was his. I understood why he lashed out; he was frustrated, but he never meant anything by it.'

I'm trying to make sense of what she's saying, but it's like a square peg being driven into a round hole, battering my brain with an idea so inconceivable that it refuses to accept it.

I remember the cigarette burns he kept hidden with shirt sleeves, the bruises on his shins concealed by trousers.

I'd always believed him.

Do I still? I cannot even begin to comprehend why he would have made it all up. Or worse still, shared his horror stories as a victim, when in fact he was the perpetrator. But had I got it all wrong? Had he spun me a yarn? Was the man I knew as Jacob really that good an actor?

'None of this is making sense,' I say. 'Are you at home? I'm coming to see you; we need to talk.'

'If you come anywhere near here, I'll call the police,' she says, sounding genuinely scared.

'I'm not who you think I am.'

'You're exactly who I think you are,' she says. 'The blood in my husband's flat is proof of that.'

'*Blood?*' I repeat.

My mouth dries up as I remember the spotlessly clean flat with no sign of any disturbance, least of all blood.

'It was all over the kitchen floor,' she says, making my stomach lurch. 'And they've found your footprint in it.'

The line goes dead, but I'm outside the address where I know the only other Michael Talbot lives within a few minutes. I look through teary eyes at the perfect family home, its neat box hedging and white window shutters giving away none of the secrets it holds within.

The thought of what I'm about to walk into almost makes me run back to the car. If I wasn't trembling so much, not trusting my legs to get me there, maybe I would. But it wouldn't make my problems go away, it would only make them worse. I'd be relinquishing all control and I'd just be left waiting, wondering when the guillotine was going to fall.

I have to do this. I have to take back my life.

My palms are clammy as I stand at the front door, knowing that just a piece of wood separates me from my apparent nemesis. I clench and unclench my hands to distract from the sudden dryness in my mouth and swallow to ease the tickle in the back of my throat.

The chrome knocker glints in the sunlight and as I raise my arm slowly towards it, I can't stop the sudden vision of my sister being on the other side of the door.

I shake my head in an effort to dislodge the preposterous thought as I lift the heavy ring, holding it high for just one second longer to ask myself if I'm definitely doing the right thing. *You have no other choice*, comes another voice from within, as I let go and watch it fall, like a hammer.

I wait for a dog to bark or the marching of feet down the hallway. But the house stands in complete silence. I ring once more, but still there's nothing, and I peer through the front window between the slats of the wooden blinds, into a perfectly appointed living room with no signs of life.

The two sofas, one navy and one cream, look pristine, the scatter cushions expertly arranged and plumped. *Horse & Hound* magazines sit comfortably alongside *Country Homes & Interiors*, fanned out on the coffee table. And there's an abundance of framed photos on the consoles in the alcoves either side of the fireplace. I shield my eyes to get a better look, but the light from the sun throws shadows across both displays. Though in the larger frames, I can definitely make out three children against a white background, as if part of a studio shoot. Another shows a young man awkwardly posing in a sash and mortarboard, no doubt eager to throw it up in the air and leave everything it represents behind. I fervently scan for a photo that shows me who the parents in this family are, but they're either too small to see or just don't exist.

I go to the house next door, whose front room is a hive of activity with the TV on and a woodwind instrument being played badly.

A cheery-looking woman comes to the door, but the tea towel in her hands tells me she's right in the middle of something.

'I'm sorry to trouble you,' I say. 'But I was hoping to find the Talbots next door. I've been knocking, but there's no response.'

Her face changes. 'Are you the police?' she asks.

I'm suddenly at a loss for breath, and reach out surreptitiously to steady myself against the porch wall.

'Y-yes,' I say, unconvincingly.

'You've just missed her,' she says.

'Ah, that's a shame,' I say.

'Is there any news?' she asks, sensing an opportunity to get the inside scoop. 'Have they found Michael yet?'

I shake my head. 'Nothing I can reveal at the moment, I'm afraid.'

She wipes her hands with the tea towel, as if it gives her something to do. 'You never think it's going to come to this, do you?'

I raise my eyebrows questioningly. 'Meaning?'

'Well, we always used to hear raised voices through the wall,' she says. 'Her screams would send shivers down my spine.'

My stomach lurches.

'Though my husband and I used to say that if it had happened to us, we'd probably be at each other's throats as well.' Her eyes glaze over. 'I mean, how do you get over something like that?'

My phone shrills in my hand, demanding my attention. 'I'm sorry,' I say, seeing that it's Detective Robson. 'I need to take this.'

'Mrs Chandler?' she barks.

'Yes,' I say wearily.

'I've just come from the Royal Garden hotel.'

My legs wobble beneath me as I imagine her scouring

the CCTV footage, desperately searching for the indisputable proof that I was there, drinking with Jacob, flirting with him; luring an innocent man to his death.

'I spoke to Andy Kerridge, the General Manager there,' she goes on.

I stay silent, not trusting myself to speak.

'He says that you *were* at the hotel.'

My head feels as if it's about to explode as I try to second-guess what she knows and what she doesn't. Is there any point in me continuing with this charade, if she's just biding her time, ready to pounce with the ace up her sleeve?

What if I hadn't wiped all the incriminating scenes from the CCTV? Had I been clever enough to leave no trace of Leon and me whatsoever? Not even a lingering suggestion in the corner of a frame; perhaps the back of my head, or a flash of his booted foot. Even if I had, there's every chance that Andy would have it all backed up onto a hard drive. His anger, confusion, and ultimately disappointment in what I'd done when he'd trusted me leaves a bitter taste in my mouth.

'He says you asked to see the CCTV from the night of June twenty-first – the night Michael Talbot went missing.'

'Yes,' I squeak, terrified that I might give something away that Andy hasn't.

'So why did you think he was going to be there?'

'I didn't, but it's a place I advise my clients to go to

if they ever feel in danger. So I made the assumption that he might have done.'

She's giving nothing away. No sign of what she saw on the CCTV and no clue as to what Andy has told her.

'Mr Talbot took a call that evening that lasted forty-five seconds.'

I know. I'd seen him on the CCTV, looking terrified as he no doubt listened to his wife telling him what she was going to do when she tracked him down. The sickening realization that the real danger might have been there in the bar with him threatens to wind me.

'Do you want to know where the call was made from?' she asks.

I wish I could say no.

'The burner phone we found hidden in your house,' she goes on, without waiting for me to answer.

It feels as if the sky is closing in on me. I fall heavily onto the closed door of my car.

'And do you want to know what else was on the phone?' says Robson, her voice sounding as if she's underwater – or maybe it's me that's drowning.

'Message after message from you to Michael. And message after message from him telling you that it was over and to leave him alone.'

I gasp, desperate for air.

'But here's the interesting thing; the messages stop on the night Michael Talbot went missing.'

'I told you,' I rasp. 'I've never seen that phone before.'

'I'm going to need you to come down to the station first thing in the morning,' she says. 'We're running some tests on items recovered from your house and I expect to have the results by then.'

'Is it true that you've found some prints at the flat?' I ask, seemingly unable to stop myself from putting my foot in it.

'That's not information I'm able to share with you at this juncture,' she says.

I want to say, *But you can share it with Vanessa Talbot?* but thankfully stop myself. If she finds out I've been stalking and hounding Michael's wife, it'll not work in my favour.

I get into the car and bang my hands against the steering wheel. There's no way out of this, someone has made sure of that. I'm being forced further and further into a corner, the damning evidence building against me with every passing hour.

My chest hurts and my brain is heavy with convoluted theories of who's behind this. As much as it pains me, Leon most definitely has the means; in fact he's the only person who could possibly have filmed us having sex in my office and put it on my computer, who could have hidden a phone in our house. And as insane as it sounds, I'd like to think that only he could have put my sister's bunny rabbit on my pillow, because if it wasn't him . . .

Jennifer, on the other hand, may not have the means, but she's most definitely got the motive. A tear falls onto my cheek as I wonder how far she'd go to avenge her sense of abandonment. Had she recruited Jacob to take me down? Had his whole character and backstory been created specifically for me? Has she played the part of his puppet master, expertly leaving breadcrumbs with my name on, leading the police right to my door?

I unfold the piece of paper I'd written her phone number on and look at it, my fingers drumming on the steering wheel. Are these digits all that I need to unravel what's going on? Do they hold the key to everything? It's too much of a coincidence that my sister has just happened to turn up after twenty-six years for them not to.

My hands are shaking as I tap her number on the screen. After all these years spent imagining how it was going to be, this is not the conversation I thought she and I would be having. But I can't ignore the very real possibility that she's behind what's going on.

I imagine her surprise when she hears my voice. She won't be expecting it for sure; certainly not this soon. Though if she's innocent in all this, she'll no doubt be keen to talk to me. But if she's got something to hide, I might be about to catch her off-guard.

'Hello,' she says, her accent instantly taking me back across the Pond. I try to picture her as the thirty-five-year-old woman she now is. But try as I might, all I can see is the nine-year-old child indelibly printed on my mind's eye.

'Jen, it's me,' I say shakily.

'Hi,' she says, hesitantly. 'Wow, thanks for calling me back.'

There's a moment of silence as we both feel the weight of what needs to be said hanging between us.

'What are you doing here, Jen?' I ask, needing to cut to the chase.

'I . . . I wanted to see you,' she says. 'I got your contact details from Aunt Meryl – well, not directly, but she gave me enough to go on.'

'So, you know where I live?'

'Well, I know you're in . . . Whitstable, is it? Is that how you say it?' She attempts to laugh.

'So, you've seen him?' I cut in, still unable to refer to him as my father, *our* father, all these years later.

'Yes,' she says quietly. 'We met a couple of weeks ago.'

I can hardly bear to ask. 'And?'

'And – he's very sorry,' she says. 'For everything. He says not a day has gone by when he hasn't wondered what had become of us and how his actions had impacted our lives.'

I scoff.

'And every night,' she goes on, 'just before lights out, he kissed a photo of Mom and begged for her forgiveness.'

An unexpected tear springs to my eye.

'He would love to see you,' she says. 'But he's not holding out much hope.'

A breath catches in my throat. 'So he dispatched you to bring me back?' I say bitterly.

'What?' she rasps. 'Of course not. Me coming here has got nothing to do with him. I needed to do this for me – to see if there was any way of us getting back to how we once were.'

I sigh heavily. 'That was in another lifetime.'

'It doesn't have to be,' she says, sounding wounded. 'We could be sisters again – if you'll just give me the chance.'

It's as if a dagger is piercing my heart and every word she utters is driving it in a millimetre more.

'And you thought that showing up here and turning my life upside down would achieve that?' I cry. 'Is that honestly how you thought we could build bridges?'

'N-no,' she stutters. 'I never meant to upset you. I'm so sorry if I have, but I'm just as scared as you are.'

About what? I can't help but ask myself. *That this is all going to backfire on you?*

'You have to believe me,' she goes on. 'I'm not the person I used to be. I'm not going to hurt you again.'

Something inside me breaks. She's saying all the right things. Making all the right noises. Do I dare believe that she's telling the truth and that whatever's going on has got nothing to do with her?

'Listen—' I start.

'We don't have to talk about it if you don't want to,' she says.

274

I don't know what I want any more.

'It wasn't my fault,' is all I can think to say. It's all I've wanted to say for twenty-six years.

'I know,' she says softly. 'And I'm sorry that every time you tried to reach out to me, I let you down.'

'No, I let *you* down,' I say. It had felt like I'd left no stone unturned in my quest to find and save her, but now looking back, I didn't try nearly hard enough.

'It was nobody else's fault but mine,' she says. 'I was pretty unreachable.'

'But why now, Jen?' I ask, as my suspicions rally again, refusing to be silenced. 'Why now? After all this time.'

'You're my sister,' she says, her voice breaking. 'We were torn apart when we needed each other the most. That should never have been allowed to happen, but it did and it's down to us to right the wrongs that have befallen us.'

'I'm just not sure I can do this right now,' I say. 'There's a lot going on.'

'Yes, Leon told me that you both have a lot on your plate at the moment.'

'Sorry . . . what?' I question, sure I misheard her.

'Er, Leon . . .' she says, hesitantly. 'He . . . he told me about the concert this weekend and—'

'You've spoken to my *husband*?' I say shrilly.

'I'm sorry, I thought you knew.'

'What are you doing speaking to Leon?'

'Well, I . . . I just thought . . .'

'You thought *what*?' I ask, struggling for breath.

'I . . . just wanted to test the waters without burning my bridges,' she says. 'I wanted to gauge the situation. I needed to know if you hated me, or still missed me.' Her voice cracks, but I can't afford to get caught up in the emotion of it all.

'So you thought you'd track him down and speak to him first?'

'Yes,' she says. 'And when he said that you'd spent weeks scouring the subway, a month crying when I didn't show up at the airport, and that you cuddled my pink rabbit whenever you felt down, I knew it was a risk worth taking.'

My blood runs cold at the thought of my own husband telling my intimate secrets to a woman he doesn't know. How could he do that when he doesn't even know the full story? Why would he betray my trust, risk our marriage on something he knows so little about?

But whose fault is that? asks a voice inside my head. *Perhaps if you'd been honest at the very beginning, he would have been more honest with you.*

'I'm sorry, I can't do this,' I say, as the deceit burrows under my skin.

Though whether it's mine or his, I can't tell any more.

25

Leon is sitting on a stool with his head in his hands on the kitchen worktop when I get back to the house.

'You need to start talking,' I say, throwing my bag onto the counter. It takes all my resolve not to launch myself at him. 'What the hell do you think you're doing talking to my sister, without speaking to me first? You had no right to do that.'

He puffs out his cheeks, looking visibly relieved. 'You honestly think that's our biggest problem right now?'

'I don't know,' I shout. 'You tell me. All this stuff happens – Jacob goes missing, my estranged sister turns up, I'm under suspicion for something I know nothing about, and all the while, *you*' – I jab a finger aggressively in his direction – 'you're right slam dunk in the middle of it all.'

'I thought I was doing the right thing,' he says quietly. 'You call her name out in your sleep; she's obviously on your mind all the time, so when she got in touch with me, I wasn't going to turn her away because that's not what you would have wanted me to do.'

'You should have told me,' I seethe. 'You have no idea what you've done.'

'What I've *done*?' he exclaims. 'She's your sister and yes, she may have been in a bad place for a while, but I made sure that she was well out of that before agreeing to anything. Did you know she's been to rehab?'

'You just don't get it, do you?' I yell. 'I think she's got something to do with Jacob, and is setting me up for it.'

Leon shakes his head vehemently. 'You're not thinking straight,' he says. 'Why would she do that? What have you ever done to her to warrant that kind of revenge?'

'I let her go,' I wail.

'You had no other choice,' he says, standing up and coming towards me. 'You were a child yourself.'

'But she needed me,' I cry, holding my hand up to warn him off coming any nearer. 'And I wasn't there.'

'She's got nothing to do with Jacob,' he says.

'How do you know?'

'Because I've just had a call from his wife,' he says.

I narrow my eyes as I watch him watching me. 'Vanessa?' I ask needlessly.

He nods.

'Well, why?' I ask, as all the guilty parties and their motivations merge into one in my head. 'What did she want? How did she get your number?'

He shrugs at the litany of questions. 'It seems that she's in exactly the same position as me.'

'Meaning?' I ask, my patience too thin to be playing mind games.

'Meaning, we both seemingly have unfaithful partners.'

'*What*?' I rasp.

'Look, I'm trying really hard to believe you but everyone and everything is telling me the same story – that you two are having an affair.'

'I swear I'm telling you the truth.'

He looks like he wants to come to me, but he stops himself. 'You have to understand. You've been holding back ever since this whole thing started. I'm being drip-fed information on a need-to-know-basis.'

I can't disagree with him on that.

'So until I'm sure you've told me everything, I'm going to reserve judgement.'

I look at him, aghast. 'You're supposed to be my husband,' I say.

'And you're supposed to be my wife,' he bats back.

'What do you want me to do?' I cry.

'I want you to be honest,' he says. 'About everything.'

'I've told you all there is to know,' I say.

'So you're sticking with the story that you didn't send me that text last night?'

'It's not a story, it's the truth. You must be able to tell it wasn't sent from my phone.'

'No, it wasn't,' he says resignedly.

'Well, there you go then.'

'But that doesn't mean you didn't send it from the burner phone,' he says, looking me in the eye, his gaze unwavering.

'The burner phone?' I ask, wondering when this

nausea-inducing rollercoaster will ever end. 'How do you know about the burner phone?'

He slams his hands down on the granite. 'So it's true then!' he says, his nostrils flaring.

'The police found a phone here this morning,' I say. 'But it wasn't mine.'

'Of course it wasn't.' He makes a self-satisfied clicking sound with his mouth.

'How do you know there was a phone?' I ask again.

'Vanessa told me that's how you and he communicated, with secret phones.'

My ears go hot, muffling everything he says. I can see his lips moving, but it doesn't correlate with what he's saying. All I can think about is how he and Vanessa seem to know more about the phone found in my bathroom than I do. And suddenly, it all becomes clear.

'Oh my god,' I gasp.

He looks at me with a perplexed expression.

'It's . . . it's you and her, isn't it?'

'What?' he says, but I know he knows I'm on to him. I can see it in his eyes.

'You and Michael's wife, that's what this is all about.' I hit my forehead with the base of my palm. 'How can I have been so fucking stupid?'

He watches me carefully as my brain pulls it all together. 'You and her are in this together,' I say, my voice high-pitched. 'You wanted to get rid of Michael and frame me for it.'

'This is getting more absurd by the minute,' he says.

I pace up and down as all the pieces fall into place. 'That's it!' I exclaim, thinking aloud. 'You did it because you wanted to be together. You wanted us both out of the picture and this is how you thought you'd make that happen.'

Leon laughs. 'Oh, I've heard it all now.'

I go towards him, desperate to lash out, but as soon as I'm an inch away, I stop myself, ashamed that I came so close. 'What have you done with him, you bastard?' I scream. 'Tell me what you've done with him.'

He looks at me wide-eyed, as if he can't believe that our relationship has sunk to such depths. Him and me both.

'This is crazy,' he yells. '*You're* crazy!'

He storms out, making the house shake as the door slams and rebounds against the frame.

One of us had to leave, before something was said that we'd never recover from. Though right now, it doesn't feel like we'll ever be able to get back to the normal we used to think was boring. It was only a week ago that life had seemed so mundane, but I'd go back there in an instant. How have our lives been turned upside down in such a short space of time? How has the implicit trust I had in my husband, and him in me, been eroded so deeply?

I'm still pulling myself together when, a few minutes later, a voice calls out down the hall. 'Hello?'

With the concert starting in a couple of hours' time, I knew that we'd most likely have visitors; friends excitedly passing by on their way to the ground, with picnic hampers and clinking bottles of wine. But of all the days to have an open house . . .

I quickly wipe under my eyes and pull at my blouse. 'In here,' I say, popping my head around the kitchen door.

'Hey, sorry to just show up,' comes an American drawl.

Of all the people it could be, Anna is my most preferred. Not least because it means she's OK after last night.

'I just wanted to say sorry about yesterday,' she says, proffering a bottle of wine and a small bouquet of flowers.

'What's this?' I ask.

'It's just a little thank you,' she says, as the corners of her mouth turn up.

As I take them from her, I realize that I've never seen her smile before.

'For what?'

'You have no idea how much you've helped me these past couple of months,' she says. 'And after yesterday, I finally think I've turned a corner.'

'What happened?' I ask.

'So I went back home after seeing you and told Nick, very calmly, that we couldn't go on the way we were and that I was going to leave him unless we sorted things out.' Her eyes light up. 'We had a really good talk and he admits that he lets his anger and frustrations get the better of him, and that none of it is my fault. He doesn't want me to leave and says he will do everything he can to make it up to me.'

'That's great,' I say, tempering my misgivings. I've heard this a thousand times before.

'So I'm going to give him a chance,' she says. 'But I wanted to say thank you because without you, I wouldn't have had the courage to do it.'

'Does this mean you're ending your sessions?'

She nods. 'You've been so incredible and given me so much, but I've got everything from them that I needed.'

I smile, yet can't help but wonder if she'll be knocking on my door again in a month's time.

'Are you going to the concert?' she asks.

I want to say no. I want to tell her that whilst her life has seemingly got infinitely better, mine is imploding around me. But instead I smile and nod.

'I wouldn't miss it for the world,' I say.

26

I lock the door behind her and take my phone and my heavy heart up to 'Mom's room'. It's the only place where I feel I have someone on my side.

As I lie on the bed, I can hear the opening chords of Bach's *Adagio* drifting through the open window, as the violin section of the twenty-five-piece orchestra Leon booked flexes its strings for a soundcheck. I wonder if it even occurs to him as he's putting the final touches to the afternoon's festivities that it's the solo from our wedding, sung in the church as we signed the register.

The haunting concerto stops abruptly, much like our marriage, it seems, and the irony almost makes me cry. A few seconds later it starts up again, joined by the low pitch of the cellos.

Why am I being punished? I ask, hoping my mother can hear me. *I only ever wanted to do the right thing. Why would anyone see it any other way?*

I'm startled by the interruption of my phone ringing and sit bolt upright when I see *Ness* flashing on the screen.

'Hello?' I say, breathlessly.

There's a muffled scream at the other end of the line.

'Oh my god, Vanessa, is that you?' I shout.

'If you think you're going to get away with this . . . I'll . . . if it's the last thing I do,' comes the sporadic buffeting of a man's voice, which sounds a lot like Jacob's.

There's a sinister silence. 'Vanessa!' I bellow. 'Can you hear me?'

There's heavy breathing and a rustling sound, but as I press the phone tightly to my ear, there's something else. I close the window, shutting out the sporadic melodies of the string section on the other side of the copse. But I can still hear it, coming down the line.

'Fuck,' I say aloud, almost dropping the phone. I open the window, listen to the dulcet tones and slam it shut again. The music is playing, as if in stereo; because whoever's at the other end of the line is listening to the same thing as me.

Vanessa Talbot's phone is here, on the estate. But with two thousand people expected for the concert, it's going to be like looking for a needle in a haystack, especially when I don't even know who I'm looking for.

My legs don't feel like my own as I sprint across the meadow and through the copse of trees towards the concert ground. The tuning of instruments and the holler of 'Testing . . . testing,' all adds to the cacophony resounding in my head.

My lungs are burning by the time the woodland opens out to the manicured lawns that roll down towards the stage. I'm buoyed to see just a couple of hundred people at most, milling about within the confines of the fences surrounding the site, so I'm confident that even if I'm not able to identify Vanessa, I'll certainly know Jacob.

I need to be quick though, as the drive leading down from the main house is already teeming with people making their way to what they hope is going to be a pleasurable evening in the sun. Until a few days ago, I thought I was going to be one of them, looking forward to my own Lady of the Manor moment with excitement as I proudly watched my husband arrange the biggest event Whitstable has ever seen.

Yet now, I doubt I'll even be able to get into the grounds, as a man wearing an all-black ensemble, with a lanyard hanging around his neck, puts a hand out to stop me passing through the gate.

'I'm . . .' I start, barely able to catch my breath. 'I'm . . . I'm the organizer's wife.'

I may as well have said I'd just been dug up. 'Have you got your pass?' he says, looking me up and down with bemusement.

'No, I left it back at home,' I say. 'I live over there.' I point blindly through the trees I've just come through. 'I live on the estate.'

'You need a pass,' he says bluntly.

'Oh, for God's sake, I live here! I'm Leon's wife.'

'Well, then you'll be able to get another one easily enough,' he says, holding his scanner up to a punter who's remembered their ticket.

I haven't got time for this, I want to scream, reaching for my phone in my back pocket to call Leon. I try the other one and helplessly pat myself down, but I already know it's not there. I must have left it on the bed when I raced out of the house.

I consider rushing him, but he's big and strong, and even if I got past him, where would I go? I don't even know what I'm looking for; I just know I've got to find it.

I turn away and run along the perimeter towards the stage. The ground is uneven underfoot as I track along the fence, but I can't look at where I'm stepping at the same time as peering in through the wire mesh, trying to see if I can spot Jacob from afar, amongst the growing queues at the Pimm's tent and the strawberries and cream kiosk.

I wonder what I'll do if I spot him. Will I scream and shout, demanding to know what's going on? Or will I just be so relieved to see him alive and well that I'll want to hug him?

There's a hub of activity behind the stage, as musicians, crew members and engineers make the final preparations before the show starts. I look for Leon among the melee, knowing this is most likely where he'll be, but even if I spot him, he's not who I need to find. It's only Jacob who can save me.

The perimeter goes way beyond the stage, every step taking me further and further away from where I need to be; every second allowing more people through the gates. I should have gone in the opposite direction; perhaps I would have found a more affable security guard.

I'm just about to turn back along the fence, daunted and panicked by the length of it, unable to see an access point, when something catches my eye.

Over by the old stables, which are just visible through an opening in the trees, a flurry of pigeons flap and squawk out of a gaping hole in the moss-covered slate roof. It's as if they've heard a shotgun, yet the only sound I can hear is the distant hum of the burgeoning crowd.

I'm momentarily rooted to the spot, my body waiting to catch up with the fanciful theories racing through my brain.

Without even acknowledging I'm going to do it, my feet are walking down the slope, away from the fence, and through the wildflowers towards the outbuildings. It's as if something is pushing me, propelling me forwards, and I couldn't stop even if I wanted to. By the time the leaning flintstone stable block comes into full view, I'm almost running, desperately needing to quash the macabre movie that is playing out in my head.

As I squeeze through the barriers around the site, I can hear a loud clanging sound coming from inside. It may just be builders clearing the place up, but I don't recall Leon saying he'd instructed anyone to start working on it seeing as they're awaiting planning permission. Besides, I can't imagine he'd choose this weekend to do so.

The incessant drumming of metal against metal is getting louder as I pass by the disused swimming pool, the faded tiles on the top step just visible above the stagnant green water that fills it. Pieces of wood, discarded drink cans and what looks like an old overall litter the surface, and I shudder at the thought of what has become of the items that don't float.

I creep forward as if I'm a sniper in training, sprinting the last few metres and pushing my back up against the jagged wall. I imagine what I'll say if Tom, the head gardener, comes around the corner to see me playing a grown-up game of hide and seek. Or even worse, if Tristan is watching this all unfold in real-time on the cameras up in the security lodge. Though that concern is allayed when I remember him telling me that Leon had limited the coverage to the immediate concert site this week.

I instinctively crouch down as I enter the stable block, staying below the line of the half-height walls of the stalls, not knowing what I'm about to encounter. Suddenly the banging that had been reverberating around the stone walls stops and I can't help but gasp as I hear a low groan.

'Hello, is someone there?' comes a voice.

I hold a hand to my mouth, willing myself to stop and think before I answer.

'Please,' says the voice. 'Please help me.'

'Jacob?' I breathe, rounding the corner of the stall on my hands and knees.

'Naomi!' he cries out. 'Oh my god, please help me.'

I can't help but recoil at the sight of him, bloodied and bruised. His ankles are tied to chair legs and his wrists handcuffed to the bars of the stable stool. I instinctively want to go to him and set him free, but something's holding me back and he can sense my reticence.

'You have to hurry,' he says. 'She's only just left, but she won't be long.'

'Who?' I ask, as I crawl through the dark brown sludge puddles on the slimy stone floor.

'Who do you think?' he says bitterly. 'I told you what she was capable of. I told you what she'd do if she found me.'

'Vanessa's done this to you?'

He nods, his normally piercing blue eyes darkened by fear.

'But how did you get here?' I ask, as I set about untying the rope that is bound tightly around his ankles.

'She lured me here,' he says. 'Pretending to be you.'

'What?' I ask, looking around for something to prise the handcuffs apart. 'When?'

'After I met you at the hotel on Monday night,' he says. 'I got a text about ten minutes after you left, asking me to come to Tattenhall as you thought I'd be safer here.'

'But I would never have done that.'

'I know, and it's my own stupid fault,' he says. 'If I'm honest with myself, I was hoping you'd changed your mind . . .'

'About what?' I ask.

He looks away as if ashamed, and I realize what he means. 'But *she* was here waiting for me instead,' he says.

'So you've been here all this time?'

He nods. 'I thought she was going to kill me.'

A stable door creaks and we look at each other, wide-eyed and terrified.

'Hurry, there's a hammer over there,' he says. 'If you dislodge this bar, I'll be able to free myself.'

'Why didn't you tell me you were really called Michael Talbot?' I ask, as I hit the bars of the stool with all my might, the metal curling an inch with every strike.

'I was too scared to give you my real name in the beginning,' he says. 'And by the time I realized I could trust you, I knew if I told you the truth, you probably wouldn't trust *me*.'

He takes a sharp intake of breath and I can feel his body going rigid.

'No!' screams a woman's voice.

I freeze, unable to look up for fear of seeing a madwoman standing there, pointing a gun in my face.

'Oh my god,' she shouts. 'No.'

I slowly bring my head up, steeling myself. But nothing could prepare me for what I see.

Even with her dishevelled blonde hair falling onto her face and my brain's refusal to see what's there, there's no denying who it is.

'Anna?'

27

My heart stops. The blood being pumped around my body seems to suspend in mid-flow.

Of all the conspiracy theories that have been rattling around my head these past few days, Anna being involved in any way was just not on my radar. *Why would it be?*

'I-I don't understand,' I falter. 'What are *you* doing here?'

She backs herself up against the stall wall. 'When they said it was you, I didn't believe them, but they were right.' She covers her mouth in a futile attempt to stifle her sobs.

My head feels as if it's about to explode as I try to make sense of what's going on. 'What are you talking about? Who told you it was me?'

'The police,' she cries. 'They've told me everything; the emails, the hotel CCTV, the phone . . .'

'The police think this is *your* doing?' asks Michael incredulously, looking at me.

I nod numbly, whilst still trying to work out what Anna's doing here and why she's been talking to the police.

'They've even found her footprint in your blood,' cries Anna.

'Jesus Christ,' says Michael. 'She's set you up.'

'But . . . you . . . you . . .' I say, waiting for one of them to change into someone else because it just doesn't make sense for these two people who have been paying me to listen to their life stories to be here together. 'What the hell is going on here?' I say. 'How do you even know each other?'

'She's my wife,' says Michael bluntly.

'Anna's your *wife*?' I gasp.

I think of all the stories he'd told me about the violence he'd endured and can't even begin to compute that he was talking about the woman in front of me; the woman I've known for the past two months.

'But how? H-how can that be?' I stutter. 'You told me your wife beat you. That she abused and humiliated you. That she . . . she . . .' I can't list everything he's accused her of; there are too many to mention.

'She did all of that,' he exclaims. 'She's still doing it.'

'He told you *I* was abusing *him*?' asks Anna incredulously.

I shake my head, unable to make any sense of what either of them are saying. I'd believed them both wholly and unequivocally when they were sitting on my couch, each telling me their own story. Why wouldn't I, because why would they be making it up? But now, I have no idea who was telling the truth.

'You have proof in front of you that I've been telling the truth. I've been kept here for five days!'

294

'But how . . . I mean, how can this even be possible?' I turn to look at the woman who just yesterday was going to end it all. The same woman, I suddenly realize, who was screaming down the phone at me this morning, accusing me of having an affair with her husband.

'So *you're* Vanessa?'

She looks at me; the eyes that had appeared to be dead with grief are now burning with a ferocious fire. Her mouth, with which only words of shame and self-reproach had been uttered, is pulled tight. She looks nothing like the woman I've come to know as Anna.

In the madness of the moment, I find myself searching her face for any resemblance to the little girl I haven't seen for twenty-six years. Could Jennifer be in there? Has she been in there all this time without me realizing it?

My shredded brain runs over every conversation we've had, desperately looking for clues that she's the sister I left behind. Does she have my mother's eyes? Or the ravaged features of her drug-taking past? It seems she certainly has my father's psychotic gene.

It could be her . . . and oh my god. Even as I'm thinking it, I'm wondering how I've missed it. It's the biggest clue I could possibly have been given, yet it's only now, as I'm piecing it all together, that it occurs to me what's been staring me in the face all this time. Her New York accent; a characteristic so hard to disguise that she'd had to invent a whole backstory to pass it off without me realizing.

I remember the picture of New York that she'd given me, thinking it was Anna's sweet attempt to make me feel more at home. But could it have been Jennifer's warped endeavour to take me back there; to relive the horrors we endured?

No, I refuse to believe it. My own sister would never do this to me. Plus, I'm sure I would have recognized her in one of our many sessions together, that she would have slipped up.

'I'm going to call the police,' says Vanessa, edging herself away from me, looking terrified.

'You know I'm not behind this,' I say. 'You know that's not who I am.'

'I don't know who you are any more,' she says tearfully. 'I trusted you. I told you everything and you repay me by having an affair and . . . and doing *this* to him.'

'Don't listen to her, Naomi,' bellows Michael, as he raises himself onto his feet. I immediately wish that I'd kept him restrained – at least until I know exactly what's going on. 'She's a goddamn liar.'

'You . . . you said that he'd hurt you . . . that he'd hurt the children,' I say, looking to her in shock and confusion. 'But how could he have when he's been here?'

'I thought he'd gone to ground because of the anniversary,' she says. 'I thought he just needed some time away – I was relieved because it's what I needed too. But when he didn't come home on Tuesday and again on Wednesday, I started to panic. I called the police because

I was scared that he'd done something stupid, but they told me that it looked like he was having an affair.'

'She's lying,' snarls Michael.

I shake my head, still unable to grasp what the hell's going on.

'I was so upset,' she goes on. 'And I desperately wanted to speak to you, *needed* to speak to you, but when you were there in front of me, I just didn't know how to. I felt so foolish and ashamed; I never expected my husband to have an affair in an attempt to drown his grief.'

'So you made up the assault?' I ask incredulously.

She nods. 'I didn't know how else to explain why I was so hurt and upset. And then you were so kind it made me feel worse, but now I know why.' Her eyes go dark and she bares her teeth. 'How could you?' she hisses. 'How could you hold my hand and rub my back when all along you've been having an affair with my husband and keeping him here?'

'Naomi,' calls out Michael, 'Naomi, you have to listen to me.'

I stand there staring into the abyss, transfixed by the insanity of the situation.

'Look at me, Naomi!' Michael yells, in an attempt to rouse me from my stupor. I numbly turn to him. 'You know you have no part to play in this. You know that what she's saying is completely untrue. She brought me here. She tied me up. And she has kept me here for the past five days.'

Vanessa snorts. 'As well as being a cruel, cold-hearted bully, you also have a vivid imagination.'

'So – what? You think I've done to this to *myself*?' he screeches, looking between us both. 'Naomi, please, just think about what she's saying. She's exactly who I've told you she is. If you'll just free me from this' – he nods towards the bars that with just one more strike will free him from restraint – 'I promise I'll prove it to you.'

I raise the hammer I'd forgotten I was holding and see the look of terror in Vanessa's eyes. She screams as I bring it down with all my might and strike the bar one more time.

'You're making a big mistake,' she cries, as Michael's still handcuffed wrists are released. 'You have no idea what he's capable of.'

For a moment, I'm poleaxed, waiting for him to run or lunge at me, but he does neither. He just stands there with his shackled hands hanging in front of him.

'We need to call the police,' he says, looking at me.

I nod. 'I haven't got a phone,' I say, struggling to think clearly. 'But there are police on site, just a few hundred metres away.'

Vanessa stumbles backwards out of the stables as I move towards the door, her face frozen in fear of what I might be about to do to her.

'Please,' she says, blinking rapidly as her eyes adjust to the sunlight. 'Please don't hurt me. I won't stand in your way if you want to be together. I'll do whatever you want, but please don't hurt me.'

The smile she'd displayed less than an hour ago is replaced with a look of abject terror as I get closer. I have to make her understand that she's got it all wrong.

'You came to my house with thank-you presents,' I say, suddenly remembering. 'You bought me wine and flowers. Why would you have done that if you'd already been told that I was having an affair with your husband and was the prime suspect in his disappearance?'

'I wanted to look you in the eye and give you a chance to tell me the truth.'

I shake my head, struggling to believe a word she says.

'But you did better than that,' she goes on. 'You led me here, so I could see for myself.'

'So you followed me?'

'Well, how else would I have known where he was?'

'Because *you* brought me here,' yells Michael.

'We're going to the police,' I say, raising the hammer to my chest in an attempt to ward either of them off trying anything. 'Then we'll find out which one of you is the liar.'

I can just make out the opening bars of the *Adagio* as the soft strings drift on the breeze, and I turn towards the copse that leads to the concert site. It's just a split-second lapse in awareness, but in that moment there's a sudden whoosh of air and an animalistic roar; a feral battle cry that reverberates around my core, shaking my very foundations. I don't even have time to lift the hammer before a looming mass of limbs reaches out towards me.

Michael's weight falls onto me, his arms going around my neck, locking on my throat as he pushes me forwards. I try to stay upright, but he's dragging me down and I stumble.

All I can see, as I desperately try to right myself, is the deep green algae-topped water of the swimming pool in front of me. I know that if I go in there, I'll never come back out again.

I try to turn, thrashing out with my hands, aiming for whatever part of him I can hit, but he pins my arms down by my side, giving me no way to protect myself as the ground comes up to meet me.

My head jolts backwards as my chin makes impact and I groan as the air in my diaphragm is forced out of me. I can't help but wonder if I'm already dead as everything around me seems to have stopped, the silence deafening.

There were never going to be any winners in this, but the shock that Michael is not the man I thought he was assaults me. That I'd allowed his alter-ego, Jacob, to manipulate and play with my good intentions and malleable heart – right to the very end. How had I not seen the chink in his armour? That tiny tell-tale sign that he was the abuser and not the abused.

'Please,' I whisper, just to test if I'm still alive. 'Just think about what you're doing. Think of your boys.'

He makes a grunting sound as his weight shifts, and for a second I dare to believe that he's really listening to what I'm saying.

'You're their father. The man who is supposed to protect them at all costs. But how can you if you're not here?'

'He's never protected them,' hisses Vanessa.

'Don't,' bellows Michael, lifting himself off me. I slowly roll over to see his silhouette rising up into the sky, moving towards Vanessa. She backs herself up against the stables, cowering in his shadow.

'Shall I tell her what you did to Ben?' she says. 'That you left the door open for him to wander off. That you were too drunk to know if he was in his bed or not.'

'*You* were there as well,' chokes Michael. 'It wasn't just my fault.'

'You told me you'd locked the door,' screeches Vanessa. 'You led me to believe that you'd checked – like any self-respecting father would have done. It was your responsibility to ensure the safety of our children and I was foolish to believe that you'd put them first – instead of the bottle. How could I have been so stupid?'

'I swear I locked the door,' cries Michael, with tears running down his face.

'So how come our little boy was able to let himself out and wander down to the sea in the dark?'

I push myself up onto my elbows, listening in abject horror at the events that had led to Ben's untimely death. So *that* had been the catalyst that Jacob had alluded to – the magical day that had turned into a nightmare, after which nothing had ever been the same again. How could it?

'If it weren't for you, he would still be alive,' yells Vanessa, as a guttural cry escapes from somewhere deep inside her. 'My little boy would still be with me, holding my hand, giving me cuddles.'

'He wouldn't be a little boy any more,' whispers Michael. 'He'd be a young man.'

I look between them, not knowing whose version of the child they lost is true; is Michael looking to distance himself from the son he let down just last year? Or is Vanessa clinging on to the boy she lost a decade ago?

'But he'll never get to be that man now, will he?' she wails. 'Because the daddy who professed to love him so much—'

'Stop!' yells Michael, bearing down over Vanessa as she presses herself into the flintstone wall. 'Just stop.'

I want to run, knowing that this could be my only chance, but how can I? Vanessa needs me, just like my mother needed me, and I'm not going to make the same mistake twice.

There's a glint of something in the melee of limbs; a shimmer of silver as it slices through the air.

'No!' I scream, forcing myself up off the ground and going towards them.

But before I can get there, Vanessa cries out, and I watch helplessly as she falls like a timbered tree. The thud when she hits the ground is sickening, her head taking the full brunt.

She lies there motionless and I look at Michael, open-mouthed, as he stands over her with a knife in his hand.

'Oh my god,' I breathe, backing away. 'Is she . . . ?'

'Naomi!' says Michael, turning to face me.

'No!' I say, shaking. 'Don't come any nearer.'

'But it wasn't my fault,' he says. 'You saw how she was. You saw what she did.'

He looks at me, and I search his eyes for the man I thought he was, and for just a split second he's there, imploring me to believe him.

'You've . . . you've killed her,' I cry.

He comes towards me and I turn and run, as fast as the pain in my body will allow.

'Naomi, stop!' he calls out.

My lungs burn as I fight for every breath I take. My legs turn to jelly, as adrenaline and the desire to survive courses through me.

'Naomi!'

Brambles hit my face but still my legs work in unison, powering forward over the uneven ground.

I'm almost through the woodland; I can see the perimeter fence of safety, hear the banging drums of *The*

Marriage of Figaro, when my ankle buckles. I cry out as I fall forwards, not least because I was so close to saving myself.

As I hit the ground, my ribs feel as if they've left imprints in the soil. I lie there in the dense undergrowth, forcing my panting breaths down into my diaphragm, making my chest feel as if it's about to explode. I can't make a sound. I can't tell him where I am. Because I've no doubt that he'll kill me too.

How have I become embroiled in this nightmare? Been sucked into the vortex of another couple's toxic marriage?

Because that's what you do, I hear Leon's voice saying in my head. *You can't say I didn't warn you.*

Salty tears make tracks down my cheeks as it occurs to me how close he might be. I let them fall onto the undergrowth for fear that wiping them away will tell Michael where I am.

I freeze as I hear twigs snapping underfoot. It sounds as if he's right here, so close that I can hear his laboured breaths. Or is it just my own exhalation whistling through the trees?

The stones beneath me are beginning to feel as if I'm lying on a bed of nails. I clench my eyes tightly to shut off the pain.

Too scared to move yet, I strain my ears, listening for any clue as to where Michael might be.

There's a splash of water, as if someone has jumped

into the pool, and my heart stops, frozen in time as I try to work out what's going on.

The realization creeps up slowly, but once it does, I can't get to my feet quickly enough. The pain sears through me, but I have to get away from here – I can't waste another second.

I'm a moving target as twigs crack and my breaths come in short, sharp, audible gasps. I can't risk looking back to see if he's heard me. This is my only chance to get help for Vanessa, even though it already seems too late to save her.

As I run away, towards the opening in the trees, I can't help but picture her lifeless body floating down to the bottom of the pool. She looks so serene, but then I imagine her eyes opening as the water starts to choke her; her desperate attempt to get to the surface for air, only to be met by Michael's forceful arm, pushing her back under.

I feel like I'm drowning myself as I push on, but I can't stop. Not while Vanessa might still be fighting for her life.

28

I'm wrapped in a blanket, shivering in the first aid tent as uniformed police come and go, several of them checking that I'm OK but none of them brave enough, or perhaps qualified enough, to ask or answer any questions.

'Shh, it's OK,' soothes Leon, as he pulls me into him. I wince from the pain; every grain of dirt stabs like a needle. Every tear I've cried stings like acid.

'You're going to be OK,' he says, breathing me in.

'He killed her,' I cry. 'I saw him do it.'

'I'm so sorry,' he says, his lips resting on my forehead. 'I can't begin to imagine how it must feel to see that happen.' He has to stop himself from saying 'again'.

'I never thought I'd allow a man to hurt a woman after what happened to Mom, but there was nothing I could do.' I fall into him.

'To think that he's been in our house, in the office with you for all those sessions . . .' he says, almost to himself. 'Did you have any idea he was capable . . . of this?'

I shake my head. 'What have I learnt?' I wail. 'After all these years, I'm no more able to save someone than I've ever been.'

Blue lights flash by the marquee windows and I keep looking up, hoping to see an ambulance coming away from the stables with its emergency siren on, giving me a sign that skilled paramedics are miraculously bringing Vanessa's stricken body slowly back to life. But there's such a flurry of noise and lights that it's impossible to see which direction they're going in, let alone what vehicles they are.

There's a sudden shift in atmosphere as the policemen by the door, who I was assured were for my protection rather than to prevent me escaping, stand taller and cough awkwardly.

If they were wearing caps, they'd no doubt doff them as Detective Inspector Robson walks in.

'I told you I had nothing to do with it, didn't I?' I croak. 'If you'd just concentrated on finding him instead of wasting your time on me, then . . . then . . .' I'm unable to finish the sentence as an image of Vanessa, floating face down with her blonde hair swimming all around her, blindsides me.

'What happened here tonight?' she asks. Her face is oddly emotionless.

I shake my head. 'I don't know. I found him tied up in the stables, but just as I was releasing him, she came and . . . and . . .' My mouth is having trouble keeping up with the speed of the sequences that are racing through my brain. 'I had a hammer, but he came at me, throwing me onto the floor. I thought he was going to kill me but suddenly he was off me and bearing down on her. There was a knife and he must have . . .' Hot bile pushes up through my chest as I picture her falling backwards. 'She was just lying there and I ran to get help, but then I heard the splash . . .'

I pause for breath.

'You know her as Vanessa Talbot. But she was my client and called herself Anna. She talked to me about losing her son and the empty marriage his death had left behind. She always said that they were destroying each other, but I didn't think for one second he would ever go this far. They were grieving for the little boy they'd lost, blaming each other for what happened. But it seems that in his efforts to relinquish any responsibility for the part he may have played, he created such a deep and convoluted backstory that even he didn't know what was real and what wasn't. He certainly fooled me.'

I wipe a tear away as Robson scratches her head, looking genuinely perplexed. 'But you said Michael Talbot was your client.' She opens her notebook and flips over the pages until she finds what she's looking for. 'You said that he used the name Jacob.'

'He lied,' I say.

'What exactly did he lie about, Naomi?' she asks, fixing me with a steely glare.

'He lied about everything! His name, his wife, his life! No doubt he'll lie about what happened here tonight as well. But I saw what he did. I saw him kill her.'

'But Mrs Chandler,' says Robson, leaning in and tilting her head to one side. 'It wasn't her body we found. It was his.'

29

I feel like I'm falling, as if I've jumped out of an aeroplane without a parachute, turning and tumbling through the air, waiting for someone to catch me.

How can that be? That's impossible. I saw him strike Vanessa with my own two eyes.

Just like you saw your mother strike your father, says a voice from somewhere far away.

I've spent years denying it. Wanting to protect her. But despite not wanting to go there, I can see Mom trying desperately hard not to make a sound as Dad holds her by the hair and knees her in the stomach. She falls to the floor, wheezing for breath, as he kicks her with his steel-capped boots.

'Get away from her!' I scream, launching myself onto his back.

But my strength is no match for his and he throws me off, sending me crashing like a ragdoll into the Formica worktop.

'I hate you,' I scream, as he comes at me with a raised hand.

'No!' yells my mother, rushing at us, with a fear in

her eyes unlike anything I've ever seen before. 'If you *ever* touch my children, I'll kill you.'

My father momentarily doubles over, instinctively holding a hand to his hip. I'll never forget the look on his face when he sees that his fingers are covered in blood.

'I'm sorry,' says Mom, dropping the knife and backing herself up against the kitchen wall. She looks at me with tears in her eyes. 'Go!' she says.

I shake my head, refusing to leave her side. 'Go, Naomi!' she implores. 'Now.'

The next thing I remember, I'm sitting at the bottom of the stairs while the paramedics fight to save Mom's life as she lies motionless on the kitchen floor.

I can hear the snip of the scissors as they cut her clothes away from her wound, feel the sense of urgency as they frantically try to resuscitate her. But all I can see are the red-starred sneakers that she'd promised me just minutes before, hoping and praying that they'll move.

'She came at me,' cries Dad from the next room as the tiny wound in his side is being looked at. 'I had no choice. She was going to kill me.'

Without even thinking about it, I numbly pick up the bloodied knife from where it still lies on the hall floor and wrap my fingers around it. I can't allow him to paint her as a monster and say he'd acted in self-defence. He has to pay for what he's put Mom through, and if it means I have to chance my own liberty to make sure he gets what he deserves, then I'm prepared to do whatever it takes to get justice for her.

'Naomi!' calls out Leon from somewhere far away. 'Naomi!'

As my eyes begin to focus and I see him looking down at me, I'm suddenly fearful that he's seen the movie that's been playing in my head. I've never told him what really happened that day and how my lie ensured my father went to prison for a very long time. But I vow that once this is over, I'll be honest with him from now on, about everything.

'Are you OK?' he says, gently lifting me up to a sitting position.

I nod slowly.

'Once you're feeling better, Mrs Chandler, I'm going to need you to come down to the station,' says a woman who I thought had only existed in my catatonic state.

I look at her face and it suddenly all comes back to me. Michael . . . Vanessa . . . the emails, the CCTV, the pool . . .

He can't be dead; he just can't be. They've got this wrong.

'But I saw him do it,' I say. 'She was dead.'

Robson narrows her eyes as she looks at me. 'Mrs Talbot doesn't have any injuries apart from a small cut to the back of her head when she fell. Mr Talbot, however, has a knife wound in his back, and another in his chest.'

'I don't understand,' I cry, as Leon wraps an arm around me. 'I was so sure she was dead.'

'Was that what you were hoping?' asks Robson.

I will myself to stay calm and not rise to her line of questioning.

'Tell me about the beach hut,' she presses, her gaze unwavering.

'Beach hut?' I repeat, unsure of what she means.

'Down at Tankerton.'

'Right . . . that's where I met Anna,' I say, before correcting myself. 'Vanessa, I mean. She was there yesterday, threatening to kill herself, so I went to try to talk her down.'

'You seem to have forged quite the relationship with Mrs Talbot,' says Robson.

'As I keep telling you, I will do anything I can to help my clients,' I say, tempering my frustration.

Robson nods. 'And yet she says she's never met you before tonight.'

Every single nerve ending in my body stands to attention, sending a frisson of electricity from my fingertips to my toes. I clasp my hands together to stop them from shaking, but I can't still the trembling inside.

'That's . . . that's absurd,' I mumble, whilst frantically searching for a way to prove her wrong. 'She bought me the picture in my office, knowing that as a fellow New Yorker, it would remind me of home.'

Robson seems taken aback. 'Mrs Talbot's *American*?'

I laugh because I can't not. There may be many anomalies in this case, but Vanessa's origin cannot be called into question. 'Didn't you notice her accent?'

Robson narrows her eyes as if she's having real trouble working me out. I don't know what she's finding so difficult.

'She hasn't got one,' she says eventually.

I suddenly doubt myself, wondering if I'd imagined it. I certainly can't recall Vanessa sounding American when she was in the stables, but then I was too busy trying to stay alive.

I remember the picture that's hanging on my office wall; the shared stories from back home; her memories of Mom's murder. Of course she's American, otherwise . . .

My hands grip the sides of my head, my fingernails digging into my scalp in the hope it relieves the pressure that's building.

'Why don't you describe the beach hut for me?' asks Robson. 'The one you visited yesterday with Mrs Talbot.'

I force myself to breathe, but my lungs don't seem to be working properly. 'It's something of a shrine to their son,' I say. 'He died in a tragic accident and it's full of pictures of him and the family in happier times.'

Robson nods. 'I went there today,' she says. 'But I couldn't have come across a more different scene.'

I look to Leon, wanting to fall into his arms and never wake up.

'Shall I tell you what I found?' she asks.

My throat dries up as she gives one of her colleagues a nod and he hands her a see-through plastic bag.

Leon bristles beside me; its contents are so easily identifiable.

'Is this your underwear?' asks Robson, tilting her head towards the black and pink lace bra and knicker set.

'Yes, but—'

'And this?' she asks, taking another evidence bag. 'Is this your blouse?'

Prettily decorated with red cherries and a black tie at the neck and wrists, it's not a blouse you'd wear if you wanted to be incognito. But then I didn't know I didn't want to be recognized for being the last person to have a drink with a man who is now dead.

I can do nothing but nod, because anything else would be pointless and untrue.

A shrill ringtone resounds around the tent and Robson reaches into her jacket pocket to answer her phone.

'OK,' she says dourly, after listening for a few seconds. 'You're absolutely sure? There's no room for error?'

I clasp my clammy hands together, wondering if whatever she's being told is going to work in my favour or against me.

'The lab results have just come back,' she says, as she ends the call. 'And it's been confirmed that a partial print we found in Mr Talbot's blood in his kitchen is an exact match for a pair of shoes we found in your home.'

I look at her dumbfounded as Leon calls out, 'No, that can't be true.'

'Naomi Chandler, I'm arresting you on suspicion of kidnap and murder. You do not have to say anything, but it may harm your defence if you do not mention when questioned something which you later rely on in court.'

As I'm led out of the tent in handcuffs, a woman with long blonde hair looks as if she might approach me but thinks better of it. Instead she raises her hand awkwardly as I pass by, and in that moment I realize that even after all these years, I'd know that face anywhere. She's just a grown-up version of the little girl I left behind.

EPILOGUE

The two police officers, who I've come to despise for their ineptitude, are staring at me across the desk in the interview room. It surely can't be hard to see what's going on here – it should be an open and shut case, yet still they persist in asking me stupid questions.

'So you have never encountered Naomi Chandler before last night,' says Robson, for the umpteenth time.

'Not in person, no,' I say, careful to give them everything they need without them even realizing they need to know it.

'Yet you obviously knew of her?'

I nod. 'Only when Michael eventually admitted that they'd had an affair, but that it had been a terrible mistake and she wouldn't leave him alone.'

'We've recovered a file that Mrs Chandler says she discovered on her laptop,' says Harris, his beady little eyes alight. 'Of herself in a rather compromising position.' He licks his lips and I almost feel sorry for her. 'Engaged in a sexual act.'

I cover my eyes theatrically. 'Oh, please don't tell me she's with Michael,' I say. 'I couldn't bear it.'

Robson clears her throat. 'No, I can assure you she

isn't, but we weren't quite able to work out how it had been filmed.'

Robson and Naomi both, I imagine. I hadn't meant to use the video. I hadn't expected to get it, if I'm honest – it was something of a surprise bonus that I thought might come in handy to drive a wedge between Naomi and Leon. Not that I needed to – I had more than enough evidence to use against her – but I knew it would all work much more in my favour if a bit of discord was created in their relationship as well.

'Well, I would assume on a phone,' I offer, unable to believe that they couldn't have worked that one out. 'It's quite a big thing amongst couples these days; they set up a tripod and away they go.'

'Yes, I suppose so,' muses Robson. 'But we've spoken to Mr Chandler and he has no knowledge of any such recording taking place.'

I shrug my shoulders.

'So we checked out his wife's office,' she says. I don't like the way she's looking at me. 'As that's where they were at the time, and we found a camera, hidden in the back of a picture of New York.'

'I don't understand what this has got to do with me or Michael,' I say, careful to maintain eye contact.

'Well, Mrs Chandler insists that it's a picture you bought her,' says Robson. 'To remind her of where you both come from.'

I look at her as if she's mad and give a little snigger.

'I'm not quite sure which of those statements is more preposterous. I neither gave it to her, nor am I, as I hope you can tell, even remotely American.'

Robson smiles as if she's onside.

'Are you familiar with the Royal Garden hotel in Canterbury?' she asks.

'Yes, I've been there a few times over the years,' I say. 'Why? Is that where they used to meet?'

'Your husband and Naomi Chandler?' asks Robson.

I nod meekly, as if I don't want to know, yet am resigned to having to.

'Mrs Chandler is quite adamant that she's never had an improper relationship with Michael,' she says.

'I don't know how she expects anyone to believe that when all the evidence proves otherwise,' I say. 'He was living in her flat – and didn't you say you had doorbell footage of her being there?'

They give each other a sideways glance and sweat instantly springs to my armpits. Had they told me about the video on Michael's phone? Or have I just implied that I'd already seen it before leaving it for them to find? I need to be more careful.

'So what's the relevance of the hotel then?' I say, eager to turn it back onto them.

'Well, we had a reported sighting of your husband and someone who resembles Naomi Chandler there on the night he disappeared.'

I make a show of having a bad taste in my mouth,

although in reality I'm licking my lips with satisfaction. The anonymous tip-off had served me well.

'They must have CCTV,' I say, assuming they've already seen Naomi and Michael walking in together.

'Well, *unfortunately the hotel manager informed us that there was a slight technical glitch for a while that evening.*'

Really?

'*So there's no record of either Mrs Chandler or your husband entering or leaving the hotel.*'

'Well, *check the surrounding area,' I say, my frustration at their incompetence growing. 'There must be other CCTV that would have captured them.*'

'*We could do, except we've spoken to Shelley Jenkins, a friend of Mrs Chandler's, and she has confirmed that she* was *with her at that time.*'

It takes all my willpower to stop my eyes from narrowing and my nostrils from flaring. That's impossible. I saw Naomi go in with my own two eyes – closely followed by her suspicious husband, but there's no need to bring him into it and complicate matters.

'So *where does that leave us?' I ask, conscious that my voice is wavering for the first time.*

'Well, *we obviously have your statement alleging that Naomi Chandler was keeping your husband captive on the Tattenhall estate, and that when you came across them she assaulted you, causing you to lose consciousness.*'

I nod.

'In which time you presume that she also attacked your husband, inflicting a fatal blow to his chest and leaving him for dead in the swimming pool.'

I allow my shoulders to convulse and squeeze out a tear for extra effect. 'I'll just never understand why she had to kill him,' I sob. 'She didn't need to kill him.'

I look up quickly to make sure my amateur dramatics aren't going to waste.

They both study me as if waiting for a crack to appear, but they'll be waiting a long time because I've plastered over everything.

Robson closes the folder in front of her to signal that we're getting close to the end of the interview and I slip my arms into my jacket.

'Mmm,' she says. 'It doesn't seem to make sense.'

If she were me, it would make perfect sense. It was always going to end this way once there was a chance Michael was going to find out what really happened on the night Ben died.

I was waiting for Naomi to take him back, to trawl through his memories, daring to spark a recollection that would be my undoing. But as I watched the videos of their sessions, she only ever got close once; when she asked him when he'd been at his happiest and he'd talked about the last day we spent with Ben. I'd held my breath as she pressed him, watching his eyes as they searched for the truth, all the time knowing what I'd have to do

321

if he found it. Because I haven't spent the past ten years blocking the reality out and expending all my energy into convincing both Michael and myself that he hadn't locked the door – the door that Ben had so innocently walked out of – just for someone like Naomi to come along and unlock the proof that he did.

Though ironically, in the end, it wasn't Naomi who had threatened to release him from his guilt, and damn me to perdition.

It was Kyle.

He was the only one who could really destroy the glass house I'd put myself in. Because only he knew I'd left the cottage to meet him that night.

I couldn't let him tell Michael that whilst he'd been torturing himself for all these years, unable to understand how his youngest child had managed to slip out of a door that he was so sure he'd secured, his wife had unlocked it to spend an illicit hour with another man. He couldn't ever know that all the time our little boy was wandering aimlessly in the dark, his mother was wondering how long she could be out for. Or that when the water was lapping above him, she was fantasizing that without children, she'd be able to live the life she wanted.

I paid the ultimate price for my wicked thoughts and actions – but if Kyle told Michael the truth, I'd have to take the blame as well, and I've spent far too long apportioning that to someone else.

So the game's up, and Michael lost. Naomi too, unluckily for her. She was, quite literally, in the wrong place at the wrong time. But, luckily for me, she played right into my hands – even though the police still seem to be questioning her motive.

'Maybe she really did mean, "If I can't have you, no one will,"' I offer, trying to steer them in the right direction.

Robson looks at me questioningly and my pores prickle.

'I thought she'd written something like that in a letter to him?' I say, my throat drying up as I scramble to remember whether they'd told me that, or if I've once again allowed my growing sense of unease to trip me up.

I have to keep my nerve. I'm so close to walking out of here as a free woman. Free of the constraints Michael has made me feel bound by. Free of the fear that one day he would find out what I did. Now, there's only Kyle standing between me and the lie that I'll take to my grave – but by this time tomorrow he will no longer be a liability either.

'I didn't know you were aware of the contents of Mrs Chandler's emails to your husband,' says Robson, eyeing me intently.

I picture the unsightly blotches that must surely be spreading up from my neck, their red tentacles creeping onto my face. 'He showed them to me,' I say, as my right leg trembles uncontrollably. 'Because he was so scared of what she might do.'

'So he really thought she was capable of something like this?'

'Oh, absolutely,' I say, far too enthusiastically. 'She'd threaten him on the phone as well.' I look between the two officers, hoping that direct eye contact will distract from the other parts of my body that are letting me down. 'I tried to reassure him that she'd never follow through, but . . .' I choke, allowing a tear to fall.

'It certainly all seems to point to Mrs Chandler being culpable,' says Robson. 'But there's just one thing that doesn't quite add up.'

'What's that?' I ask, forcing my face to look as if I care.

'It's the shoe print,' says Robson, her annoying face begging to be punched.

'What about it?' I say. 'I thought you said it matched a pair of trainers you found at Naomi's house.'

'Yes, but they're the same size as all the shoes we found at your house, Mrs Talbot.'

'So?' I ask, finding it incredibly difficult to disguise my irritability. 'Thirty-eight is the average shoe size for British women.'

'Yes . . . it is,' she muses, frustratingly slowly.

'But . . . ?'

'But Naomi Chandler is a forty-one, so she couldn't possibly have been wearing them.'

What? *I think frantically of the lengths I've gone to, to pull this off, leaving no stone unturned or a single detail to chance. She's calling my bluff. Of course they're Naomi's shoes; they were in her wardrobe in the spare bedroom.*

'Wh-what do you mean?' *I ask, willing the involuntary spasm in my jaw to stop.*

'They're her mother's,' *says Robson, her eyes boring into mine.* 'You took the only pair that weren't hers.'

ACKNOWLEDGEMENTS

This is my fifth book . . . my fifth book! If you'd have told me five years ago that I'd publish just one novel, I would have talked you out of it. My ideas weren't good enough. I didn't have the imagination. I certainly didn't have the time. And anyway, what was the point? There was a million-to-one chance that it would be picked up – that kind of thing only ever happened to other people, *younger* people, *cleverer* people, *better-connected* people . . .

Except I'm proof that you don't need to be any of those.

Now, I'm firmly of the belief that if you want to write a book, what have you got to lose by giving it a whirl? Get the words down on the page, find yourself a fabulous agent like Tanera Simons @ Darley Anderson to champion you, brilliant editors like Catherine Richards at Minotaur and Vicki Mellor at Pan Macmillan to impart their wisdom, and you'll be surprised how quickly the wonderous team around you grows . . . Nettie Finn, Joseph Brosnan, Hector deJean, Dakota Cohen, Amber Cortes, Rebecca Lloyd, Rebecca Needes, Mary Darby, Georgia Fuller, Kristina Egan, Sheila David, Rosanna

Bellingham . . . all go the extra mile to get their author's words read by as many people as possible.

Another reason I held back from writing fiction for so long was that I didn't think I was well-travelled enough. But then I listened to a famous author talk about his novel set in America's deep south. I'd read the book and had been transported there myself; blinded by the writer's knowledge and memories of a place and time he must surely have experienced personally. Except he then admitted that he'd never travelled south of New York! Proving that now, with the power of the internet and the connectivity we're all able to create, you can go anywhere, experience anything and get answers to questions you don't know. To this end, I'll be forever grateful to my army of American friends who helped me out with references and memories that made Naomi the woman she is:

Debbie Anderson
Jessica Baxter
Carol Bibb
Donna Block
Cindy Bokma
Lisa Boris
Kimberley Brewer
Jasmin Brodie
Erin Christiansen
Sarah Deaner
Maria Denmark

Samantha Fugate
Trisha Glenn
Jordan Gomez
Kristina Hayes
Jennifer Herkert
Mallory Knott
Amber Laurito
Briana Miceli
Leah Mossor
Christine Mott
Kimberley Mussell
Emily Ostlund
Heather Starr
Sarah Yum

Big thanks also to my friends on home soil who continue to support and encourage me, and to Rob, Oliver, Lucy and Oscar who continue to put up with me! I couldn't do this without you.

Thank you so much for reading *The Blame Game* – I know how many books there are out there and I will never take it for granted that you chose mine. I hope you enjoyed it. And for any aspiring writers, who have been wanting to do this for ages: I look forward to reading your work soon!

Best wishes,
Sandie x

THE OTHER WOMAN

If you loved B. A. Paris' *Behind Closed Doors* or Michelle Frances' *The Girlfriend*, you will devour Sandie Jones' page-turning thriller.

When Emily meets Adam she knows he is the one. That together they can deal with anything that is thrown at them. But lurking in the shadows is another woman, Pammie. Emily chose Adam, but she didn't choose his mother. There's nothing a mother wouldn't do for her son, and now Emily is about to find out just how far Pammie will go to get what she wants . . .

PRAISE FOR SANDIE JONES

'Thoroughly entertaining!'
Michelle Frances, author of *The Girlfriend*

'A compulsive, claustrophobic read'
Emma Kavanagh, author of *The Killer on the Wall*

The First Mistake is the stunning novel from *The Other Woman* author Sandie Jones, who delivers twist after heart-stopping twist, in this addictively readable domestic suspense about a wife, her husband, and her best friend.

For Alice, life has never been better. After the death of her first husband, she has remarried, with a successful business, two children and a beautiful house. In Beth, she also has the best friend she has always wanted. A friend without judgement, she is the most trustworthy and loyal person Alice knows. So when Alice begins to suspect her husband Nathan is having an affair, she turns to Beth to help her find the truth. She can trust Beth, can't she . . . ?

PRAISE FOR SANDIE JONES

'A twisty, deliciously fun read'
Sarah Pekkanen, author of *The Wife Between Us*

'Skilful twists' *Sunday Mirror*

THE HALF SISTER

The Half Sister is the third heart-pounding thriller from
Sandie Jones, perfect for fans of Sally Hepworth's *The
Mother-in-Law* and Michelle Frances' *The Daughter*. Have
you read it yet?

Kate and Lauren. Sisters who are always there for each other.
But as they gather for their weekly Sunday lunch, a knock
on the door changes everything.

The new arrival, Jess, claims to be their half sister, but that
would mean the unthinkable . . . that she's the secret
daughter of their beloved, recently deceased father Harry.
Their mother Rose is devastated, and Kate and Lauren refuse
to believe Jess's lies.

But as the fall-out starts, it's clear that each is hiding secrets,
and that perhaps this family isn't as perfect as it appears.

Where there was truth, now there are lies, and only one
thing is certain – their half sister's arrival has ruined
everything . . .

PRAISE FOR SANDIE JONES

'Wickedly relatable story, wonderful characters and
a great twist' T. M. Logan, author of *The Holiday*

'Psychological suspense at its most addictive'
Michele Campbell, author of *It's Always the Husband*

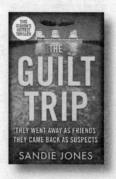

The Guilt Trip is the compelling, twisty novel from Sandie Jones, the author of *The Other Woman*, and perfect for fans of T. M. Logan's *The Holiday*.

Jack and Rachel. Noah and Paige. Will and Ali. Five friends who've known each other for years. And Ali, Will's fiancée.

Now it's Ali and Will's wedding, and all three couples are going on a weekend getaway together in Portugal. It's a chance to relax and get to know Ali a little better, perhaps. A newcomer to their group, she seems perfectly nice – and Will seems happy after years of bad choices. But Ali is hiding more than one secret . . .

By the end of the weekend there'll be one dead body – and five people with guilty consciences, wondering if they really know each other so well after all. Because one of them has to be the killer. . .

PRAISE FOR SANDIE JONES

'An absolute corker'
T. M. Logan, bestselling author of *The Holiday*

'Plot twists galore! Totally addictive' *The Sun*

PUBLISHING AUGUST 2023

THE TRADE OFF

Would you print a lie across a front page?

For Stella, deputy editor of *The Globe*, the choice
has always been clear. There is no stone she will
leave unturned in her pursuit of the best story.
It's what she's built her reputation on.

For Jess, the *Globe*'s rookie reporter, the story stops when
the truth does. But she knows that the dirty tricks of the
tabloids will be hard to overturn.

And when the subject of the story Jess is working
on pays the ultimate price, she suspects that the
paper may have had more to do with it than
they're letting on . . .

*What price would you pay to uncover the truth
if someone is prepared to kill to bury it?*

Read on for an exclusive extract . . .

1

Jess

'So, what would you bring to *The Globe*?' The revered editor of the country's top-selling newspaper is perched on the edge of his desk, making himself at least two feet taller than me as I sit before him.

'Er, I've got lots of ideas,' I say, desperate for saliva to moisten my mouth. 'I'm a team player, my research skills are exemplary and I'm eager to learn.'

He exaggerates a yawn. 'Bor-ing.'

I shift in my chair, fearing I've blown the only chance I'll ever get to learn from the best.

He looks at me with even less interest than ten seconds ago. 'That's what every kid who comes through that door says, and it's why they all leave the same way – without a job.'

My throat clenches and my head throbs as I search desperately for something more exciting to offer.

'You're going to have to sell yourself,' my boss at the local newspaper that I work on had advised. 'Max Forsythe is a man of great means, but he has exceptionally high standards. That's why I've recommended you for the position, as much as it will pain me to lose you.'

'Well, I must be exactly what you want, otherwise I wouldn't have got this far,' I say to Mr Forsythe, squirming in my seat.

He looks at me with an amused expression, his interest piqued.

'And what is it I want?' he asks.

'Me,' I say resolutely, whilst trying to quash the colour that I can feel flooding my cheeks. 'You must have approached the *Essex Gazette* for a reason. A million junior reporters would kill for this opportunity if you'd advertised it, but you didn't. Why not?'

My ears grow hot as I pretend to be the person I think he wants: assertive, driven, hungry, not afraid to step out of my comfort zone.

'I need someone I can trust,' he says, getting up and walking round to his side of the desk. 'And your editor seems to think I can trust *you*.' He narrows his eyes as he sits down and looks at me.

I nod and swallow, conscious not to break eye contact, because I imagine he's someone who can tell a lot from the way you look at him.

'It's a whole different ball game to working on a local rag,' he says. 'There's no such thing as office hours; you work until the paper's put to bed, until I'm happy with every single word and picture in it.'

I nod fervently before pulling back, not wishing to come across like an over-excited puppy.

'And then you'll go straight out and get me stories for the next edition.'

'OK,' I say, unable to stop myself smiling at the thought of me and my notepad venturing out onto the streets of London in search of the next big exclusive. 'I can do that.'

'Do you have a boyfriend?' he asks, changing tack abruptly.

'Erm, well . . .' I stutter, taken aback, unable to see why that's relevant.

Mr Forsythe's eyes are wide with anticipation, making me feel as if my answer's the difference between me getting this job and not. But something in the way he's looking at me makes me think it's not just the job at stake here.

'Well, yes, actually I do,' I lie.

For some reason it makes me feel safer; gives me a false sense of security.

He can't hide his disappointment in my answer. 'Shame, it would be a whole lot easier if you were single.'

My hackles stand on end in sudden indignation. Is he suggesting what I think he is?

'Do you live together?' he asks, seemingly oblivious to my discomfort.

'Well, yes . . . we . . .'

'Are you faithful to him?' He asks the question without even looking at me.

I instinctively pull the coat on my lap tighter to me and reach for my handbag, from where it sits on the floor. I want to turn round to check that the almost deserted open-plan newsroom I'd walked through, to get to this office, still has a few people milling about. But I don't want to show my nerves and make him think he's got the upper hand. Though I almost laugh at my own naive thoughts. Of course he's got the upper hand; he always has – he's one of the most powerful men in media.

'I don't think that's a question I need to—'

'It gives me an insight into who you really are,' he says, cutting me off.

I straighten myself up, hoping it will strengthen my resolve.

'My personal relationships have no bearing on my suitability for employment,' I say, desperately trying to keep my voice steady.

'Well, they do if it stops the man employing you from getting what he wants,' he replies, looking at me suggestively; daring me to ask him to quantify what his statement actually means. Though I know he'll only deny what we both realize he's implying, if I challenge him.

The phone on his desk buzzes and I'm grateful that the tension is broken, but as soon as the tightness in my shoulders begins to dissipate, his assistant sends me into free fall again.

'I'm about to leave,' she says through the intercom. 'Is there anything you need before I go?'

He raises his eyebrows at me in question, and I want to scream at her, 'Yes, take me with you', but my lips feel as if they've been glued shut.

'Is anyone else still here?' asks Max, looking out through the glass walls of his office.

I follow his gaze to the fifty or so desks that stretch out across the floor, desperately wanting to see activity, but even the harsh strip lighting that had shone so brightly when I arrived has been reduced to a low-level night light.

'Only Bill on the back bench,' says the voice through the intercom. 'But I think he's packing up as we speak.'

'Thanks, Gail,' says Max, smiling and widening his eyes. 'I'll see you in the morning.'

I go to stand up. 'Thank you for your time,' I say. 'I really should be going as well.'

He looks at his watch. 'Why? Do you turn into a pumpkin at nine thirty?'

I force a smile, but alarm bells are going off inside my head. When Gail told me it was a 9 p.m. interview or nothing at all, I'd not even questioned it. Max Forsythe had a daily newspaper to run, a nightly deadline to meet; I was just ridiculously grateful for the opportunity. But now that tomorrow's edition has been put to bed and I'm sitting here, alone with the man whose reputation precedes him, I wonder whether he has me down as being *too* eager to please.

'Sit down, relax,' he says, walking over to the drinks

trolley, which I'd assumed was merely for show. 'I only mention it because not many relationships survive this newsroom. You need to be sure that yours is strong enough.'

'Women can work hard *and* hold down a relationship,' I say.

'Good to hear,' he says, lifting a cut-glass decanter in mid-air. 'Now, what can I get you?'

'I'm fine,' I say tartly, still standing with my coat over my arm and wondering if I have time to catch the same lift as Max's assistant. 'I'm not much of a drinker.'

He smirks. 'Not even when we've got something to celebrate?'

If that's his way of telling me I've got the job, I'm no longer sure I want it.

I shake my head. 'Not even then.'

'A word to the wise,' he says, taking a sip of his drink. 'You'll be nobody's friend if you abstain. People won't feel like you're one of them. They'll have their guard up. And that'll get you nowhere. *But* if you can perfect the art of making them believe you're drunk when you're actually stone-cold sober, it could put you at quite the advantage.'

He smiles, more to himself than to me as he warms to his theme. 'In fact if you're able to pull that off, it could set you head and shoulders above the rest. While all my other journalists are matching their marks shot for shot, line for line, *you* could be getting the story.'

'I'm not sure that sounds like me,' I offer, still unsure what he's suggesting.

'Do you *want* to be a journalist or not?' he asks, moving towards me, invading my personal space.

I force myself to stand firm, not to allow my feelings of intimidation to show.

'Well, yes, but . . .'

'Then you *have* to get used to being in uncomfortable situations, because no story worth having will come your way without you being backed up against the wall, having your loyalty questioned and your ethics challenged. If you're not prepared to be put under that kind of pressure, then you either get out now or you find a way to fake it, because I don't need a rookie-shaped liability around my neck.'

'Are you offering me the job?' I ask.

'Only if your moral compass is pointing as far north as it appears to be,' he says with a smile, moving back to his desk.

It's then that the penny drops. 'Was . . . was that some kind of *test*?' I ask, feeling relieved and foolish at the same time.

'I need to know that your core values are gold-standard,' he replies. 'That your sense of what is right and wrong is imbued in your very being.'

I nod enthusiastically.

'Because it's time that tabloid journalism cleaned up its act.'

'I won't be trading my morals for a byline,' I say, a coil of excitement swirling in the pit of my stomach.

'Then I think we're going to get along just fine,' he says, finishing off his drink in one. 'Now, as much as I'd like to sit here and discuss the merits of your morality all night, I have a prior engagement with the prime minister.'